ONCE

(A RILEY PAIGE M

C000136704

BLAKE PIERCE

ISBN: 978-1-63291-801-7

BOOKS BY BLAKE PIERCE

RILEY PAIGE MYSTERY SERIES
ONCE GONE (Book #1)
ONCE TAKEN (Book #2)
ONCE CRAVED (Book #3)
ONCE LURED (Book #4)

MACKENZIE WHITE MYSTERY SERIES
BEFORE HE KILLS (Book #1)

AVERY BLACK MYSTERY SERIES
CAUSE TO KILL (Book #1)

PROLOGUE

The man worried as he sat in his car. He knew he had to hurry. Tonight, it was important to keep everything on track. But would the woman come along this road at her usual hour?

It was eleven o'clock at night, and he was cutting it close.

He remembered the voice he had heard, reverberating in his head, before he'd come here. Grandpa's voice.

"You'd better be right about her schedule, Scratch."

Scratch. The man in the car didn't like that name. It wasn't his real name. It was a folktale name for the Devil. As far as Grandpa was concerned, he was a "bad seed."

Grandpa had called him Scratch for longer than he could remember. Although everybody else called him by his real name, Scratch had stuck in his own mind. He hated his grandpa. But he couldn't pull him out of his head.

Scratch reached up and slapped his own skull several times, trying to get the voice out.

It hurt, and for a moment he had a sense of calm.

But then came Grandpa's dull laughter, echoing somewhere in there. It was a little fainter now, at least.

He looked anxiously at his watch. A few minutes past eleven. Would she be late tonight? Would she go somewhere else? No, that wasn't her style. He'd scouted her movements for days. She was always punctual, always stuck to the same routine.

If only she understood how much was at stake. Grandpa would punish him if he botched this. But there was much more to it than that. The world itself was running out of time. He had a huge responsibility, and it weighed on him heavily.

Car lights appeared, far back along the road, and he sighed with relief. That must be her.

This country road only led to a few houses. It was usually deserted at this hour except for the woman who always drove from her job straight to the house where she rented a room.

Scratch had turned his car around to face hers and stopped it right in the middle of this little gravel road. He stood outside, hands trembling, using a flashlight to peer under his hood, hoping it would work.

His heart slammed as the other vehicle drove by.

Stop! he pleaded silently. *Please stop!*

1

Soon, the other vehicle pulled to a stop a short distance from him.

He bit back a smile.

Scratch turned and looked toward the lights. Yes, it was her shabby little car, just as he had hoped.

Now, he just had to lure her to him.

She lowered her window, and he looked over at her and smiled his most pleasant smile.

"I guess I'm stranded," he called out.

He turned the flashlight briefly on the driver's face. Yes, it was definitely her.

Scratch noticed that she had a charming, open face. More importantly, she was very thin, which suited his purposes.

It seemed a shame, what he was going to have to do to her. But it was like Grandpa always said: *"It's for the greater good."*

It was true, and Scratch knew it. If the woman could only understand, perhaps she'd even be willing to sacrifice herself. After all, sacrifice was one of the finest features of human nature. She ought to be glad to be of service.

But he knew that was too much to expect. Things would get violent and messy, just like they always did.

"What's the problem?" the woman called.

He noticed something appealing in how she spoke. He didn't yet know what it was.

"I don't know," he said. "She just died on me."

The woman craned her head out of the window. He looked straight at her. Her freckled face framed by bright red curly hair was open and smiling. She didn't seem to be the least bit dismayed by the inconvenience he'd caused her.

But would she be trusting enough to get out of the car? Probably, if the other women had been any indication.

Grandpa was always telling him how horribly ugly he was, and he couldn't help thinking of himself that way. But he knew that other people—women especially—found him rather pleasant to look at.

He gestured toward the open hood. "I don't know anything about cars," he yelled back to her.

"I don't either," the woman called back.

"Well, maybe the two of us together can figure out what's wrong," he said. "Do you mind giving it a try?"

"Not at all. Just don't expect me to be much help."

She opened her door, got out, and walked toward him. Yes, everything was going perfectly. He had lured her out of her car. But time was still of the essence.

"Let's take a peek," she said, stepping beside him and looking at the engine.

Now he realized what he liked about her voice.

"You've got an interesting accent," he said. "Are you Scottish?"

"Irish," she said pleasantly. "I've only been here two months, got a green card especially so I could work with a family here."

He smiled. "Welcome to America," he said.

"Thanks. I love it so far."

He pointed toward the engine.

"Wait a minute," he said. "What do you think that is?"

The woman bent over for a closer look. He tripped the release and slammed the hood on her head with a thunk.

He opened the hood, hoping not to have to hit her again. Luckily, she was out cold, her face and torso stretched limp across the engine.

He looked all around. Nobody was in sight. Nobody had seen what had happened.

He shook with delight.

He gathered her up in his arms, noticing that her face and the front of her dress were now smeared with grease. She was as light as a feather. He carried her around to the side of his car and stretched her out on the back seat.

He felt certain that this one would serve his needs well.

*

Just as Meara began to regain consciousness, she was jolted by a deafening barrage of noise. It seemed like every kind of sound she could imagine. There were gongs, bells, chimes, birdcalls, and sundry melodies as if from a dozen music boxes. They all seemed deliberately hostile.

She opened her eyes, but nothing came into focus. Her head was splitting with pain.

Where am I? she wondered.

Was it somewhere in Dublin? No, she was able to put together just a bit of chronology. She'd flown here two months ago, started working as soon as she got settled. She was definitely in Delaware.

With an effort, she remembered stopping to help a man with his car. Then something had happened. Something bad.

But what was this place, with all its horrible noise?

She became aware that she was being carried like a child. She heard the voice of the man who was carrying her, speaking above the racket.

"Don't worry, we got here on time."

Her eyes began to focus. Her vision was filled by a staggering number of clocks of every conceivable size, shape, and style. She saw massive grandfather clocks flanked by smaller clocks, some of them cuckoo clocks, others with little parades of mechanical people. Still smaller clocks were ranged across shelves.

They're all sounding the hour, she thought.

But in all the noise, she couldn't begin to pick out the number of gongs or bells.

She turned her head to see who was carrying her. He looked down at her. Yes, it was him—the man who had asked for her help. She'd been a fool to stop for him. She'd fallen into his trap. But what was he going to do to her?

As the noise from the clocks died away, her eyes went out of focus again. She couldn't keep them open. She felt her consciousness fading.

Got to stay awake, she thought.

She heard a metallic rattling, then felt herself lowered gently to a cold, hard surface. There was another rattling, followed by footsteps, and finally by a door opening and closing. The multitude of clocks kept ticking.

Then she heard a pair of female voices.

"She's alive."

"Too bad for her."

The voices were hushed and hoarse. Meara managed to open her eyes again. She saw that the floor was gray concrete. She turned painfully and saw three human forms seated on the floor near her. Or at least she thought they were human. They seemed to be young girls, teenagers, but they were gaunt, little more than skeletons, their bones showing clearly beneath their skin. One seemed barely conscious, her head hanging forward and eyes staring at the gray floor. They reminded her of photos she'd seen of prisoners in concentration camps.

Were they even alive? Yes, they must be alive. She'd just heard them both speak.

4

"Where are we?" Meara asked.
She barely heard the hissed response.
"Welcome," one of them said, "to hell."

CHAPTER ONE

Riley Paige didn't see the first punch coming. Still, her reflexes responded well. She felt time slow down as the first jab flashed toward her stomach. She backed away from it perfectly. Then a broad left hook came toward her head. She jumped to the side and dodged it. When he closed in with a final jab to her face, her guard went up and she took the punch to her gloves.

Then time resumed its normal pace. She knew the combination of blows had come in less than two seconds.

"Good," Rudy said.

Riley smiled. Rudy was dodging and weaving now, more than ready for her attack. Riley did the same, bobbing, faking, trying to keep him guessing.

"No need to hurry," Rudy said. "Think it through. Think of it like a game of chess."

She felt a twinge of annoyance as she kept her lateral motion going. He was going easy on her. Why did he have to go easy on her?

But she knew that it was just as well. This was her first time in the sparring ring with an actual opponent. Until now, she'd been testing her combinations on a heavy bag. She had to remember that she was just a beginner at this form of fighting. It really was best not to hurry.

It had been Mike Nevins's idea for her to take up sparring. The forensic psychiatrist who consulted with the FBI was also Riley's good friend. He had gotten her through a lot of personal crises.

She'd recently complained to Mike that she was having trouble controlling her aggressive impulses. She was losing her temper frequently. She felt on edge.

"Try sparring," Mike had said. *"It's a great way to let off steam."*

Right now she felt pretty sure that Mike was right. It felt good to be thinking on her feet, dealing with real threats instead of imagined ones, and it was relaxing to be dealing with threats that weren't actually deadly.

It was also good that she'd joined a gym that got her away from Quantico headquarters. She spent too much time there. This was a welcome change.

But she had dawdled too long. And she could see in Rudy's eyes that he was preparing for another attack.

She mentally chose her next combination. She popped abruptly toward him for her attack. Her first punch was a left jab, which he dodged and countered with a right cross that grazed her sparring helmet. She followed in less than a second with a right jab, which he took to his glove. In a flash she launched a left hook, which he dodged by lurching to the side.

"Good," Rudy said again.

It didn't feel good to Riley. She hadn't landed a single punch, while he had clipped her a little even while defending himself, and she was starting to feel irritation building up. But she reminded herself of what Rudy had told her at the very start ...

"Don't expect to land a lot of punches. Nobody really does. Not with sparring, anyway."

She was watching his gloves now, sensing that he was about to launch another attack. But just then, a strange transformation took place in her imagination.

The gloves turned into a single flame—the white hissing flame of a propane torch. She was caged in darkness again, the prisoner of a sadistic killer named Peterson. He was toying with her, making her dodge the flame to escape its searing heat.

But she was tired of being humiliated. This time she was determined to strike back. When the flame leaped toward her face, she simultaneously ducked and launched a fierce jab that didn't connect. The flame hooked around to her, and she countered with a cross that also didn't connect. But before Peterson could make another move, she threw an uppercut, and she felt it smash into his chin ...

"Hey!" Rudy shouted.

His voice brought Riley back to her present reality. Rudy was stretched out on his back on the mat.

How did he get down there? Riley wondered.

Then she realized that she'd hit him—and hit him hard.

"Oh my God!" she shouted. "Rudy, I'm sorry!"

Rudy was grinning and getting back on his feet.

"Don't be," he said. "That was good."

They resumed sparring. The rest of the session was uneventful, and neither of them landed any punches. But now the whole thing felt good to Riley. Mike Nevins was right. This was just the therapy she needed.

All the same, she kept wondering when she'd ever be able to shake off those memories.

Maybe never, she thought.

*

Riley cut enthusiastically into her steak. The chef at Blaine's Grill did a great job with several less conventional dishes, but today's workout at the gym had left her hungry for a good steak and a salad. Her daughter, April, and her friend Crystal had ordered burgers. Blaine Hildreth, Crystal's father, was in the kitchen, but he would be back any moment now to finish up his mahi-mahi.

Riley gazed around the comfortable dining room with a deep feeling of satisfaction. She realized that her life didn't include enough warm evenings like this with friends, family, and a nice meal. The scenes her job presented were more often ugly and unsettling.

In a few days she would testify at a parole hearing for a child-killer who hoped to get out of jail early. And she needed to make sure that he didn't get away with that.

Several weeks ago she'd closed a disturbing case in Phoenix. She and her partner, Bill Jeffreys, had caught a killer who murdered prostitutes. Riley was still having trouble feeling that she'd done much good in solving that case. Now she knew too much for her own comfort about a whole world of exploited women and girls.

But she was determined to keep such thoughts out of her mind right now. She felt herself relaxing little by little. Eating out at a restaurant with a friend and both of their kids reminded her what it could be like to live a normal life. She was living in a nice home and growing closer to a nice neighbor.

Blaine returned and sat down. Riley couldn't help observing yet again that he was attractive. His receding hairline gave him a pleasantly mature look, and he was lean and fit.

"Sorry," Blaine said. "This place runs fine without me when I'm not here, but if I'm in view everybody decides they need my help."

"I know what that's like," Riley said. "I'm hoping that if I keep out of sight, BAU will forget me for a while."

April said, "No chance of that. They'll call soon. You'll be headed off to some other part of the country."

Riley sighed. "I could get used to not being on constant call."

Blaine finished a bite of his mahi-mahi.

"Have you thought about changing careers?" he asked.

Riley shrugged. "What else would I do? I've been an agent most of my adult life."

"Oh, I'm sure there are lots of things a woman of your talents could do," Blaine said. "Most of them safer than being an FBI agent."

He thought for a moment. "I could picture you being a teacher," he added.

Riley chuckled. "Do you think that's safer?" she asked.

"Depends on where you do it," Blaine said. "What about college?"

"Hey, that's an idea, Mom," April said. "You wouldn't have to travel all the time. And you'd still get to help people."

Riley said nothing as she mulled it over. Teaching at a college would surely be something like the teaching she'd done at the academy in Quantico. She'd enjoyed doing that. It always gave her a chance to recharge. But would she want to be a full-time teacher? Could she really spend all her days inside a building with no real activity?

She poked at a mushroom with her fork.

I might turn into one of these, she thought.

"What about becoming a private investigator?" Blaine asked.

"I don't think so," Riley said. "Digging up dirty secrets about divorcing couples doesn't appeal to me."

"That's not all that PIs do," Blaine said. "What about investigating insurance fraud? Hey, I've got this cook who's collecting disability, says he's got a bad back. I'm sure he's faking it, but I can't prove it. You could start with him."

Riley laughed. Blaine was joking, of course.

"Or you could look for missing people," Crystal said. "Or missing pets."

Riley laughed again. "Now *that* would make me feel like I was doing some real good in the world!"

April had dropped out of the conversation. Riley saw that she was texting and giggling. Crystal leaned across the table toward Riley.

"April's got a new boyfriend," Crystal said. Then she silently mouthed, "I don't like him."

Riley was annoyed that her daughter was ignoring everybody else at the table.

"Stop doing that," she told April. "It's rude."

"What's rude about it?" April said.

"We've talked about this," Riley said.

April ignored her and typed a message.

"Put that away," Riley said.

"In a minute, Mom."

Riley stifled a groan. She'd long since learned that "in a minute" was teen talk for "never."

Just then her own phone buzzed. She felt angry with herself for not turning it off before leaving the house. She looked at the phone and saw that it was a message from her FBI partner, Bill. She thought about leaving it unread, but she couldn't make herself do that.

As she brought up the message, she glanced up and saw April grinning at her. Her daughter was enjoying the irony. Silently seething, Riley read Bill's text message.

Meredith has a new case. He wants to discuss it with us ASAP.

Special Agent in Charge Brent Meredith was Riley's boss, and Bill's too. She felt tremendous loyalty to him. Not only was he a good and fair boss, he'd gone to bat for Riley many times when she was in trouble with the bureau. Even so, Riley was determined not to let herself get drawn in, at least for the time being.

I can't go traveling right now, she texted back.

Bill replied, *It's right here in the area.*

Riley shook her head with discouragement. Standing her ground wasn't going to be easy.

She texted back to him, *I'll get back to you.*

No reply came, and Riley put the phone back in her bag.

"I thought you said that was rude, Mom," April said in a quiet, sullen voice.

April was still texting.

"I'm through with mine," she said, trying not to sound as annoyed as she felt.

April ignored her. Riley's own phone buzzed again. She cursed silently. She saw that the text was from Meredith himself.

Be at BAU meeting tomorrow 9 AM.

Riley was trying to think of a way to excuse herself when another text followed.

That's an order.

CHAPTER TWO

Riley's spirits sank as she looked at the two images looming on screens above the BAU conference room table. One was a photo of a carefree girl with bright eyes and a winning smile. The other was her corpse, horribly emaciated and lying with her arms pointed in odd directions. Since she had been ordered to attend this meeting, Riley knew there must be other victims like this one.

Sam Flores, a savvy lab technician with black-rimmed glasses, was running the multimedia display for the four other agents seated around the table.

"These pictures are of Metta Lunoe, seventeen years old," Flores said. "Her family lives in Collierville, New Jersey. Her parents reported her missing in March—a runaway."

He added a huge map of Delaware to the display, indicating a location with a pointer.

He said, "Her body turned up in a field outside of Mowbray, Delaware, on May sixteenth. Her neck had been broken."

Flores brought up another pair of images—one showing another vibrant young girl, the other showing her almost unrecognizably withered, her arms stretched out in a similar way.

"These pictures are of Valerie Bruner, also seventeen, a reported runaway from Norbury, Virginia. She disappeared in April."

Flores pointed to another location on the map.

"Her body was found stretched out in a dirt road near Redditch, Delaware, on June twelfth. Obviously the same MO as the earlier killing. Agent Jeffreys was brought in to investigate."

Riley was startled. How could Bill have worked on a case that hadn't involved her? Then she remembered. In June, she had been hospitalized, recovering from her horrible ordeal in Peterson's cage. Even so, Bill had visited her frequently in the hospital. He'd never mentioned that he was also working this case.

She turned toward Bill.

"Why didn't you tell me about this?" she asked.

Bill's face looked grim.

"It wasn't a good time," he said. "You had troubles of your own."

"Who was your partner?" Riley asked.

"Agent Remsen."

Riley recognized the name. Bruce Remsen had transferred out of Quantico before she had come back to work.

Then after a pause, Bill added, "I couldn't crack the case."

Now Riley could read his expression and tone of voice. After years of friendship and partnership, she understood Bill as well as anybody did. And she knew that he was deeply disappointed with himself.

Flores brought up the medical examiner's photos of the girls' naked backs. The bodies were so wasted away that they barely seemed real. Both backs bore old scars and fresh welts.

Riley felt a gnawing discomfort all over now. She was taken aback by the feeling. Since when had she gotten queasy about photos of corpses?

Flores said, "They were both starved almost to death before their necks were broken. They were also severely beaten, probably over a long period of time. Their bodies were moved to where they were found postmortem. We have no idea where they were actually killed."

Trying not to let her rising unease get the best of her, Riley mulled over similarities with cases she and Bill had solved during the last few months. The so-called "dolly killer" had left his victims' bodies where they could be easily found, posed naked in grotesque doll-like positions. The "chain killer" hung the bodies of his victims up off the ground, wildly decked in heavy chains.

Now Flores brought up the image of another young woman—a cheerful-looking redhead. Alongside the photo was one of a beat-up, empty Toyota.

"This car belonged to a twenty-four-year-old Irish immigrant named Meara Keagan," Flores said. "She was reported missing yesterday morning. Her car was found abandoned just outside an apartment building in Westree, Delaware. She worked there for a family as maid and nanny."

Now Special Agent Brent Meredith spoke. He was a daunting, big-boned African-American with angular features and a no-nonsense demeanor.

"She got off her shift at eleven o'clock the night before last," Meredith said. "The car was found early the next morning."

Special Agent in Charge Carl Walder leaned forward in his chair. He was Brent Meredith's boss—a babyish, freckle-faced man with curly, copper-colored hair. Riley didn't like him. She didn't think he was especially competent. It didn't help that he'd once fired her.

"Why do we think this disappearance is linked with the earlier murders?" Walder asked. "Meara Keagan is older than the other victims."

Now Lucy Vargas chimed in. She was a bright young rookie with dark hair, dark eyes, and a dark complexion.

"You can see by the map. Keagan disappeared in the same general area where the two bodies were found. It might be coincidence, but it seems unlikely. Not over a period of five months, all so close together."

Despite her increasing discomfort, Riley was pleased at the sight of Walder wincing a little. Without meaning to, Lucy had put him in his place. Riley hoped he wouldn't find some way to get back at Lucy later on. Walder could be petty that way.

"That's correct, Agent Vargas," Meredith said. "Our guess is that the younger girls were abducted while hitchhiking. Very likely along this highway that runs through the area." He pointed out a specific line on the map.

Lucy asked, "Isn't hitchhiking banned in Delaware?" She added, "Of course, that can be hard to enforce."

"You're right about that," Meredith said. "And this isn't an interstate or even the main state highway, so hitchhikers probably do use it. Apparently the killer does too. One body was found alongside this road and the other two are less than ten miles from it. Keagan was taken about sixty miles north along that same route. With her he used a different ruse. If he follows his usual pattern, he'll keep her until she's almost starved to death. Then he'll break her neck and leave her body the same way as before."

"We're not going to let that happen," Bill said in a tight voice.

Meredith said, "Agents Paige and Jeffreys, I want to you to get right to work on this." He pushed a manila folder stuffed with photos and reports across the table toward Riley. "Agent Paige, here's all the info you need to bring you up to speed."

Riley reached toward the folder. But her hand jerked back with a spasm of horrible anxiety.

What's the matter with me?

Her head was spinning, and out-of-focus images started to take shape in her brain. Was this PTSD from the Peterson case? No, it was different. It was something else entirely.

Riley got up from her chair and fled the conference room. As she hurried down the hallway toward her office, the images in her head came into sharper focus.

They were faces—faces of women and girls.

She saw Mitzi, Koreen, and Tantra—young call girls whose respectable attire masked their degradation even from themselves.

She saw Justine, an aging whore hunched over a drink at a bar, tired and bitter and fully prepared to die an ugly death.

She saw Chrissy, virtually imprisoned in a brothel by her abusive pimp husband.

And worst of all, she saw Trinda, a fifteen-year-old girl who had already lived a nightmare of sexual exploitation, and who could imagine no other life.

Riley arrived in her office and collapsed into her chair. Now she understood her onslaught of revulsion. The images she'd seen just now had been a trigger. They'd brought to the surface her darkest misgivings about the Phoenix case. She'd stopped a brutal murderer, but she hadn't brought justice to the women and girls she'd met. A whole world of exploitation remained. She hadn't even scratched the surface of the wrongs they endured.

And now she was haunted and troubled in a way she'd never known before. This seemed worse than PTSD to her. After all, she could give vent to her private rage and horror in a sparring gym. She had no way to get rid of these new feelings.

And could she bring herself to work another case like Phoenix?

She heard Bill's voice at the door.

"Riley."

She looked up and saw her partner looking at her with a sad expression. He was holding the folder Meredith had tried to give her.

"I need you on this case," Bill said. "It's personal for me. It makes me crazy that I couldn't crack it. And can't help wondering if I was off my game because my marriage was falling apart. I got to know Valerie Bruner's family. They're good people. But I haven't stayed in touch with them because … well, I let them down. I've got to make things right with them."

He put the folder on Riley's desk.

"Just look at this. Please."

He left Riley's office. She sat staring at the folder in a state of indecision.

This wasn't like her. She knew she had to snap out of it.

As she mulled things over, she remembered something from her time in Phoenix. She had been able to save one girl named Jilly. Or at least she had tried.

She took out her phone and dialed the number for a shelter for teenagers in Phoenix, Arizona. A familiar voice came on the line.

"This is Brenda Fitch."

Riley was glad that Brenda took the call. She'd gotten to know the social worker during her previous case.

"Hi, Brenda," she said. "This is Riley. I just thought I'd check in on Jilly."

Jilly was a girl that Riley had rescued from sex trafficking—a skinny, dark-haired thirteen-year-old. Jilly had no family except for an abusive father. Riley called every so often to find out how Jilly was doing.

Riley heard a sigh from Brenda.

"It's good of you to call," Brenda said. "I wish more people showed some concern. Jilly's still with us."

Riley's heart sank. She hoped that someday she'd call and be told that Jilly had been taken in by a kindly foster family. This wasn't going to be that day. Now Riley was worried.

She said, "The last time we talked, you were afraid you'd have to send her back to her father."

"Oh, no, we've got that legally sorted out. We've even got a restraining order to keep him away from her."

Riley breathed a sigh of relief.

"Jilly asks about you all the time," Brenda said. "Would you like to talk to her?"

"Yes. Please."

Brenda put Riley on hold. Riley suddenly wondered whether this was such a good idea. Whenever she talked to Jilly, she wound up feeling guilty. She couldn't understand why she felt that way. After all, she had saved Jilly from a life of exploitation and abuse.

But saved her for what? she wondered. What kind of life did Jilly have to look forward to?

She heard Jilly's voice.

"Hey, Agent Paige."

"How many times do I have to tell you not to call me that?"

"Sorry. Hey, Riley."

Riley chuckled a little.

"Hey, yourself. How are you doing?"

"Okay, I guess."

A silence fell.

A typical teenager, Riley thought. It was always hard to get Jilly talking.

"So what are you up to?" Riley asked.

"Just waking up," Jilly said, sounding a bit groggy. "Going to eat breakfast."

Riley then realized that it was three hours earlier in Phoenix.

"I'm sorry to call so early," Riley said. "I keep forgetting about the time difference."

"It's okay. It's nice of you to call."

Riley heard a yawn.

"So are you going to school today?" Riley asked.

"Yeah. They let us out of the joint every day to do that."

It was Jilly's little running joke, calling the shelter the "joint" as if it were a prison. Riley didn't find it very funny.

Riley said, "Well, I'll let you go have breakfast and get ready."

"Hey, wait a minute," Jilly said.

Another silence fell. Riley thought she heard Jilly choke back a sob.

"Nobody wants me, Riley," Jilly said. She was crying now. "Foster families keep passing me over. They don't like my past."

Riley was staggered.

Her "past"? she thought. *Jesus, how can a thirteen-year-old have a "past"? What's the matter with people?*

"I'm sorry," Riley said.

Jilly spoke haltingly through her tears.

"It's like … well, you know, it's … I mean, Riley, it seems like *you're* the only one who cares."

Riley's throat ached and her eyes stung. She couldn't reply.

Jilly said, "Couldn't I come to live with you? I won't be much trouble. You've got a daughter, right? She could be like my sister. We could look after each other. I miss you."

Riley struggled to speak.

"I … I don't think that's possible, Jilly."

"Why not?"

Riley felt devastated. The question struck her like a bullet.

"It's just … not possible," Riley said.

She could still hear Jilly crying.

"Okay," Jilly said. "I've got to head over to breakfast. Bye."

"Bye," Riley said. "I'll call again soon."

She heard a click as Jilly ended the call. Riley bent over her desk, tears running down her own face. Jilly's question kept echoing through her head ...

"Why not?"

There were a thousand reasons. She had her hands full with April as it was. Her job was too consuming, both of her time and energy. And was she in any way qualified or prepared to deal with Jilly's psychological scarring? Of course she wasn't.

Riley wiped her eyes and sat upright. Indulging in self-pity wasn't going to help anybody. It was time to get back to work. Girls were dying out there, and they needed her.

She picked up the folder and opened it. Was it time, she wondered, to get back in the arena?

CHAPTER THREE

Scratch sat on his front porch swing watching the kids come and go in their Halloween costumes. He usually enjoyed having trick-or-treaters come around. But it seemed a bittersweet occasion this year.

How many of these kids will be alive in just a few weeks? he wondered.

He sighed. Probably none of them. The deadline was near and no one was paying attention to his messages.

The porch swing chains were creaking. There was a light, warm rain falling, and Scratch hoped that the kids wouldn't catch cold. He had a basket of candy on his lap, and he was being pretty generous. It was getting late, and soon there would be no more kids.

In Scratch's mind Grandpa was still complaining, even though the cranky old man had died years ago. And it didn't matter that Scratch was grown now, he was never free from the old man's advice.

"Look at that one in the cloak and the black plastic mask," Grandpa said. *"Call that a costume?"*

Scratch hoped that he and Grandpa weren't about to have another argument.

"He's dressed up as Darth Vader, Grandpa," he said.

"I don't care who the hell he's supposed to be. It's a cheap, store-bought outfit. When I took you trick-or-treating, we always made your costumes for you."

Scratch remembered those costumes. To turn him into a mummy, Grandpa had wrapped him up in torn-up bed sheets. To make him into a knight in shining armor, Grandpa had decked him out in cumbersome poster board covered with aluminum foil, and he'd carried a lance made out of a broomstick. Grandpa's costumes were always creative.

Still, Scratch didn't remember those Halloweens fondly. Grandpa would always curse and complain while getting him into those outfits. And when Scratch got home from trick-or-treating ... for a moment, Scratch felt like a little boy again. He knew that Grandpa was always right. Scratch didn't always understand why, but that didn't matter. Grandpa was right, and he was wrong. That was just the way things were. It was the way things had always been.

Scratch had been relieved when he got too old for trick-or-treating. Ever since then, he'd been free to sit on the porch dispensing candy to kids. He was happy for them. He was glad that they were enjoying childhood, even if he hadn't.

Three kids clambered up onto the porch. A boy was dressed as Spiderman, a girl as Catwoman. They looked about nine years old. The third kid's costume made Scratch smile. A little girl, about seven years old, was wearing a bumblebee outfit.

"Trick-or-treat!" they all shouted as they gathered in front of Scratch.

Scratch chuckled and rummaged around in the basket for candy. He gave some to the kids, who thanked him and went away.

"Stop giving them candy!" Grandpa growled. *"When are you going to stop encouraging the little bastards?"*

Scratch had been quietly defying Grandpa for a couple of hours now. He'd have to pay for it later.

Meanwhile, Grandpa was still grumbling. *"Don't forget, we've got work to do tomorrow night."*

Scratch didn't reply, just listened to the creaking porch swing. No, he wouldn't forget what had to be done tomorrow night. It was a dirty job, but it had to be done.

*

Libby Clark followed her big brother and her cousin into the dark woods that lay behind all the neighborhood backyards. She didn't want to be here. She wanted to be home snugly in bed.

Her brother, Gary, was leading the way, carrying a flashlight. He looked all weird in his Spiderman costume. Her cousin Denise was following Gary in her Catwoman outfit. Libby was trotting along behind both of them.

"Come on, you two," Gary said, pushing ahead.

He slid between two bushes just fine, and so did Denise, but Libby's costume was all puffy and got caught on some branches. Now she had something new to be scared about. If the bumblebee costume got ruined, Mommy would have a fit. Libby managed to get untangled and scurried to catch up.

"I want to go home," Libby said.

"Go right ahead," Gary said, moving right along.

But of course Libby was too scared to go back. They had come way too far already. She didn't dare go back alone.

20

"Maybe we all should go back," Denise said. "Libby's scared."

Gary stopped and turned around. Libby wished she could see his face behind that mask.

"What's the matter, Denise?" he said. "Are you scared too?"

Denise laughed nervously.

"No," she said. Libby could tell she was lying.

"Then come on, both of you," Gary said.

The little group kept on moving. The ground was soggy and slimy, and Libby was up to her knees in wet weeds. At least it had stopped raining. The moon was starting to show through the clouds. But it was also getting colder, and Libby was damp all over, and she was shivering, and she was really, really scared.

Finally the trees and bushes opened onto a large clearing. Steam was rising up from the wet ground. Gary stopped right up to the edge of the space, and so did Denise and Libby.

"Here it is," Gary whispered, pointing. "Lookit—it's square, just like there was supposed to be a house or something here. But there's not a house. There's nothing. Trees and bushes can't even grow here. Just weeds is all. That's because it's cursed ground. Ghosts live here."

Libby reminded herself of what Daddy said.

"There's no such thing as ghosts."

Even so, her knees were shaking. She was afraid she was going to pee herself. Mommy sure wouldn't like that.

"What are those?" Denise asked.

She pointed to two shapes rising up out of the ground. To Libby they looked like big pipes that were bent over at the top, and they were almost completely covered with ivy.

"I don't know," Gary said. "They remind me of submarine periscopes. Maybe the ghosts are watching us. Go take a look, Denise."

Denise let out a scared-sounding laugh.

"*You* have a look!" Denise said.

"Okay, I will," Gary said.

Gary stepped none too boldly out into the clearing and walked toward one of the shapes. He stopped in his tracks about three feet away from it. Then he turned around and came back to rejoin his cousin and sister.

"I can't tell what it is," he said.

Denise laughed again. "That's because you didn't even look!" she said.

"Did so," Gary said.

"Did not! You didn't even get near it!"

"I did so get near it. If you're so curious, go check it out yourself."

Denise didn't say anything for a moment. Then she trotted out onto the bare patch. She got a little closer to the shape than Gary, but she trotted straight back without stopping.

"I don't know what it is either," she said.

"It's your turn to look, Libby," Gary said.

Libby's fear was creeping up in her throat just like that ivy.

"Don't make her go, Gary," Denise said. "She's too little."

"She's not too little. She's growing up. It's time she acted like it."

Gary gave Libby a sharp shove. She found herself a couple of feet out into the space. She turned around and tried to go back again, but Gary stretched his hand out to stop her.

"Huh-uh," he said. "Denise and I went. You've got to go too."

Libby gulped hard and turned around and faced the empty space with its two bent things. She had the creepy feeling that they could be looking back at her.

She remembered her daddy's words again ...

"There's no such thing as ghosts."

Daddy wouldn't lie about a thing like that. So what was she scared of, anyway?

Besides, she was getting mad at Gary for being a bully. She was almost as mad as she was scared.

I'll show him, she thought.

Her legs still shaking, she took step after step out into the big square space. As she walked toward the metal thing, Libby actually felt braver.

By the time she got close to the thing—closer than even Gary or Denise had gotten—she was feeling pretty proud of herself. Still, she couldn't tell what it was.

With more courage than she even thought she had, she reached her hand out toward it. She pushed her fingers among the ivy leaves, hoping that her hand wouldn't get snatched or eaten or maybe something worse. Her fingers came up against the hard, cold metal pipe.

What is it? she wondered.

Now she felt a slight vibration in the pipe. And she heard something. It seemed to be coming from the pipe.

She leaned really close to the pipe. The sound was faint, but she knew that it wasn't her imagination. The sound was real, and it was just like a woman weeping and moaning.

Libby jerked her hand away from the pipe. She was too frightened to move or speak or scream or do anything. She couldn't even breathe. It felt like that time when she'd fallen out of a tree on her back and the wind got knocked out of her lungs.

She knew that she had to get away. But she stayed frozen. It was like she had to tell her body how to move.

Turn and run, she thought.

But for a few terrifying seconds she just couldn't do it.

Then her legs seemed to start running all on their own, and she found herself dashing back toward the edge of the clearing. She was terrified that something really bad would reach out and grab her and yank her back.

When she arrived at the edge of the woods, she bent over, gasping for breath. Now she realized that she hadn't even been breathing all this time.

"What's the matter?" Denise asked.

"A ghost!" Libby gasped out. "I heard a ghost!"

She didn't wait for a reply. She tore away and ran as fast as she could back the way they'd come. She heard her brother and cousin running behind her.

"Hey, Libby stop!" her brother called out. "Wait up!"

But there was no way she was going to stop running until she was safe at home.

CHAPTER FOUR

Riley knocked on April's bedroom door. It was noon, and it seemed high time for her daughter to get up. But the answer she got wasn't what she had been hoping for.

"What do you want?" came the muffled, sullen retort from inside the room.

"Are you going to sleep all day?" Riley asked.

"I'm up now. I'll be down in a minute."

With a sigh, Riley walked back down the stairs. She wished Gabriela was here, but she always took some time away on Sundays.

Riley plopped herself down on the couch. All day yesterday April had been sullen and distant. Riley hadn't known how to relieve the unidentified tension between them, and she'd been relieved when April had gone to a Halloween party in the evening. Since it had been at a friend's house a couple of blocks away, Riley hadn't worried. At least not until it got to be after one a.m. and her daughter wasn't home.

Fortunately, April had showed up while Riley was still undecided whether or not to take some kind of action. But April had come in and stalked off to bed with barely a word to her mother. And so far, she didn't sound any more inclined to communicate this morning.

Riley was glad that she was home to try to sort out whatever was wrong. She hadn't committed herself to the new case, and she was still feeling torn about it. Bill kept reporting to her, so she knew that yesterday he and Lucy Vargas had gone out to investigate Meara Keagan's disappearance. They'd interviewed the family Meara had been working for, and also her neighbors in her apartment building. They'd gotten no leads at all.

Today Lucy was taking charge of a general search, coordinating several agents who were passing out flyers with Meara's picture on them. Meanwhile, Bill was none too patiently waiting for Riley to decide whether to take the case or not.

But she didn't have to decide right away. Everybody at Quantico understood that Riley wouldn't be available tomorrow. One of the first killers she'd ever brought to justice was up for parole in Maryland. Not testifying at that hearing was simply out of the question.

As Riley sat mulling over her choices, April came bounding down the stairs, fully dressed. She charged into the kitchen without even giving her mother so much as a glance. Riley got up and followed her.

"What have we got to eat?" April asked, looking inside the refrigerator.

"I could fix you some breakfast," Riley said.

"That's okay. I'll find something."

April took out a piece of cheese and closed the refrigerator door. At the kitchen counter she cut off a slice of cheese and poured herself a cup of coffee. She added cream and sugar to the coffee, sat down at the kitchen table, and began to nibble on the cheese.

Riley sat down with her daughter.

"How was the party?" Riley asked.

"It was okay."

"You got home kind of late."

"No, I didn't."

Riley decided not to argue. Maybe one o'clock really wasn't late for fifteen-year-olds to be out at parties these days. How would she know?

"Crystal told me you have a boyfriend," Riley said.

"Yeah," April said, sipping her coffee.

"What's his name?"

"Joel."

After a few moments of silence, Riley asked, "How old is he?"

"I don't know."

Riley felt a knot of anxiety and anger rise up in her throat.

"How old is he?" Riley repeated.

"Fifteen, okay? The same as me."

Riley felt sure that April was lying.

"I'd like to meet him," Riley said.

April rolled her eyes. "Christ, Mom. When did you grow up? The fifties or something?"

Riley felt stung.

"I don't think that's unreasonable," Riley said. "Have him stop by. Introduce him to me."

April set down her coffee cup so hard it spilled a little onto the table.

"Why do you try to control me all the time?" she snapped.

"I'm not trying to control you. I just want to meet your boyfriend."

25

For a few moments, April just stared sullenly and silently into her coffee. Then she suddenly got up from the table and stormed out of the kitchen.

"April!" Riley yelled.

Riley followed April through the house. April went to the front door and grabbed her bag, which was hanging on the hat stand.

"Where are you going?" Riley said.

April didn't reply. She opened the door and went out, slamming the door behind her.

Riley stood in stunned silence for a few moments. Surely, she thought, April would come right back.

She waited for a whole minute. Then she went to the door, opened it, and looked up and down the street. There was no sign of April anywhere.

Riley felt the bitter taste of disappointment in her mouth. She wondered how things had gotten like this. She'd had tough times with April in the past. But when the three of them—Riley, April, and Gabriela—had moved to this townhouse during the summer, April had been very happy. She'd made friends with Crystal and had been fine when school started in September.

But now, just two months later, April had gone from a happy teenager back to being a sullen one. Had her PTSD kicked back in? April had suffered a delayed reaction after the killer named Peterson had caged her and tried to kill her. But she had been seeing a good therapist and had seemed to be working her way through those problems.

Still standing in the open doorway, Riley took her cell phone out of her pocket and texted April.

U come back here. Right now.

The text was marked as "delivered." Riley waited. Nothing happened. Had April left her own cell phone at home? No, that was not possible. April had grabbed her bag on the way out, and she never went anywhere without her cell phone.

Riley kept looking at the phone. The message was still marked as "delivered," not "read." Was April simply ignoring her text?

Just then, Riley felt pretty sure she knew where April had gone. She picked up a key from a table near the door and stepped out onto her little front porch. She went down the stairs from her townhouse and across the lawn to the next unit, where Blaine and Crystal lived. Again staring at her cell phone, she rang the doorbell.

When Blaine answered the door and saw her, a wide smile spread across his features.

"Well!" he said. "This is a nice surprise. What brings you over?"

Riley stammered awkwardly.

"I was wondering if ... Does April happen to be here? Visiting Crystal?"

"No," he said. "Crystal's not here either. She went to the coffee shop, she said. You know, the one close by."

Blaine knitted his brow with concern.

"What's the matter?" he asked. "Is there some kind of problem?"

Riley groaned. "We had a fight," she said. "She stormed out. I was hoping she'd come over here. I think she's ignoring my text."

"Come on in," Blaine said.

Riley followed him into his living room. The two of them sat down on the couch.

"I don't know what's going on with her," Riley said. "I don't know what's going on with us."

Blaine smiled wistfully.

"I know the feeling," he said.

Riley was a bit surprised.

"Do you?" she asked. "It always looks to me like you and Crystal get along perfectly."

"Most of the time, sure. But since she's gotten to be a teenager, it gets pretty rocky sometimes."

Blaine looked at Riley sympathetically for a moment.

"Don't tell me," he said. "It's got something to do with a boyfriend."

"Apparently," Riley said. "She won't tell me anything about him. And she refuses to introduce him to me."

Blaine shook his head.

"They're both at that age," he said. "Having a boyfriend is a life-and-death matter. Crystal doesn't have one yet, which is fine with me, but not with her. She's absolutely desperate about it."

"I guess I was the same at that age," Riley said.

Blaine chuckled a little. "Believe me, when I was fifteen, girls were just about all I ever thought about. Would you like some coffee?"

"I would, thanks. Black will be fine."

27

Blaine went to the kitchen. Riley looked around, noticing yet again how nicely decorated the place was. Blaine definitely had good taste.

Blaine came back with two cups of coffee. Riley took a sip. It was delicious.

"I swear, I didn't know what I was getting into when I became a mother," she said. "I guess it didn't help that I was way too young for it."

"How old were you?"

"Twenty-four."

Blaine threw back his head and laughed.

"I was younger. Got married at twenty-one. I thought Phoebe was the most beautiful girl I'd ever seen. Sexy as hell. I kind of overlooked that fact that she was also bipolar and already drank a lot."

Riley was more and more interested. She'd known that Blaine had been divorced, but little else. It seemed that she and Blaine had youthful mistakes in common. It had been too easy for them to see life through the rosy glow of physical attraction.

"How long did your marriage last?" Riley asked.

"About nine years. We should have ended it long before. *I* should have ended it. I kept thinking I could rescue Phoebe. It was a stupid idea. Crystal was born when Phoebe was twenty-one and I was twenty-two, a student in chef school. We were too poor and too immature. Our next baby was stillborn, and Phoebe never got over it. She became a complete alcoholic. She got abusive."

Blaine's look was farther away now. Riley sensed that he was reliving bitter memories that he didn't want to talk about.

"When April came along, I was in training to be an FBI agent," she said. "Ryan wanted me to give it up, but I wouldn't. He was dead set on becoming a successful lawyer. Well, we both got the careers we wanted. We just didn't have anything in common for the long haul. We couldn't make the real foundations of a marriage."

Riley fell silent under Blaine's sympathetic gaze. She felt relieved to be able to talk to another adult about all this. She was starting to realize that it was almost impossible to feel uncomfortable around Blaine. She felt as if she could talk to him about anything.

"Blaine, I'm really torn right now," she said. "I'm really needed on an important case. But things are such a mess at home. I feel like I'm not spending enough time with April."

Blaine smiled.

"Oh, yeah. The old work-versus-family dilemma. I know it well. Believe me, owning a restaurant is awfully time consuming. Making time for Crystal is a challenge."

Riley looked into Blaine's gentle blue eyes.

"How do you find a balance?" she asked.

Blaine shrugged slightly.

"You don't," he said. "There's not enough time for everything. But there's no point in punishing yourself for not being able to do the impossible. Believe me, giving up your career isn't a solution. I mean, Phoebe tried being a stay-at-home mom. It was part of what drove her crazy. You just have to make peace with it."

Riley smiled. It sounded like a wonderful idea—making peace with it. Maybe she could do that. It really did seem possible.

She reached over and touched Blaine's hand. He took her hand and squeezed it. Riley felt a delicious tension between them. For a moment, she thought that maybe she could stay with Blaine for while, now that both their children were occupied elsewhere. Maybe she could …

But even as the thoughts began to form in her mind, she felt herself drawing away from him. She wasn't ready to act on these fresh new feelings.

She gently pulled her hand away.

"Thanks," she said. "I'd better go home. For all I know, April's back already."

She exchanged goodbyes with Blaine. As soon as she stepped out the door, her phone buzzed. It was a text from April.

Just got ur text. Really sorry I acted like that. I'm at the coffee shop. Be back soon.

Riley sighed. She simply had no idea what to text back. It seemed best not to reply at all. She and April were going to have to have a serious talk later on.

Riley had just stepped back into her house when the phone buzzed again. It was a call from Ryan. Her ex was just about the last person in the world she wanted to hear from. But she knew that he'd keep leaving messages if she didn't talk to him now. She accepted the call.

"What do you want, Ryan?" she asked curtly.

"Am I catching you at a bad time?"

Riley wanted to say that no time was a good time as far as he was concerned. But she kept her thought to herself.

"Now's okay, I guess," she said.

"I was thinking about dropping by to see you and April," he said. "I'd like to talk to both of you."

Riley stifled a groan. "I'd rather you didn't do that."

"I thought you said this isn't a bad time."

Riley didn't reply. This was just like Ryan, twisting her words to try to manipulate her.

"How's April doing?" Ryan asked.

She almost snorted with laughter. She knew he was just trying to get some kind of conversation going.

"Nice of you to ask," Riley said sarcastically. "She's doing fine."

It was a lie, of course. But bringing Ryan into things was the last way to make them better.

"Listen, Riley …" Ryan's voice trailed off. "I've made a lot of mistakes."

No kidding, Riley thought. She kept silent.

After a few moments Ryan said, "Things haven't been going so well for me lately."

Riley still said nothing.

"Well, I just wanted to make sure that you and April are all right."

Riley could hardly believe his nerve.

"We're doing fine. Why do you ask? Has one of your new girlfriends left, Ryan? Or are things going badly at the office?"

"You're being awfully hard on me, Riley."

As far as she was concerned, she was being as gentle as she could manage. She understood the whole situation. Ryan must be alone right now. The socialite who had moved in with him after the divorce must have left, or some newer affair had gone sour.

She knew that Ryan couldn't stand being alone. He'd always turn back to Riley and April as a last resort. If she let him come back, it would only last until another woman caught his eye.

Riley said, "I think you ought to patch things up with your last girlfriend. Or the one before that. I don't even know how many you've been through since we've been divorced. How many, Ryan?"

She heard a slight gasp on the phone. Riley had definitely called it right.

"Ryan, the truth is this *isn't* a good time."

It was the truth. She'd just paid a nice visit to a man she liked. Why spoil it now?

"When will be a good time?" Ryan asked.

"I don't know," Riley said. "I'll let you know. Bye."

She ended the call. She'd been pacing since she'd started talking to Ryan. She sat down and took a few deep breaths to calm herself.

Then she sent a text message to April.

U'd better get home right now.

It only took a few seconds before she got a reply.

OK. I'm on my way. I'm sorry, Mom.

Riley sighed. April sounded fine now. She would probably be all right for a little while. But something was off.

What was going on with her?

CHAPTER FIVE

In his dimly lit lair, Scratch dashed frantically back and forth among the hundreds of clocks, trying to get everything ready. It was just a few minutes before midnight.

"Fix the one with the horse on it!" Grandpa yelled. *"It's a whole minute behind!"*

"I'll get to it," Scratch said.

Scratch knew he'd be punished anyway, but it would be especially bad if he didn't get everything ready on time. Right now he had his hands full with other clocks.

He fixed the clock with the curling metal flowers, which had fallen a full five minutes behind. Then he opened a grandfather clock and moved the minute hand just a little to the right.

He checked the big clock with deer antlers on top. It often fell behind, but it looked okay right now. Finally he was able to fix the one with the rearing horse on it. It was a good thing, too. It was all of seven minutes behind.

"That'll have to do," Grandpa grumbled. *"You know what to do next."*

Scratch obediently went to the table and picked up the whip. It was a cat o' nine tails, and Grandpa had started beating him with it when he was too young to remember.

He walked toward the end of the lair that was separated by a chain-link fence. Behind the fence were the four female captives, with no furnishings except wooden bunks without mattresses. There was a closet behind them where they went to relieve themselves. The stench had stopped bothering Scratch quite a while back.

The Irish woman he had fetched a couple of nights back was watching him carefully. After their long diet of crumbs and water, the others were wasted and weary. Two of them seldom did anything more than weep and moan. The fourth was just sitting on the floor near the fence, shrunken and cadaverous. She made no noise at all. She barely looked alive.

Scratch opened the door to the cage. The Irish woman leaped forward, trying to escape. Scratch lashed fiercely at her face with the whip. She cringed back, turning away. He whipped her back over and over again. He knew from experience that it would hurt plenty even through her tattered blouse, especially over the welts and cuts he'd given her already.

Then an uproar of noise filled the air as all the clocks began to strike the midnight hour. Scratch knew what he was supposed to do now.

As the racket continued, he hurried back to the weakest and skinniest girl, the one who seemed barely alive. She looked up at him with a strange expression. She was the only one who had been here long enough to know what he was about to do next. She looked almost as if she were ready for it, maybe even welcomed it.

Scratch had no choice.

He crouched beside her and snapped her neck.

As life ebbed out of her body, he stared up at an ornate antique clock just on the other side of the fence. A hand-carved Death was marching back and forth across the front of it, clad in a black robe, his grinning skull face peering out from beneath his cowl. He was cutting down knights and kings and queens and paupers alike. It was Scratch's favorite of all the clocks.

The surrounding noise slowly died away. Soon there was no sound at all except the chorus of ticking clocks and the whimpering of the women who still survived.

Scratch slung the dead girl over his shoulder. She was so feather-light that it took no effort at all. He opened the cage, stepped outside, and locked it behind him.

The time, he knew, had come.

CHAPTER SIX

A pretty good act, Riley thought.

Larry Mullins's voice was shaking a little. As he finished up his prepared statement to the parole board and the families of his victims, he sounded like he was on the verge of tears.

"I've had fifteen years to look back," Mullins said. "Not a day goes by when I'm not filled with regret. I can't go back and change what happened. I can't bring Nathan Betts and Ian Harter back to life. But I still have years to make a meaningful contribution to society. Please give me a chance to do that."

Mullins sat down. His lawyer handed him a handkerchief, and he wiped his eyes—although Riley didn't see any actual tears.

The hearing officer and case manager conferred with each other in whispers. So did the members of the parole board.

Riley knew it would soon be her turn to testify. Meanwhile, she studied Mullins's face.

She remembered him well and thought that he hadn't changed much. Even back then, he had been well-scrubbed and well-spoken with an earnest air of innocence about him. If he was more hardened now, he hid it behind his expressions of abject sorrow. Back then he had been working as a nanny—or a "manny," as his lawyer preferred to say.

What struck Riley most was how little he'd aged. He'd been twenty-five when he'd gone to prison. He still had the same amiable, boyish expression that he'd had back then.

The same wasn't true of the victims' parents. The two couples looked prematurely old and broken in spirit. Riley's heart ached for all their years of grief and sorrow.

She wished she'd been able to do right by them from the beginning. So had her first FBI partner, Jake Crivaro. It had been one of Riley's first cases as an agent, and Jake had been a fine mentor.

Larry Mullins had been arrested on a charge of the death of one child on a playground. During their investigation, Riley and Jake found that another child had died under almost identical circumstances while in Mullins's care in a different city. Both children had been suffocated.

When Riley had apprehended Mullins, read him his rights, and cuffed him, his smirking, gloating expression had all but admitted his guilt to her.

"Good luck," he had said to her sarcastically.

Indeed, luck turned against Riley and Jake as soon as Mullins was in custody. He had firmly denied committing the murders. And despite Riley's and Jake's best efforts, the evidence against him remained dangerously thin. It had been impossible to determine just how the boys had been suffocated, and no murder weapon had been found. Mullins himself only admitted to letting them out of his sight. He'd denied murdering either of them.

Riley remembered what the chief prosecutor had said to her and Jake.

"We've got to be careful, or the bastard will walk. If we try to prosecute him on all possible charges, we'll lose the whole thing. We can't prove that Mullins was the only person who had access to the children when they were killed."

Then came the plea-bargaining. Riley hated plea bargains. Her hatred for them had started with that case. Mullins's lawyer offered the deal. Mullins would plead guilty to both murders, but not as premeditated killings, and his sentences would run simultaneously.

It was a lousy deal. It didn't even make sense. If Mullins had really killed the children, how could he have also been merely negligent? The two conclusions were completely contradictory. But the prosecutor saw no choice but to accept the deal. Mullins finally faced thirty years in prison with the possibility of parole or early release for good behavior.

The families had been crushed and horrified. They'd blamed Riley and Jake for not doing their job. Jake had retired as soon as the case was over, a bitter and angry man.

Riley had promised the boys' families she would do everything she could to keep Mullins behind bars. A few days ago, Nathan Betts's parents had called Riley to tell her about the parole hearing. The time had come for her to keep her promise.

The general whispering came to an end. Hearing Officer Julie Simmons looked at Riley.

"I understand that FBI Special Agent Riley Paige would like to make a statement," Simmons said.

Riley gulped hard. The moment she had spent fifteen years preparing for had arrived. She knew the parole board was familiar with all of the evidence already, as incomplete as it was. There was no point in going over it again. She had to make a more personal appeal.

She stood up and spoke.

"As I understand it, Larry Mullins is up for parole because he is an 'exemplary prisoner.'" With a note of irony, she added, "Mr. Mullins, I congratulate you on your achievement."

Mullin nodded, his face showing no expression. Riley continued.

"'Exemplary behavior'—what does that mean, exactly? It seems to me that it has less to do with what he has done than with what he *hasn't* done. He hasn't broken prison rules. He's behaved himself. That's all."

Riley struggled to keep her voice steady.

"Frankly, I'm not surprised. There aren't any children in prison for him to kill."

There were gasps and murmurs in the room. Mullins's smile turned into a steady glare.

"Pardon me," Riley said. "I realize that Mullins never pleaded to premeditated murder, and the prosecution never pursued that verdict. But he pleaded guilty nonetheless. He killed two children. There is no way he could have done so with good intentions."

She paused a moment, choosing her next words carefully. She wanted to goad Mullins into showing his anger, showing his true colors. But of course the man knew that if he did, he'd ruin his record of good behavior and would never get out. Her best strategy was to make the board members face the reality of what he had done.

"I saw Ian Harter's lifeless four-year-old body the day after he was killed. He looked like he was asleep with his eyes open. Death had taken all expression away, and his face was slack and peaceful. Even so, I could still see the terror in his lifeless eyes. His last moments on this earth were filled with terror. It was the same for little Nathan Betts."

Riley heard both mothers begin to cry. She hated bringing back those awful memories, but she simply had no choice.

"We mustn't forget their terror," Riley said. "And we mustn't forget that Mullins showed little emotion during his trial, and certainly no sign of remorse. His remorse came much, much later—if it was ever real at all."

Riley took a long, slow breath.

"How many years of life did he take away from those boys if you add them together? Much, much more than a hundred, it seems to me. He got a sentence of thirty years. He's only served fifteen. It's not enough. He'll never live long enough to pay back all those lost years."

Riley's voice was shaking now. She knew she had to control herself. She couldn't break down in tears or shout with rage.

"Has the time come to forgive Larry Mullins? I leave that up to the boys' families. Forgiveness really isn't what this hearing is about. It's just not the point. The most important matter is the danger he still presents. We can't risk the likelihood that more children will die at his hands."

Riley noticed that a couple of people on the parole board were checking their watches. She panicked a little. The board had already reviewed two other cases this morning, and they had four more to finish before noon. They were getting impatient. Riley had to wrap this up immediately. She looked straight at them.

"Ladies and gentleman, I implore you not to grant this parole."

Then she said, "Perhaps someone else would like to speak on the prisoner's behalf."

Riley sat down. Her final words had been double-edged. She knew perfectly well that not one single person was here to speak in Mullins's defense. Despite all his "good behavior," he still didn't have a friend or defender in the world. Nor, Riley was sure, did he deserve one.

"Would anybody like to speak?" the hearing officer asked.

"I would just like to add a few words," a voice said from the back of the room.

Riley gasped. She knew that voice well.

She whirled around in her seat and saw a familiar short, barrel-chested man standing in the back of the room. It was Jake Crivaro—the last person she expected to see today. Riley was delighted and surprised.

Jake came forward and stated his name and rank for the board members, then said, "I can tell you that this guy is a master manipulator. Don't believe him. He's lying. He showed no remorse when we caught him. What you are seeing is all an act."

Jake stepped right up to the table and leaned across it toward Mullins.

"Bet you didn't expect to see me today," he said, his voice full of contempt. "I wouldn't have missed it—you child-killing little prick of a weasel."

The hearing officer banged her gavel.

"Order!" she shouted.

"Oh, I'm sorry," Jake said mock-apologetically. "I didn't mean to insult our model prisoner. After all, he's rehabilitated now. He's a *repentant* child-killing little prick of a weasel."

Jake just stood there, looking down at Mullins. Riley studied the prisoner's expression. She knew that Jake was doing his best to provoke an outburst from Mullins. But the prisoner's face remained stony and calm.

"Mr. Crivaro, please take your seat," the hearing officer said. "The board may make their decision now."

The board members huddled together to share their notes and thoughts. Their whispering was animated and tense. Meanwhile, there was nothing for Riley to do but wait.

Donald and Melanie Betts were now sobbing. Darla Harter was weeping, and her husband, Ross, was holding her hand. He was staring straight at Riley. His look cut through her like a knife. What did he think of the testimony she just gave? Did he think it made up for her failure all those years ago?

The room was too warm, and she felt sweat breaking on her brow. Her heart was beating anxiously.

It only took a few minutes for the huddle to break up. One of the board members whispered to the hearing officer. She turned toward everybody else who was present.

"Parole is denied," she said. "Let's get started on the next case."

Riley gasped aloud at the woman's bluntness, as if the case were about nothing more than a parking ticket. But she reminded herself that the board was in a hurry to move on with the rest of their morning work.

Riley stood up, and both couples rushed toward her. Melanie Betts threw herself into Riley's arms.

"Oh, thank you, thank you, thank you ..." she kept saying

The three other parents crowded around her, smiling through their tears and saying "thank you" over and over again.

She saw that Jake was standing aside in the hallway. As soon as she could, she left the parents and ran to him.

"Jake!" she said, giving him a hug. "How long has it been?"

"Too long," Jake said with that sideways smile of his. "You kids today never write or call."

Riley sighed. Jake had always treated her like a daughter. And it really was true that she should have stayed in better touch.

"So how have you been?" she asked.

"I'm seventy-five years old," he said. "I've had both knees and a hip replaced. My eyes are shot. I've got a hearing aid and a pacemaker. And all my friends except you have croaked. How do you think I've been?"

Riley smiled. He'd aged quite a lot since she'd last seen him. Even so, he didn't seem nearly as frail as he was making himself out to be. She was sure he could still do his old job if he was ever needed again.

"Well, I'm glad you were able to talk yourself in here," she said.

"You shouldn't be surprised," Jake said. "I'm at least as smooth a talker as that bastard Mullins."

"Your statement really helped," Riley said.

Jake shrugged. "Well, I wish I could've gotten a rise out of him. I'd love to have seen him lose it in front of the parole board. But he's cooler and smarter than I remember. Maybe prison has taught him that. Anyway, we got a good decision even without getting him to freak out. Maybe he'll stay behind bars for good."

Riley didn't say anything for a moment. Jake gave her a curious look.

"Is there something you're not telling me?" he asked.

"I'm afraid it's not that simple," Riley said. "If Mullins keeps racking up points for good behavior, his early release will probably be mandatory in another year. There's nothing you or I or anybody can do about it."

"Jesus," Jake said, looking as bitter and angry as he had all those years before.

Riley knew just how he felt. It was heartbreaking to imagine Mullins going free. Today's small victory now seemed much more bitter than sweet.

"Well, I've got to be going," Jake said. "It was great seeing you."

Riley sadly watched her old partner walk away. She understood why he wasn't going to hang around to indulge in negative feelings. That just wasn't his way. She made a mental note to get in touch with him soon.

She also tried to find a bright side to what had just happened. After fifteen long years, the Bettses and the Harters had finally forgiven her. But Riley didn't feel as if she deserved forgiveness, any more than did Larry Mullins.

Just then, Larry Mullins was led out in handcuffs.

He turned to look at her and smiled wide, mouthing his evil words silently.

"See you next year."

CHAPTER SEVEN

Riley was in her car and headed back home when she got the call from Bill. She put her phone on speaker.

"What's going on?" she asked.

"We've found another body," he said. "In Delaware."

"Was it Meara Keagan?" Riley asked.

"No. We haven't identified the victim. This is just like the other two, only worse."

Riley let the facts of the situation sink in. Meara Keagan was still being held captive. The killer might be holding other women captive as well. It was all but certain that the killings would continue. How many killings was anybody's guess.

Bill's voice was agitated.

"Riley, I'm losing my mind here," he said. "I know I'm not thinking straight. Lucy's a great help, but she's still awfully green."

Riley understood perfectly how he felt. The irony felt palpable. Here she was beating herself up about the Larry Mullins case. Meanwhile in Delaware, Bill felt as if his own past failure had cost a third woman her life.

Riley thought about the drive to wherever Bill was. It would probably take nearly three hours to get there.

"Are you finished there?" Bill asked.

Riley had told both Bill and Brent Meredith that she would be in Maryland today for the parole hearing.

"Yeah," she said.

"Good," Bill said. "I've sent a helicopter to pick you up."

"You what?" Riley said with a gasp.

"There's a private airport near where you are. I'll text you the location. The chopper is probably there already. There's a cadet on board who'll drive your car back."

Without another word, Bill ended the call.

Riley drove in silence for a moment. She had been relieved when the hearing had ended during the morning. She wanted to be home when her daughter got out of school. There had been no more arguments yesterday, but April hadn't said much at all. This morning Riley had left before April was awake.

But the decision had obviously been made for her. Ready or not, she was on the new case. She would have to talk to April later.

But she didn't have to think long before it seemed perfectly right. She turned her car around and followed the directions Bill had sent her. The surest cure for her feeling of failure would be to bring another killer to justice—*real* justice.

It was time.

*

Riley stared down at the dead girl lying on the wooden bandstand floor. It was a bright, cool morning. The bandstand was housed in a gazebo right in the center of the town square, surrounded by nicely kept grass and trees.

The victim looked shockingly like the girls in the photos Riley had seen of the two victims from earlier months. She was lying face up and so emaciated that she appeared to be positively mummified. Her dirty, torn clothing might have once fit but now looked grotesquely large on her. She bore old scars and more recent wounds from what looked like the lashes of a whip.

Riley guessed that she was about seventeen, the age of the other two murder victims.

Or maybe not, she thought.

After all, Meara Keagan was twenty-four. The killer might be changing his MO. This girl was too wasted away for Riley to be able to determine her age.

Riley was standing between Bill and Lucy.

"She looks like she was starved more than the other two," Bill remarked. "He must have kept her for a lot longer."

Riley heard a world of self-reproach in Bill's words. She looked at her partner. The bitterness showed in his face as well. Riley knew what Bill was thinking. This girl had surely been alive and held captive when he'd investigated this case and come up with nothing. He was blaming himself for her death.

Riley knew that he shouldn't blame himself. Even so, she didn't know what to say to make him feel better. Her own regrets about the Larry Mullins case still left a bad taste in her mouth.

Riley turned around to take in her surroundings. From here, the only completely visible structure was the courthouse across the street—a large brick building with a clock tower. Redditch was a charming little colonial town. Riley wasn't really surprised that the body could have been brought here in the dead of night without anybody noticing. The whole town would have been fast asleep. The square was lined with sidewalks, so the killer hadn't left any footprints.

42

The local police had taped off the square and were keeping onlookers away. But Riley could see that some press had gathered outside the tapes.

She was worried. So far, the press hadn't caught on that the two previous murders and Meara Keagan's disappearance had all been connected. But with this new murder, somebody was liable to connect the dots. The public would know sooner or later. Then the investigation would become a lot more difficult.

Standing nearby was Redditch's police chief Aaron Pomeroy.

"How and when was the body found?" Riley asked him.

"We've got a street cleaner who goes out to work before dawn. He found her."

Pomeroy looked badly shaken. He was an overweight, aging man. Riley figured that even in a little town like this, a cop his age had handled a murder or two somewhere along the line. But he'd probably never dealt with anything this disturbing.

Agent Lucy Vargas crouched beside the corpse and studied it closely.

"Our killer's awfully confident," Lucy said.

"How do you figure?" Riley asked.

"Well, he's putting the bodies out for display," she said. "Metta Lunoe was found in an open field, Valerie Bruner by the side of a road. Only about half of all serial killers transport their victims away from the murder site. Of those who do, about half conceal them. And most bodies that are left in view are just dumped. This kind of display suggests that he's pretty cocky."

Riley was pleased that Lucy had paid good attention in class. But somehow she didn't think that cockiness was this killer's point. He wasn't trying to show off or taunt the authorities. He was up to something else. Riley didn't yet know what it was.

But she was pretty sure it had something to do with the way the body was laid out. It was both awkward and deliberate. The girl's left arm was stretched straight above her head. Her right arm was also straight but placed slightly to one side of her body. Even the head, with its broken neck, had been straightened to align as well as possible with the rest of the body.

Riley thought back to the photos of the other victims. She noticed that Lucy was carrying a tablet computer.

Riley asked her, "Lucy, could you bring up the photos of the other two corpses?"

It took Lucy only a few seconds to comply. Riley and Bill crowded next to Lucy to look at the two images.

Bill pointed and said, "Metta Lunoe's corpse was a mirror image of this one—right arm raised, left arm to the side of the body. Valerie Bruner's right arm was raised but her left arm was placed across the body, pointed downwards."

Riley stooped down and took hold of the corpse's wrist and tried to move it. The whole arm was immobile. Rigor mortis had fully set in. It would take a medical examiner to determine the exact time of death, but Riley felt pretty sure that the girl had been dead for at least nine hours. And like the other girls, she'd been moved to this spot shortly after she'd been killed.

The more she looked, the more something nagged at Riley. The killer had gone to so much trouble to arrange the corpse. He'd carried the body across the square, up six stairs, and had meticulously manipulated it. Even so, its overall position didn't make sense.

The body wasn't aligned with any of the gazebo walls. It wasn't related to the opening of the gazebo or to the courthouse or anything else that Riley could see. It seemed to be laid out at a random angle.

But this guy doesn't do anything random, she thought.

Riley sensed that the killer was trying to communicate something. She had no idea what it might be.

"What do you make of the poses?" Riley asked Lucy.

"I don't know," Lucy said. "Not many killers actually pose their bodies. It's weird."

She's still really new to this job, Riley reminded herself.

Lucy hadn't caught on that the weird cases were exactly the ones they routinely got called in for. For seasoned agents like Riley and Bill, weirdness had long since become numbingly normal.

Riley said, "Lucy, let's take a look at the map."

Lucy brought up the map that showed where the other two bodies had been found.

"The bodies have been placed in a pretty tight cluster," Lucy said, pointing again. "Valerie Bruner was found less than ten miles from where Metta Lunoe was found. And this one is less than ten miles from where Valerie Bruner was found."

Riley could see that Lucy was right. However, Meara Keagan had disappeared quite a few miles to the north in Westree.

"Does anybody see any connections among the locations?" Riley asked Bill and Lucy.

"Not really," Lucy said. "Metta Lunoe's body was in a field outside of Mowbray. Valerie Bruner's was just along the edge of a highway. And now this one right in the middle of a small town. It's almost as if the killer was looking for places that have nothing in common."

Just then Riley heard shouting from among the onlookers.

"I know who did it! I know who did it!"

Riley, Bill, and Lucy all turned to look. A young man was waving and shouting from behind the tape.

"I know who did it!" he cried again.

CHAPTER EIGHT

Riley took a careful look at the man who was shouting. She could see that several people around him were nodding and murmuring in agreement.

"I know who did it! We all know who did it!"

"Josh is right," a woman next to him said. "It's got to be Dennis."

"He's a weirdo," another man said. "That guy has always been a ticking bomb."

Bill and Lucy hurried toward the edge of the square where the man was shouting, but Riley held her position. She called out to one of the cops beyond the tape.

"Bring him over here," she said, pointing to the man who was doing the yelling.

She knew it was important to separate him from the group. If everybody started pitching in with stories, the truth would be impossible to untangle. If there was any truth in what everybody was yelling about.

Besides, reporters were starting to cluster around him. It wouldn't do for Riley to interview the guy right under their noses.

The cop lifted the tape and escorted the man toward them.

He was still yelling, "We all know who did it! We all know who did it!"

"Calm down," Riley said, taking him by the arm and leading him far enough away from the onlookers to be able to talk to him unheard.

"Ask anybody about Dennis," the agitated man was saying. "He's a loner. He's weird. He scares girls. He annoys women."

Riley got out her notepad, and so did Bill. She saw the intense interest in Bill's eyes. But she knew they'd better take things slowly. They barely knew anything just yet. Besides, this man was so agitated that Riley felt wary of his judgment. She needed to hear from somebody more neutral.

"What's his full name?" Riley asked.

"Dennis Vaughn," the man said.

"Keep talking to him," Riley told Bill.

Bill nodded and kept taking notes. Riley walked back to the gazebo, where Police Chief Aaron Pomeroy was still standing beside the body.

"Chief Pomeroy, what can you tell me about Dennis Vaughn?"

Riley could tell by his expression that the name was all too familiar.

"What do you want to know about him?" he asked.

"Do you think he might be a viable suspect?"

Pomeroy scratched his head. "Now that you mention it, maybe so. At least he might be worth talking to."

"Why is that?"

"Well, we've had a lot of trouble with him for years. Indecent exposure, lewd behavior, that kind of thing. A couple of years ago it was window peeping, and he spent some time in the Delaware Psychiatric Center. Last year he got obsessed with a high school cheerleader, wrote letters to her and stalked her. The girl's family got a court injunction, but he ignored it. So he did six months in prison."

"When was he released?" she asked.

"Back in February."

Riley was getting more and more interested. Dennis Vaughn had gotten out of prison shortly before the killings had started. Was it merely a coincidence?

"Local girls and women are starting to complain," Pomeroy said. "Rumor has it that he's been snapping pictures of them. It's nothing we can arrest him for—at least not yet."

"What else can you tell me about him?" Riley asked.

Pomeroy shrugged. "Well, he's kind of a bum. He's maybe thirty years old and he's never held down a job that anybody can remember. Sponges off family he's got here in town—aunts, uncles, grandparents. I hear that he's been real sullen lately. Holds it against the whole town that he had to do prison time. He keeps telling folks, 'One of these days.'"

"'One of these days' what?" Riley asked.

"Nobody knows. Folks have started calling him a ticking bomb. They don't know what he might do next. But he's actually never been violent that we know of."

Riley's mind was racing, trying to make sense of this possible new lead.

Meanwhile, Bill and Lucy had finished talking to the man and were walking toward Riley and Pomeroy.

Bill's face looked bright and confident—a sudden change from his recent gloomy demeanor.

"Dennis Vaughn's our killer, all right," he told Riley. "Everything the guy just told us fits the profile perfectly."

Riley didn't reply. It was starting to seem likely, but she knew better than to jump to conclusions.

Besides, the certainty in Bill's voice made her nervous. Ever since she'd arrived here this morning, she'd felt like Bill was teetering on the brink of really erratic behavior. It was understandable given his personal feelings about the case, especially his guilt over not solving it sooner. But it could also get to be a serious problem. She needed him to be his usual rock-solid self.

She turned toward Pomeroy.

"Could you tell us where to find him?"

"Sure," Pomeroy said, pointing. "Walk straight along Main Street until you get to Brattleboro. Turn left, and his house is the third one to the right."

Riley told Lucy, "You stay and wait for the medical examiner's team. It's fine for them to take the body right away. We've got lots of photographs."

Lucy nodded.

Bill and Riley walked toward the police tape, where reporters craned toward them with cameras and microphones.

"Does the FBI have a statement to make?" asked one.

"Not yet," Riley said.

She and Bill ducked under the tape and pushed their way among the reporters and onlookers.

Another reporter yelled, "Does this killing have anything to do with the murders of Metta Lunoe and Valerie Bruner?"

"Or with Meara Keagan's disappearance?" another asked.

Riley bristled. It wouldn't be long before the news was widespread that there was a serial killer in Delaware.

"No comment," she snapped at the reporters. Then she added, "If you keep following us I'll arrest you for interfering with an investigation. It's called obstruction of justice."

The reporters backed away. Riley and Bill disentangled themselves from the small crowd and continued on their way. Riley knew they wouldn't have a lot of time on this case before other, more aggressive reporters arrived on the scene. They were likely to have a lot of media attention to deal with.

It was a short walk to Dennis Vaughn's house. After just three blocks, they got to Brattleboro and turned left.

Vaughn's house was a dilapidated little ruin with a heavily dented tin roof, peeling white paint, and a sagging front porch. The lawn was knee-deep with grass and weeds, and an old, decrepit-looking Plymouth Valiant was parked in the driveway. The vehicle was certainly large enough for the transportation of emaciated corpses.

Bill and Riley walked up onto the porch and knocked on the screen door.

"Whaddya want?" called a voice from inside.

"Are we speaking to Dennis Vaughn?" Bill answered.

"Yeah, maybe. Why?"

Riley said, "We're with the FBI. We want to talk to you."

The front door opened. Dennis Vaughn stood behind the screen door, which was still hooked shut. He was an unsavory-looking young man, overweight, with a shaggy beard. Excessive body hair showed under his torn, food-stained undershirt.

"What's this all about?" Vaughn asked in a petulant, quavering voice. "Are you here to arrest me or what?"

"We've just got some questions," Riley said, showing her badge. "Could we come inside?"

"Why should I let you in?" Vaughn asked.

"Why shouldn't you let us in?" Riley asked. "You don't have anything to hide, do you?"

"We could come back with a warrant," Bill added.

Vaughn shook his head and growled. He unhooked the screen door and Bill and Riley stepped inside.

The house was even more of a wreck inside. The wallpaper was peeling, and there were broken gaps in the floorboards. There was hardly any furniture—just a couple of battered straight-back chairs and a couch with its stuffing hanging out. Plates and bowls were scattered everywhere, some of them filled with moldy food. Disagreeable smells filled the air.

What caught Riley's eye were dozens of photographs randomly thumbtacked to the walls. All of them were of women and girls in casual, unsuspecting poses.

Vaughn noticed Riley's interest in the pictures.

"It's my hobby," he said. "Is there anything wrong with that?"

Riley didn't reply, and Bill said nothing. Riley doubted there was anything illegal about the pictures themselves. It looked as if they'd all been taken outdoors in public places in broad daylight, and none were actually indecent. Even so, the very act of snapping pictures of girls and women without their knowledge or consent struck Riley as deeply creepy.

Vaughn sat down on a wooden chair that creaked under his weight.

"You're here to accuse me of something," he said. "So why don't you get on with it?"

Riley sat down on another rickety chair facing him. Bill stood beside her.

"What do you think we're here to accuse of you of?" she asked.

It was an interview technique that had worked well for her in the past. Sometimes it was best not to start with direct questions about a case. Sometimes it was better to get a potential suspect talking until he tripped himself up with his own words.

Vaughn shrugged.

"One thing or another," he said. "It's always something. Everybody always misunderstands."

"Misunderstands what?" Riley asked, still trying to coax him along.

"I like girls, okay?" he said. "What guy my age doesn't? Why do people think everything I do is wrong just because *I* do it?"

He glanced around at some of the pictures, as if he hoped they'd say something to defend him. Riley just waited for him to keep talking. She hoped that Bill would do the same, but her partner's impatience was tense and palpable.

"I try to be friendly with girls," he said. "Can I help it if they don't understand?"

His voice was slow, even a bit sluggish. Riley felt pretty sure he wasn't drunk or drugged. Perhaps he was a bit mentally slow or had some neurological problem.

"Why do you think people treat you differently?" Riley said, trying to sound almost sympathetic.

"How should I know?" Vaughn said, shrugging again.

Then in an almost inaudible sullen voice he added ...

"One of these days."

"'One of these days' what?" Riley asked.

Vaughn shrugged yet again. "Nothing. I don't mean anything. But one of these days. That's all I'm saying."

Riley felt encouraged that his talk was becoming nonsensical. That often happened before a suspect really betrayed himself.

But before Vaughn could say anything else, Bill stepped toward him menacingly.

"What do you know about the murders of Metta Lunoe and Valerie Bruner?"

"I never heard of them," Vaughn said.

Bill bent uncomfortably close to him and peered into his eyes. Riley was worried now. She wanted to tell Bill to knock it off. But interfering might make things worse.

"What about Meara Keagan?" Bill asked.

"Never heard of her either."

Bill was talking more loudly now.

"Where were you last Thursday night?"

"I don't know."

"You mean you weren't at home?"

Vaughn was sweating nervously. His eyes were wide with alarm.

"Maybe I wasn't. I don't keep track. I go out sometimes."

"Where do you go?"

"I go driving around. I like to get out of town. I hate this town. I wish I could live someplace else."

Bill spat his next question in Vaughn's face.

"And where were you driving around last Thursday?"

"I don't know. I don't even know if I was driving around that night."

"You're lying," Bill shouted. "You were driving around Westree, weren't you? You found a nice lady there, didn't you?"

Riley shot out of her seat. Bill was clearly out of control now. She had to stop him.

"Bill," she said quietly, grabbing him by the shoulder.

Bill shoved away her hand. He pushed Vaughn over in the chair. Already on the verge of breaking, the chair fell to pieces. Vaughn was sprawled on the floor for a moment. Then Bill grabbed him by the undershirt and hauled him across the room, pushing him back first against the wall.

"Bill, stop it," Riley shouted.

Bill was pressing Vaughn against the wall. Riley was afraid he might pull his gun at any second.

"Prove it!" Bill snarled.

Riley managed to get between Bill and Vaughn. She pushed Bill back forcefully.

"That's enough!" she snapped loudly. "We're leaving!"

Bill was staring at her, his eyes wild with rage.

Riley turned to Vaughn and said, "I'm sorry. My partner's sorry. We'll go now."

Without waiting for Vaughn to say anything, Riley shoved Bill toward the front door, then out onto the porch.

"What the hell's the matter with you?" she hissed at him.

"What's the matter with *you*? Let me back in there. We've got him. I know we've got him. We'll make him show us his driver's license, find out what his middle name is."

"No," Riley said. "We're not going to make him do anything. Jesus, Bill, you could lose your badge for acting like that. You know better."

Bill looked like he couldn't believe his ears. "Why?" he demanded. "We've got him. We could get a confession."

Riley felt like shaking him.

"We don't know that. Maybe he is our guy, but I don't think so."

"Why the hell not?"

"For one thing, that car of his is too easily spotted and remembered."

Bill thought for a moment.

"So he used a different car."

"Maybe, but I don't think he's organized enough to carry out this many murders without getting caught."

"That could be just an act."

Riley was getting impatient at Bill's resistance.

"Bill, think of how carefully all these bodies were placed. Stretched out so neatly. Arms placed in exact positions."

"He could have done that."

Riley groaned aloud. Bill was really being stubborn.

"I don't think he could," Riley said. "Think about his house. Nothing is placed neatly, not even the photographs. Nothing looks intentional. Absolutely nothing."

"Except maybe that he intends to kill," Bill said. He was still angry, but Riley could see that he was settling down.

"Bill," she said. "There's some purpose driving this killer, some rationale for what he's doing. So far, we can't guess his reasons, but that's what I intend to find out."

Neither Riley nor Bill said a word during the short walk back. As the town square came into sight, Riley saw that the medical examiner's vehicle had arrived and the body was being taken away.

52

Riley felt badly shaken. The interview had been a disaster, and she had no idea whether Dennis Vaughn was their suspect or not.

Riley's worry now bordered on panic.

If I can't count on Bill, who can I count on?

CHAPTER NINE

Riley was anxious to get Bill away from Redditch without any further trouble. Luckily, she had no problem finding a good reason to go elsewhere. She always wanted to visit crime scenes in person, even after the victims' bodies had long since been removed. She often got her best hunches that way. Sometimes she could even get into the killer's mind.

So just an hour after the disastrous interview, Bill was driving her to see the locations where the first two bodies had been found. He was focused on the road ahead, clutching the wheel and not talking.

During the drive she'd tried a couple of times to get him to talk about what had just happened. He'd refused to say a single word, obviously angry with Riley for pulling him away from Dennis Vaughn a little while ago.

She had no idea what her partner thought he'd accomplished by terrorizing Vaughn.

Riley felt pretty sure that Dennis Vaughn wouldn't complain to the police about the abuse he'd suffered. He was much too despised in Redditch for anyone to believe him. But that didn't make Riley feel any better about what had happened.

They were heading eastward from Redditch, making their way along rural roads. When they reached a highway crossing, Bill finally spoke.

He said, "The locals call this the 'Six O'clock Highway,' because it goes straight north and south."

Riley felt relieved that he'd finally said something.

Bill turned right onto the highway. He soon slowed and pulled the car over onto the shoulder. He and Riley both got out of the car, and he walked directly to a particular spot.

He pointed to the ground and said, "This is where Valerie Bruner's body turned up."

Riley was impressed at his precision. This stretch of highway didn't have any distinguishing landmarks to speak of. Bill must have memorized every bush or tree along here. He had obsessively noted every detail.

She wasn't surprised. Bill had been here before Valerie Bruner's corpse was taken away in June. Riley knew that the scene was still extremely vivid in his mind.

As she studied the location, she remembered the photograph that Lucy had shown them earlier. Valerie Bruner's body had been laid out about six feet away from the pavement, her limbs arranged in the position that suggested a D in semaphore code.

"The killer stretched her out exactly parallel to the pavement," Riley said. "The body we just saw back in Redditch wasn't laid out like that. It wasn't lined up with anything in particular."

"So what?" Bill muttered almost inaudibly.

Riley paced back and forth, examining the place closely. Then she stopped and shut her eyes, trying to get some feeling of the killer's presence. She took a few long, deep breaths. It was no good. She was coming up blank.

"Let's go," she told Bill.

They got back into the car. Bill drove back the way they'd come, then turned east onto a county road. The silence continued.

"Bill, if we can't even talk about the case, we've got a problem," she said.

"Who says we can't talk about the case?" Bill said. "I'm fine talking about the case. It just doesn't seem like there's much to say yet."

Riley sighed. She wondered how long his defensiveness could go on. She and Bill had been seriously at odds a few times in the past, but it was very rare for friction between them to interfere with their work.

As the car neared the Atlantic coast, the colorful leaves of autumn gave way to more barren surroundings—most of it sandy with patches of tall grass. Some distance ahead, Riley saw strange towering structures that looked to her like the gigantic skeleton of some long-extinct beast. She wondered if Delaware's sand dunes hid other skeletons, remnants of crimes committed just a few miles from the Atlantic Ocean.

She knew that those structures were actually a perfectly ordinary Ferris wheel and a rollercoaster. There was an amusement park in the beachside tourist town of Mowbray.

Just when they reached the outskirts of town, Bill pulled over again and stopped.

"This is the place," he said. "Out here in the sand."

They both got out of the car and walked out across a broad stretch of sand. A hint of calliope music drifted eerily across the way from the amusement park. They followed a windbreak fence that ran perpendicular to the highway. There were a few houses not far away on the other side of the fence. After about a hundred yards, they stopped walking. Bill pointed to a tattered handkerchief that was tied to the fence.

"This marks the spot," he said.

Bill's eyes darkened as he stared at the spot on the ground. Riley could imagine what he was thinking and feeling. Although he hadn't yet been on the case when Metta Lunoe's body had been found here in May, he had been here since then. Riley knew that he had pored over the place with utmost care. This location must have been haunting him for months now.

Riley closed her eyes and breathed long and deep, trying to get a feeling of the killer's presence. The sound of music tangled up in the wind made it easier to do this time. Doubtless the killer had heard the same sounds on the night when he had brought the body here.

She could see him park his car about where Bill had parked. He opened his trunk, lifted out Metta Lunoe's emaciated corpse, slung it across his shoulder, then trudged to this spot in the sand.

Was the moon out that night? she wondered.

She should have checked before coming out here. But even if there had been moonlight, he surely was carrying a flashlight. She imagined the kinds of weird shadows the fence would have cast. It all seemed very clear.

And the music—the song was old and familiar, and he probably knew it. Did he hum or whistle along with it as he went about his grisly task? No. She felt sure that he didn't. He wasn't gloating or even playful like some other killers she'd hunted. He took his job as seriously as she and Bill did theirs.

But there were houses nearby, on the far side of the fence. At night, their lights would be on. Somebody sitting on a back porch might even see what he was doing. Did this worry him? It must have, but not enough to make him seek out a more out-of-the-way spot. He had his reasons to be exactly here. He wasn't going to vary from his plan.

And he had the body's exact position in his head—right arm raised, left arm to the side of the body.

But when Riley imagined the killer laying the body on the ground, something odd happened. He *must* have had an impulse to arrange it neatly in relation to the surroundings—the fence, especially. It would only feel natural to lay it out parallel to the fence, or perhaps perpendicular to it.

But he hadn't done that. She remembered from the photos. The body's feet had been almost right next to the fence. The head had been angled away from the fence a little. A tuft of weeds had poked out from behind the head, making the position look all the more awkward.

Why? Riley wondered.

In her gut, she felt a hunch taking shape.

It wasn't his idea, she thought.

She felt sure of it somehow. *None* of this was his idea. Not the meticulous poses, the peculiar angles, or perhaps even the murders themselves.

He was following orders.

Riley's eyes snapped open. She saw that Bill was looking at her.

"Did you get anything?" Bill asked.

Riley knew that Bill was long since used to her crime scene meditations. He understood how productive they could sometimes be.

Riley asked, "Are we sure there's only one murderer? I mean, one man acting alone?"

Bill thought for a moment.

"Pretty sure," he said. "The only time he left any footprints was here. The sand shifted overnight, so we couldn't get anything from them. Still, there was only one set of footprints, coming and going. Why?"

Riley didn't reply. Maybe she was wrong. It was only a hunch, after all. It was nothing she could prove. Even so, the feeling had been really strong.

"Riley, I'm sorry," Bill said suddenly.

Riley felt relieved. It was about time for Bill to snap out of it.

"I was wrong," he continued. "I don't know what got into me back there."

"*I* know what got into you," Riley said. "You feel absolutely crazed to solve this case. You feel like you owe it to the victims—both the ones who are already dead, and the ones who aren't. You feel like you've let them down so far. I understand. I've been there."

Bill nodded.

Riley said, "But Bill, if we get it wrong, if we only *think* we've solved it and we bring in the wrong man, it'll be worse than doing nothing. More women could die. We know he's already holding at least one captive. We've got to get it right. And we've got to do things by the book."

"I know," Bill said. "I won't let it happen again."

Riley hoped not. But there was nothing more to say about it right now.

"Come on," she said. "I've seen enough here. Let's head back to Redditch."

They walked back to the car, and Bill started to drive. Riley got out her phone and checked the text messages she'd been sending to April all day. They were still only marked "delivered," not "read."

She was worried. She dialed the home phone. Gabriela answered.

"Hi, Gabriela, I'm just checking in. Is everything all right?"

Gabriela's voice sounded agitated.

"*Señora* Riley, I am glad you called! I was just going to call you. I got a call from April's school. She skipped out of school early. She hasn't gone back. I keep trying to call her, but she won't answer. I don't know where she is or what she's doing. And she's supposed to have a meeting with her therapist this afternoon after school."

"*Un momentito,* Gabriela," she said.

She covered the phone and turned to Bill.

"Is the helicopter that brought me to Redditch still here?" she asked.

Bill nodded. "Sure. Why?"

Riley didn't answer Bill. She got back on the phone.

"Don't worry, Gabriela. I'm coming right home."

Riley's heart sank. She didn't know whether to be furious or terrified. But she knew she had to get home to find out what was wrong with April.

But I'd better wrap things up at home fast, she thought.

Her head was filled with terrible images of what the killer might do in her absence.

CHAPTER TEN

When Riley opened her front door, she was greeted by Gabriela's anxious face. Riley knew that things must be serious. The Guatemalan woman had been through a lot of difficulties in her life and wasn't easily alarmed. She was glad she had decided to return to Quantico with the FBI helicopter and drive home right away.

"Is April here?" Riley asked.

"Sí," Gabriela said. "She is upstairs in her room."

Riley walked inside and put down her bags.

"Did she go to the appointment?" Riley asked.

"No," Gabriela said. "Somebody at the doctor's office called, wanted to know where she was." Gabriela's eyes widened. *"Señora* Riley," she said, "April won't talk to me. I don't know what's wrong."

That really worried Riley. April adored Gabriela and almost never shut her out. "I'll see what I can find out," she said, patting Gabriela's shoulder and heading for the stairway.

As Riley hurried up the stairs, she heard music playing in April's room. She knocked on the door.

She heard April call out, "Come in."

She walked inside. April was sitting on her bed with her cell phone in her hand. She actually smiled at Riley.

"Hey, Mom!" she said loudly over the music. "I didn't expect you back so soon! Did you get the case solved early?"

Riley knew this teenage tactic well. April was trying to act as if everything was all right. As though this was just a normal day.

"Turn down the music," Riley said.

April did so, and Riley sat down on the bed with her.

"Gabriela said that you left school early," Riley said.

April was trying to look surprised now.

"Wow, is that why you came home early?" she said. "Look, it was just a misunderstanding. I had a pass to go to the local library. For research. So I left. The office got mixed up and called Gabriela. I explained it to her. I thought she understood. I had no idea that she'd call you. What was she thinking, huh?"

April was lying and Riley knew it. But she'd learned from past confrontations not to say so outright. She just sat there.

"Aren't you going to say anything?" April asked, sounding more defensive now.

Riley still said nothing.

"Jesus, you don't even believe me, do you?" April said, trying to sound righteously indignant. "Can I help it if you don't even believe anything I say? Can I help it if you don't trust me?"

It was a familiar manipulative trick of April's. But Riley wasn't going to fall for it this time.

"Should I believe you, April?" Riley said quietly. "Should I trust you? Can I?"

Riley could tell by April's expression that she'd just punched a hole in her defenses. April jumped up from the bed, stomped toward the door, and swung it open.

"If you can't even trust me, there's no point in talking," April said, her voice trembling with rage. "Just go. Just leave me alone, okay?"

Riley didn't speak or move. She kept her eyes locked on April's. She realized that she was using one of her own interview methods—the very tactic she'd tried to use on Dennis Vaughn before Bill had made a wreck of things.

Just get her talking, Riley thought. *Let her trip herself up.*

It felt weird, treating her daughter the same way she'd treat a murder suspect. But she could feel that it was working.

Still standing by the door, April burst into tears.

"Leave me alone! Please!"

April stood there sobbing. Riley sensed that she was crying more out of guilt and shame than anger.

Riley patted the mattress next to her and said quietly, "Come back over here and sit down."

April stood staring through her tears for a moment. Then she stomped back and sat down on the bed so hard that the frame shook. Riley handed her a handkerchief.

"I'm working on a case in Delaware, April," Riley said, sounding a lot calmer than she felt. "Women are being killed. But when I heard from Gabriela that you'd skipped school, I came straight home. I flew back by helicopter. That's how much I worry about you."

April choked down a sob.

"Things will go a lot better if you just tell me the truth," Riley said. As soon as the words were out of her mouth, she realized that she'd said exactly the same thing to countless suspects. Had she really learned her parenting skills from years of detective work? It seemed bitterly ironic.

"I skipped out of school, Mom," April finally said. "I'm sorry, I don't know what I was thinking. I got so bored."

Riley's heart melted a little. She remembered what it was like. She, too, had sometimes skipped school as a teenager. She'd been living with an aunt and uncle during those years. She'd driven them crazy with her wayward behavior. Was she being a hypocrite to expect anything different from her own daughter?

No, she told herself. *I'm being a parent, that's all.*

"Were you with Joel?" Riley asked.

"Yeah, I guess," April said.

Riley sighed. She'd used that same lamely evasive phrase herself as a teenager—*"Yeah, I guess."* She didn't like it that her daughter had a boyfriend who encouraged her in bad behavior. But at least April more or less admitted it.

"Where did you go?" Riley asked.

"To the mall," April said.

A telltale catch in April's voice made Riley wonder if this was true.

"And what about your appointment with Dr. Sloat?" Riley asked.

"What about it?"

"Gabriela says you missed it."

April dabbed her eyes and cleared her throat.

"I'm sorry," she said. "I should have called and canceled it."

"I don't want you canceling appointments with your therapist."

April shook her head.

"Mom, Dr. Sloat's great, and I really like her, but I don't need her help anymore. I really don't."

Riley patted her daughter's hand.

"I'll decide when you don't need her anymore. And that will depend on what Dr. Sloat thinks. Promise me you'll keep your next appointment."

"I promise," April said.

"And promise me that you'll bring Joel around so I can meet him," Riley said.

"I promise."

Riley had no idea whether these promises meant anything. But it seemed like the best she could do for now. She got up from the bed.

"A couple more things," Riley said. "Gabriela told me that you wouldn't talk to her. I want no more of that. Gabriela's maybe the best thing we've got right now. She's doing everything she can to hold our lives together. Always be nice to her."

"Okay," April said.

"Also, you're grounded for a week."

April let out a groan of despair.

"But Mom—"

"No 'buts.' That's final."

Riley left the room before April had time to start making another scene. She walked downstairs where Gabriela was waiting.

"How is the *chica*?" Gabriela asked worriedly.

"Grounded for a week," Riley said. "Please make sure she doesn't go anywhere except school."

Gabriela nodded.

"I will get dinner ready," she said. She disappeared into the kitchen.

Riley sat down on the couch, feeling deeply grateful for Gabriela's presence in their lives. She also felt exhausted and rattled.

She thought she'd handled things fairly well with April just now. Even so, she knew that she only barely had things under control. Things were likely to unravel in her absence. And how could she come flying back from whatever case she might be working on whenever April had a crisis?

She remembered what Blaine had said to her the other day.

"Believe me, giving up your career isn't a solution."

He was right, of course. But that didn't solve Riley's problem. Here she was struggling between this crisis with April and a killer who might take another life at any moment.

She felt as if her whole world were ripping in two.

CHAPTER ELEVEN

The cat o' nine tails struck Meara's back mercilessly. She cowered into a corner and braced herself for the next blow. Another came, and then another, and another. The clocks were chiming, ringing, and blaring out the hour.

The pain was unbearable. But Meara's throat was so dry and raw that she couldn't scream anymore. Nothing came out except a hoarse, hollow gasping sound. Even she couldn't hear herself over the din of the clocks. Not that screaming had done any good. Wherever she and the other two captives were being held, no one could hear them scream here.

The chimes and bells and other sounds slowly came to a stop. Meara felt pretty sure that they had marked the hour of six o'clock.

Then the blows stopped coming. She heard her captor say, "I'm sorry, I'll try to do better."

She turned around just in time to see him strike himself on the back with the whip.

He let out a howl of pain, then said again, "I'm sorry, I'll do better. I will."

Again he swung the devilish whip across his own shoulder, striking his own back. He was turned away from her now, and she could see that his back was bleeding as badly as hers, blotches spreading across his ragged shirt.

She took the opportunity to scurry to the far side of the enclosure, where she huddled with the two half-starved girls.

She'd seen her captor do this before. She was still shocked and baffled by it. What kind of insanity drove him to punish himself so severely?

The captor didn't stop beating himself until he was exhausted and gasping. He stepped out of the cage and locked it behind him, laying the whip down on a table. Then he turned his attention to the clocks. He seemed so absorbed by them that he forgot all about his captives.

Muttering inaudibly, he moved the hands of a clock with the face of a cat. Then he took a key out of his pocket and wound another that was shaped like a butterfly. After that, he stopped and stared raptly at a clock that had been made out of what appeared to be a real human skull.

Finally, he turned back toward his captives and spoke in a strange, almost kindly voice.

"I wish I could make you understand," he said. "But I'm not allowed to talk about it—not even to you. If I could tell you, you'd understand. You'd accept everything."

He was staring straight into Meara's eyes now.

"It's just—it's just—it's just ..."

He paused a moment and then blurted out, "It's about *time*. We're running out of *time*. You, me, everyone, the world. Your sacrifice—it means something, it's important, it's the only hope left for anyone, you should feel honored ..."

Then he winced guiltily, as if he'd been slapped in the face. He picked up the whip off the table and beat himself again.

"I'm sorry," he said. "I shouldn't have said anything."

He finally laid the cat o' nine tails on the table again. Then he went out through the door where he'd come in. Meara could hear him climbing a flight of stairs.

Meara stayed crouched in the corner with the other women for a few moments. She'd never seen anyone who was truly insane before. Sometimes he talked in a strange way. Not just like he was talking to himself. He seemed to be carrying on a conversation with someone unseen and unheard. And he had killed Chelsea so casually, barely giving any attention to his own actions.

Now she realized that there was no way to reason with this monster. He would kill them all just as cruelly, and she'd never see her family again.

She thought of her sister, who was planning to come to this country to work as soon as Meara made enough to pay her way here. Cathleen would be expecting to hear from her by now. But as things were now, nobody would ever hear from her again. Nobody would ever know what had become of her. She would just vanish off the face of the earth.

Ever since she'd been brought here, Meara had paid attention to the clocks, trying to keep track of the passage of time. She guessed that she'd been here a full five days and nights, with nothing to eat or drink except occasional scraps of bread and some water.

She drew herself away from the other trembling captives and looked at them. They looked like little more the skeletons with skin stretched over their bones. Their eyes were deep and vacant. She wondered how long it would be before she was as wasted away as they were.

She shuddered as she remembered how their captor had killed the other girl when the clocks had struck twelve before. By her count, the killing had been over a full day ago. Just a snap of the neck was all that it took. She and these others were certain to share that fate sooner or later. They were probably overdue for it.

She felt what little was left of her energy ebb away. She lowered her head and cried, her sobs forcing their way painfully up through her throat.

Then she heard a rasping voice say, "Stop that."

Meara looked up. One of the girls—the one named Kimberly—was staring at her with a renewed determination.

"Stop crying like a baby," she said. "I'm sick of crying. I'm sick of doing nothing. We've got to get out of here."

Meara was stunned. She couldn't make sense of this. Kimberly was so wasted away that she could barely move at all. The one named Elise was even more emaciated and often seemed to be barely conscious.

"But how?" Meara asked Kimberly.

"You're the one who's still got some strength," Kimberly said, croaking the words out with enormous effort. "You could still run for help."

She looked right at her, and she had never seen more passion in anyone's look, her eyes burning with intention, demanding.

"You could save us all."

CHAPTER TWELVE

Meara struggled to grasp what Kimberly was saying. Could it be possible? Was there a chance of getting out of this hell?

The other two girls had already been here when Meara was brought to this place. They had seemed completely resigned to their fate. And Meara had combed over every inch of their cage. The walls were solid, and the posts holding the strong chain-link fence were bolted to the floor and the ceiling.

"How?" Meara asked. "No windows. No doors. No openings at all on this side of the fence."

Kimberly shakily raised a cadaverous finger and pointed toward the ceiling.

"Up there," she said.

Meara looked up. It wasn't the first time she'd noticed the ventilation pipe in the ceiling, about ten feet above their heads. It was hard to see in the constant dim light that came from the other side of the fence. Sometimes faint light showed through it, but they couldn't tell what was beyond it.

But it was clear that the pipe wasn't big enough for a person to fit through, not even an emaciated girl. It couldn't be more than eight inches wide.

"You said that Chelsea tried to get out there," Meara said.

"She said she did," Kimberly said. "But she wasn't making much sense."

"Chelsea is dead," whispered Elise weakly, as if to herself. "Little Chelsea is dead now."

"If we don't do something, we'll all be dead," Kimberly said.

Meara knew almost nothing about where they were. The windowless cinderblock walls and the solid concrete ceiling told her that it must be a basement. So there could be a whole house—a house where their captor lived—above their heads or very nearby. Even if they could manage the grueling feat of getting through the vent, they'd surely find themselves in his house or some other building. The noise alone would be enough to get his attention.

"It's our last hope," Kimberly said. "The next time he comes back, he'll probably kill one of us."

Did Meara see Elise nod in agreement? It was hard to tell. The poor girl, her face scarred from beatings from the whip, looked barely alive.

Meara looked up at the vent pipe. "Can we get up there?" she asked. "We're all weak."

"*I'm* too weak," Kimberly croaked. "Elise is too weak. You've still got some strength. It's up to you. Get through there yourself. Then get help. Get us out."

Meara was almost afraid to hope. But now she felt a burden of terrible responsibility toward her two fellow captives. It felt like more than she could bear.

And yet she couldn't disagree with Kimberly. How could she pass up the only possibility of escape, no matter how dim? And whatever danger might face her up above, could it really be worse than what she'd endured already—the beatings, the starvation, the total degradation?

She looked around. She saw only one way to get to the ceiling, and that was to climb up the chain-link fence. She braced herself for the unimaginable effort. Then she clutched the links with her fingers, painfully pulling herself up little by little. She felt Kimberly's hands trying to help, pushing weakly against her. Soon she was completely off the floor, inserting her feet into the openings in the fence, making her way slowly upward. Kimberly's feeble hands steadied her legs.

Finally Meara reached the top of the fence. The vent was a couple of feet away. She saw that the pipe was set into a metal plate that appeared to be screwed into the concrete itself. How could she possibly unscrew it?

Gripping the chain links with one hand, she reached out with the other and slipped her fingernails between the metal plate and the ceiling. She tugged and thought she felt a little give. The idea of ripping the vent loose seemed impossible. But she had to try.

She pulled with all the strength she had and felt a little space open up between the metal and the concrete.

With a cry of despair, Meara let go of the wire fence and clawed at the metal plate with both hands. She was falling, but a horrible rending sound told her that something had definitely come loose. She felt her body slam into Kimberly's, and then she hit the floor. All around her metal banged and clanked into the concrete floor amid a shower of dirt and pebbles.

Everything was quiet for long moments, and then she heard Kimberly groan. Meara was dazed and in pain, her arms battered from the fall and her fingernails badly torn. But she could see what she had pulled loose scattered all around her. The vent pipe lay

67

broken on the floor, looking rather like a smashed periscope. It was surrounded by other metal scraps, dirt, rocks, and clusters of weeds.

What on earth ... ? Meara wondered.

Then she heard Kimberly gasp out, "Look!"

Kimberly was lying on the floor in the middle of the debris, pointing up. Elise was sitting a few feet away, staring upward. When Meara looked up, she could hardly believe her eyes.

Through the square hole she could see a grayish sky. Now she understood. The vent didn't connect up into the house or any other building. It opened straight into the outdoors. She'd been wrong all along in thinking that they were imprisoned in a basement. Instead, it seemed to be some kind of underground bunker. And it must be very early morning.

Kimberly said, "You can get out! Go!"

"Are you hurt?" Meara asked her.

"Not much," Kimberly replied. "Can you stand up?"

Meara got slowly to her feet. Yes, she could stand up. She could walk. For the first time in days, she dared to hope.

With renewed strength, she clambered back up the fence. Hanging onto it with her left hand, she reached upward through the opening with her right, clawing and pawing at the grass and dirt outside.

Soon she felt her fingers catch fast to some roots. She held tight and swung her other hand up, groping until it caught hold of roots as well. With more strength than she thought she possessed, she pulled herself up through the opening and out into the damp morning air.

She saw that she was in a small clearing in a wooded area. Beyond that, she had no idea where she might be.

She looked back down into the hole and saw Kimberly looking up hopefully. Elise still didn't seem to understand what had happened.

"Come on up," Meara said, reaching down through the opening.

"I can't," Kimberly said.

"I'll help you."

Kimberly looked up at her with sunken, desperate eyes.

"You'll never be able to pull me out," she said. "And not Elise either." Then she rubbed one arm. "I can't climb the fence."

Meara's pulse was pounding.

"I can't just leave you here," she said.

"You've got to," Kimberly said. "Go get help. Tell the police. They can come save us. Make it fast."

Meara hated to leave her two companions behind, but she knew that she had no choice. She stood up, almost fainting from weakness. She looked all around. To one side she saw a well-beaten path leading through the wooded area. She could see the lighted windows of houses beyond it.

She stumbled in that direction until she heard a distant door slam.

Is that him? she wondered. *Is he coming back?*

She looked down at the path. This could be the very path that he used to come and go. If she followed it, she might wind up in his clutches.

She turned the other way. Another less used path led out among the trees. She couldn't see houses or anything else in that direction. Even so, the path had to lead somewhere. It had to lead to people.

She staggered along the path, feeling weaker and dizzier with every step. She wasn't sure how long she could stay on her feet, and she felt badly disoriented. Her vision blurred, and she couldn't see clearly. Weeds and branches battered her, snatching at her hair and ragged clothes.

Then to her relief, she felt the thick underbrush end in another open space.

Where am I? she wondered.

She lurched forward and felt hard pavement beneath her feet. She'd reached the edge of a highway. She looked back and forth but saw no traffic. She had no idea which way to go. She chose a direction and staggered on her way.

Her head was swimming more and more. It was getting harder to see clearly or even to stay on her feet. She was too weak to go on.

Don't give up, she told herself. *Don't give up!*

CHAPTER THIRTEEN

Scratch stared up at the early morning sunlight coming in through the broken ceiling. He'd seen the ragged hole from outside, but he hadn't been able to make himself believe it. Now he could see that the cage was littered with dirt and rubble. One girl—the freshest one, the Irish one—was missing, and the other two were huddled together staring at him fearfully.

Grandpa was furious. *"Look how you botched it this time!"* he said. *"How could you let a thing like this happen?"*

"I didn't know it needed repair," Scratch pleaded.

"Hell, do I have to tell you every damn thing to do?"

Scratch couldn't stop staring at the hole in the ceiling. In his mind, Grandpa ranted on.

"You've got to get to work. You've got to get this place fixed up. Tight as a drum, I'm telling you."

"I'll fix it," Scratch said.

"Damn right, you'll fix it. You'll have to haul this wreckage topside. Then you'll have to mix up a batch of cement in the garage. Understand what I'm saying so far?"

"I understand," he muttered.

"I can't hear you," Grandpa said.

"I said I understand!" Scratch said, almost angry with Grandpa now. He started pushing together the heavy debris.

"What do you think you're doing?" Grandpa said.

Scratch stopped, his shoulders sagging wearily.

"What should I do?" he pleaded.

"First you've got to find the girl. Find her before somebody else does, before she gets a chance to talk."

At that moment, the clocks started to strike seven. Scratch snatched up the cat o' nine tails and entered the cage. He stood over the two captives threateningly.

"Where is she?" he said. "Where did she go?"

One of the girls barely seemed to be conscious. The other was trying to scream, but she was too weak to make much noise. The din from the clocks started to die away.

"I asked you a question!" he shouted.

He struck wildly at them with the whip. But instead of turning away, the one who looked stronger just stared at him defiantly.

"She went for the police," she said.

Scratch grabbed her by the hair and stared into her hollow eyes.

"She what?" he yelled.

"The police! They're coming! It's all over for you, you sick son of a bitch!"

Scratch slashed the whip at her again. Then he turned and rushed out through the gate. He locked it carefully behind him. Then Scratch remembered the gaping hole.

"But the other girls ..." Scratch began.

"Leave them for now. They're too weak to get out. They're too weak to scream even. Now get moving!"

Scratch ran up the stairs into the open area above the shelter. He could see footprints leading away from the hole, toward a nearby path.

"That's where she went," he told Grandpa, pointing.

Scratch took off down the little-worn path, branches and brush hitting him all over. The path ended after a few yards at the edge of the highway. He looked up and down. There wasn't any morning traffic yet, and he saw no sign of the girl.

"I don't know which way she went from here," Scratch said.

But there was no reply. Grandpa never spoke anywhere but in the house and in the fallout shelter.

Scratch was fighting down wave upon wave of panic.

He ran back toward his house to get his car. Grandpa was right. He had to find the girl who had escaped.

And when he did, he would kill her right away.

CHAPTER FOURTEEN

Riley took a sip of tea, then looked at her watch. It was 9:30 a.m.

I ought to be on my way back to Delaware by now, she thought anxiously.

Instead, she was sitting in Mike Nevins's office in Washington, DC. Mike was a forensic psychiatrist who frequently consulted the FBI. Riley had known him for more than a decade.

Mike had been a great help to her over the years, and not just on murder cases. He'd helped get her through her PTSD after her ordeal in Peterson's cage.

Riley reminded herself that Bill didn't actually expect her back this morning. She'd called him for an update last night, and he'd assured her that there had been no new developments on the case. They both agreed that there would probably be a hiatus between killings.

Meanwhile, Riley had plenty of worries of a more personal nature. So last night she had gotten in touch with Mike, who said it would be okay for her to come by this morning. April had seemed all right when Riley had dropped her off at school this morning, and Gabriela knew that Riley was planning to drive on down to Delaware from here.

"I'm sorry to bother you about all this," she told him. "I mean, family counseling is a little outside your area of expertise."

"It's okay," Mike said, sitting back in his chair and chuckling a little. "It gives me a chance to stretch my skills."

Mike was a dapper, charming little man who always wore an expensive shirt with a vest. Riley liked him a lot and considered him to be one of her closest friends.

"I shouldn't be here," she said. "I've got a killer to catch in Delaware. But I'm scared to leave right now. I feel like April's really on the brink of some crisis."

"I understand," Mike said. "I remember what happened last time."

Riley knew that Mike was referring to April's last breakdown. April had been on a week-long school field trip in Washington, DC. when she'd suffered a terrible attack of PTSD. Her ex-husband refused to be bothered, and Riley had been in Arizona working on a case. She'd almost gotten fired for rushing back to help her daughter. Was all that going to happen all over again?

"Hasn't Dr. Sloat been helpful?" Mike asked.

Mike had referred April to Dr. Lesley Sloat, a stout, good-hearted therapist that both Riley and April liked.

"I thought she was helping," Riley said. "But April blew off her appointment yesterday—right after cutting her afternoon classes at school."

Mike scratched his chin thoughtfully.

"Fifteen is a tough age," he said. "Normally the worst would be behind her. But her situation has hardly been normal. Not many girls her age have been locked in a cage and tormented by a psychopath. Add to that some less unusual stressors, like her parents' divorce, and she's bound to still be having problems."

Riley sighed worriedly.

"I can get inside the minds of psychotic killers, but my own daughter's a mystery."

Mike chuckled again.

"Well, a teenager's mind is as much of a mystery as any psychopath's," he said. "They're going through so much developmental change that they don't even understand themselves. They're physically mature with an immature brain."

"That's not very encouraging," Riley said.

"I wish I had better news."

Riley and Mike fell silent for a moment.

"What else are you worried about?" Mike asked.

"Her judgment, for one thing. She's got a new boyfriend, but I don't know anything about him, and so far she won't bring him around so I can meet him."

Mike leaned forward in his chair and looked at her with concern.

"I'm afraid you're talking circles around the real problem," he said.

"And what's that?" Riley said.

"I think you know."

Riley's throat tightened up. She did know. And it was hard for her to say it out loud. But if she didn't get it out, this would be a wasted visit. Both she and Mike knew that.

"I feel helpless, Mike," she said. "Helpless and inadequate. I feel like everything I do is wrong. I just can't do it. I can't be a mother and an FBI agent. They're both too consuming. There's not enough time for both. There's not enough of *me*."

Mike nodded.

"There," he said. "Now we're getting down to business. Well, clearly you think you're doing something wrong. That means you could be doing something better, something different. What might that be?"

Riley didn't reply. The question completely stumped her.

"I don't hear an answer," Mike said in a soothing voice. "And I suspect there's a pretty good reason for that. There *isn't* anything better you could be doing. I mean, what are your options? Turning in your badge and quitting your job? How do you think that would work out?"

Riley smiled as she remembered her conversation with Blaine about this very issue.

"Now you're sounding like my next door neighbor," she said.

"Oh?"

"His name is Blaine. He's a nice guy. A father. His daughter is a friend of April's."

Mike's smile broadened.

"Single, I take it?"

Riley blushed. "How did you guess?"

"I'm pretty good at that kind of thing," he said. "Well, maybe we should be talking about this nice guy named Blaine. How are things, uh, *progressing* with him?"

Riley grunted a little.

"Progressing? Are you kidding? They're not progressing at all."

"Why not? Do you think he's not interested?"

Riley felt her blush deepen.

"I think he's interested," she said.

"And obviously *you're* interested. So what's the problem?"

Riley's mind boggled.

"What's *not* the problem? He runs a restaurant, I chase murderers. If he knew half of what goes on in my life, he'd be scared to death. I mean, she was abducted straight out of her father's house. Could you blame him for being scared that the same thing could happen right next door? He'd probably move to another neighborhood."

"Are you so sure?"

Riley didn't reply. She'd been avoiding talking to Blaine about her work. Maybe it was time for that to change.

"Isn't this kind of off the topic?" she said. "I mean, we were talking about April."

"Maybe we still are," Mike said. "Do you really think things with your daughter would get worse if you had a nice man in your life? Considering how much you say she hates her father, she might be hugely relieved."

Riley fell silent again. Mike was giving her a lot to think about.

Just then her phone buzzed. She saw that the call was from Bill.

"I've got to take this," she told Mike.

Mike nodded. Riley accepted the call and stepped out into the hallway.

"What's going on?" she asked.

"Meara Keagan just turned up," Bill said. "She escaped captivity."

Riley's heart quickened.

"So?" she prodded. "Why the grim voice?"

There came a long pause on the other end. Finally, Bill spoke.

"She got hit by a car."

CHAPTER FIFTEEN

When Riley reached the hospital in Ohlman, she rushed inside. Bill was already there, pacing in the waiting area.

"Is she alive?" Riley asked. "Is she awake?"

"That's what they tell me," Bill said. "They haven't let me in to see her yet."

"How did they find her?" Riley asked.

Bill shook his head, as if in disbelief.

"That's what's really weird," he said. "Somebody dropped her off right outside—where you just came in. But whoever left her drove straight off."

"Do you think it was the person who hit her?"

"We're assuming that. Lucy Vargas is checking the surveillance footage right now. We'll know more about it soon. Come on, let's go find out if we can see her yet."

Bill led Riley down a hallway to a room with two cops standing outside. A stern-looking woman in a white coat met them. Her nametag said Dr. Leah Pressler.

"Can we talk to her now?" Bill asked the doctor.

"If it were up to me, I'd say no," Dr. Pressler said. "She's weak and extremely fragile. But she says she wants to talk. She really insists on it."

Dr. Pressler escorted Bill and Riley into the room. Meara Keagan was looking up at them with her sunken eyes. She was extremely thin and pale, which made her bright red hair and freckles stand out bizarrely, as if they were a wig and makeup.

One leg was in a cast, and intravenous tubes were restoring her bodily fluids. She looked like she'd been through hell. But at least she was still alive. And as thin and starved as she looked, she was nowhere near as emaciated as the three corpses had been.

"Are you from the FBI?" she asked in a tired, raspy voice. Riley immediately noticed her Irish accent. She remembered hearing that she was an Irish immigrant.

She said, "I'm Agent Riley Paige, and this is Agent Bill Jeffreys."

Riley sat down in a chair beside the patient. Bill and the doctor remained standing.

"May I call you Meara?" Riley asked in a gentle tone.

"Of course," the woman said, smiling sweetly.

76

"What can you remember?"

Meara Keagan's whole face strained with effort.

"This man—he knocked me out while I was trying to help him with his car. I'm not sure how long ago it was."

"Five days," Riley said in a reassuring tone.

"That's what I thought. The next thing I knew I was in a basement. In a cage with three girls, all of them starving. He kept us there, barely let us eat or drink at all. He killed one of the girls. Broke her neck."

Her voice started to falter. Riley knew that she was reliving the terror of that moment. Riley patted her hand reassuringly.

"What can you tell me about the basement?"

"It was ... full of clocks. All kinds of clocks. Hundreds of them. But they were behind a fence." She paused for a moment and then added softly, "We couldn't get out through the fence ... we couldn't get out ..." Her voice trailed off.

Riley looked at Bill, and he at her. She knew they both were wondering the same thing. Was the woman only imagining the clocks in her delirium?

"Could you describe the man who held you?" Riley asked.

She started to shake all over.

"He was ... he was ... I can't ..."

Riley understood. She was repressing the memory of her captor. Maybe she could remember what he looked like later on.

"It's okay," Riley told her. "How did you escape?"

Her expression became terribly confused.

"I don't have any idea. The last thing I remember is that the clocks were ringing and chiming and he was beating us with a whip, and he was beating himself. He did that a lot, whipped both himself and us. The next thing I knew, here I was. I don't remember anything about how I got here."

"Did you escape from him somehow?"

Meara looked away. Her eyes were foggier now and she seemed to be having trouble speaking.

"That's enough for now," the doctor said.

The doctor led Bill and Riley out into the hallway.

She said, "I'm not a neurologist, but I think I can explain the memory gap. It takes a while for the brain to turn a short-term memory into a long-term memory. It's called 'consolidation.' But a trauma to the brain can interfere with that process. She was unconscious when we found her. My guess is that she was knocked

77

out before the short-term memory of her escape could be consolidated."

"So she might not ever remember," Riley said.

"I don't see how she could," Dr. Pressler said, shaking her head. "That information just isn't in her brain anymore. It's long gone. But she might be able to tell us more about her captivity after a while. Right now she needs to rest."

Riley was about to thank the doctor for the explanation when Lucy came trotting toward them.

"We've found him on the surveillance video," she said excitedly. "Come have a look."

She led Bill and Riley to a room where a local cop was sitting at a computer.

"Here it is," the cop said.

Riley could see it all clearly. A rather beat-up looking medium-sized SUV pulled up to the hospital entrance. A man got out of the car. He was dark-haired and of medium height.

He ran around to the back of his vehicle, opened it, and took the unconscious woman out. He put her on the sidewalk and touched her head in what looked like an apologetic gesture. Then he ran back to the car, got in, and drove away.

"Stop it right there," Riley said.

The cop sitting at the computer stopped the video.

"The license plate is fully visible," Riley said.

Lucy was standing next to her. She grinned at Riley.

"We've already on it," she said. "The car belongs to a certain Jason Cahill, thirty years old. He lives right here in Ohlman. We've got an address."

"Agent Jeffreys and I will pick him up," Riley said. "Lucy, please keep track of things here. Call us right away if our patient manages to remember anything more."

*

Riley and Bill parked in front of Jason Cahill's house. It reminded Riley of where Dennis Vaughn lived back in Redditch— small wood-frame house with a porch. But it was in much better condition than Vaughn's ramshackle cottage, and the lawn was recently cut.

The house was on the outskirts of Ohlman, and a fair distance from neighboring houses. As she and Bill walked toward the place,

Riley noticed an SUV parked in the driveway—the same vehicle that had appeared in the surveillance video. Sure enough, the front of the vehicle was dented and a headlight was broken.

This might be it, Riley thought. *Maybe we've really got him.*

But just as they were about to step up onto the porch, Bill pointed to the foundations of the house.

"Look," he said. "No basement."

Bill was right. The house was open underneath, built on wooden posts. Meara had insisted that she had been held captive in a basement. Might the basement be at some other address?

In any case, Riley knew they had Jason Cahill dead to rights on a hit-and-run charge. Maybe the rest would follow easily.

Bill knocked on the door. The man who opened it looked nothing like the overweight, shaggy Dennis Vaughn. He was slim and clean-cut, and he was wearing jeans and a T-shirt. He looked tired and haggard.

"Are you the police?" he said.

Bill and Riley both showed their badges. The man looked only slightly surprised.

"The FBI. Jesus. I was expecting the police. But the FBI?"

"Are you Jason Cahill?" Bill asked.

"Yeah."

Riley said, "You're under arrest for a hit-and-run incident involving Meara Keagan. Turn around."

Jason Cahill cooperatively put his hands behind his back so that Bill could cuff him. Riley looked inside the little house. She saw that it was simply decorated with furniture that looked well-used but in good repair.

"How is she?" Cahill asked. "Is she okay?"

Instead of replying, Riley began to read him his rights.

"I know my rights," Cahill said. "I want a lawyer."

Bill's face turned red with anger. Riley worried. The last thing she needed was for him to get out of control again.

Bill growled, "What do you know about the deaths of Metta Lunoe and Valerie Bruner?"

Riley watched Cahill's face. She detected no change of expression.

"I don't know anything about them," he said. "I'm not saying anything else without a lawyer. I can't afford one, so you need to get me one."

"Where were you last Sunday night?" Bill said.

"I'm not saying anything else without a lawyer," Cahill said.

Bill tugged on the cuffs so that they hurt a little. Cahill winced in pain. Riley was walking behind them on the way out of the house.

"Hey," Riley said sharply.

Bill turned and looked at her. Riley didn't say anything, but tried to tell him by her expression that she wasn't going to put up with him going berserk again. Bill shook his head angrily.

Riley was worried—and not just about Bill. Cahill was taking things very coolly. If he really was their killer, he knew exactly how to handle himself. Proving a case against him wouldn't be easy.

And the girls would never be found.

CHAPTER SIXTEEN

Riley felt stranded. She and Bill were sitting outside the interview room at the local police station. They'd been there for a half hour now while Cahill had been consulting with a public defender in the room.

Cahill hadn't said a word to them so far, but the lawyer had talked to them plenty before he went in to confer with his client. He was a local public defender—a stocky, middle-aged fellow named Rudy Dunkelberg.

Riley had realized immediately that Dunkelberg wasn't just some backwoods rube with a law license. He knew exactly what he was doing. He'd picked up right away that Jason Cahill was wanted for a lot more than a hit-and-run accident. In fact, he'd guessed that Cahill was a suspect in the three murders, which were finally becoming public knowledge.

And now Riley knew what was coming next. Dunkelberg was going to make sure that Cahill said nothing about the murders—not even to him. It made Riley angry, but she knew that Dunkelberg was just doing his job.

"I hate it when they lawyer up," Bill muttered.

"So do I," Riley said. "But we've got to make do with the situation as it is."

Bill shook his head wearily.

"Riley, I don't know how much more of this I can take," he said. "I've just got to close this case. I've got to put a stop to this guy."

"*We've* got to close this case," Riley said, correcting him. "And we've got to do it by the book."

The interview room door opened. Dunkelberg looked out and said, "You can come in now."

Riley and Bill walked into the room and sat across the table from Cahill and his lawyer. Cahill still seemed oddly expressionless. Riley had seen plenty of psychopathic killers show a similar lack of affect.

A handwritten letter was lying on the table in front of Cahill.

"My client is ready to confess," Dunkelberg said.

"He's what?" Bill blurted with disbelief.

"Mr. Cahill will read his confession now," Dunkelberg said.

He nodded to his client, whose expression still hadn't changed at all. Cahill began to read in a slow, steady voice.

"Last night I was in Glenburn, about forty miles from Ohlman," he read. "I was playing poker with some friends I went to college with six years ago."

Dunkelberg interrupted, "My client will be glad to give you their names and contact information. Go ahead, Mr. Cahill."

"The game went on almost all night. I left at about five thirty in the morning. I was severely intoxicated. I had no business driving, but I decided to drive home anyway. At about six o'clock, a woman stepped in front of my vehicle. I didn't stop in time and I hit her."

Cahill paused for a moment.

"Then I panicked," he continued. "I wasn't thinking straight. I've already got a couple of DUIs and I was scared of getting another. But I didn't want to just leave the woman there. I picked her up and put her in the back of my car. I drove her straight to the hospital and left her there."

Cahill cleared his throat.

"I was sobering up by the time I got home. I was able to think more clearly. I knew I'd made a terrible mistake. I couldn't get to sleep. I had just decided to turn myself in when the FBI agents arrived."

Another silence fell.

"I am sincerely sorry for what I did," he said, concluding his statement.

Dunkelberg said, "That's all that my client wishes to say at this time. As you can see, he is placing himself at the mercy of the system." He handed Cahill a pen. "Now all he has to do is sign this confession—"

"Hold on," Bill snapped. "He's not signing that."

Riley understood Bill's protest. By confessing to a possibly bogus offense, Cahill might well put himself beyond their reach. But she knew that there was nothing that she or Bill could do to stop him.

Even so, she had an idea.

"Just a moment," she said. She got out her cell phone and cued up the pictures of the crime scenes and the murder victims.

She flashed a picture of Metta Lunoe's emaciated corpse at Cahill.

"Do you recognize this woman?" she asked.

At last she saw a change in the man's expression. It was subtle but visible. She flashed through a series of graphic images of Metta Lunoe until pictures of Valerie Bruner came up.

"Does any of this mean anything to you?" Riley said.

Cahill's face had gone slack and his eyes glazed over.

Bill yelled across the table, "Answer her question, damn it!"

Riley gave him a sharp nudge with her elbow.

"I'd like to confer with my partner alone for a moment," she said.

Dunkelberg nodded, and Riley escorted Bill out of the room.

"He's not our man," she told him.

"How do you know that?" Bill asked.

"I could see it in his face. He's never seen those murdered women in his life."

Bill looked like he could hardly believe his ears.

"I didn't see anything in his face," he said. "He looked as cold as could be. He looked just like a thousand killers we've seen."

Riley almost shouted, "He's hung over, Bill. He's numb and strung-out. That's why he looks like that. And on top of that he's in shock. He's still processing what he did to Meara Keagan."

Bill just stared at her for a moment.

"Are you sure?" he asked.

Riley didn't reply. She couldn't be absolutely sure. But her gut was telling her that Jason Cahill was not the killer.

"So are we back at square one?" Bill said wearily.

"No," Riley said. "We can still use him. All he's got to do is show us where the accident happened. That will get us closer to finding out where she was held."

*

Scratch had just heated up a frozen dinner and was sitting down to eat when he heard a car outside. He ran to the front window and lifted the blind. His stomach sank at what he saw in the evening light. Sure enough, across the street a man in a jacket that said POLICE was standing on a porch talking to one of his neighbors. Scratch looked down the block and saw two more cops at two other houses doing the same thing.

"They must be on to us," Scratch said.

"Yeah," Grandpa replied. *"And it's your fault for letting that woman escape."*

Scratch was about to protest that he'd looked everywhere for her, driving up and down the highway and along nearby streets. She'd been nowhere to be found.

But he kept quiet. He didn't want to get Grandpa riled right now.

Besides, he saw a young woman coming up the sidewalk and onto the porch, and she was wearing an FBI jacket. She knocked on the door.

"Should I pretend I'm not home?" Scratch asked.

"Of course not, you idiot. That might just make her suspicious. Let her in."

Sweat was breaking out on Scratch's brow.

"But what am I going to say? What am I going to do?"

"Just stay calm, damn it. Make like you don't know anything about whatever she asks you."

Scratch opened the front door. The agent was pleasant-looking young woman with a dark complexion. She was holding a batch of papers in her hand. She smiled at him.

"Excuse me for bothering you this evening, sir," she said. "I'm Agent Lucy Vargas with the FBI. I'm helping the local police canvass this general area. Have you seen this woman?"

She held out a flyer toward him. He immediately recognized the woman by her freckles and red hair. But except for the moment before he abducted her, he'd never seen her smile like that.

"Is she missing?" Scratch asked.

Grandpa hissed, *"Don't ask any questions, damn it! Leave that to her!"*

But Scratch's head was exploding with questions. Was the woman who escaped still missing? If so, where was she? Where had she gone? And what had led the police to this general area to look for her?

Instead of answering his question, the FBI woman said, "We just want to know if anybody has seen her around here during the last week."

Scratch shook his head dumbly.

"Are you sure?" the woman said, holding the flyer closer to him. "Please take a good look."

Grandpa whispered, *"Tell her you're sure."*

"I'm sure," Scratch said.

The FBI woman was looking at him a bit warily. He wondered why. Was it the way he was breathing? Was it the sweat that was forming on his face?

"Sir, do you have a basement?" the woman asked.

Scratch froze. Why would she be looking for a basement? What did she know?

"Yes, I do," Scratch managed to say calmly.

The woman was studying him closely.

"Might I come inside for a look, sir?" she asked.

Scratch opened his mouth but nothing came out. Grandpa was furious.

"For Christ sake, let her come in. We've got nothing to hide here. Let her look to her heart's content. And smile! Stop acting like some kind of goddamn criminal!"

Scratch managed to force a smile.

"Sure," he told the agent. "Come on in."

The woman stepped inside and looked all around. Scratch hoped nothing suspicious was in sight. The front room had once been Grandpa's clockmaker's shop. But Scratch had moved all of Grandpa's clocks out to the shelter years ago. Otherwise, the house was furnished much as it had been when Grandpa had died and left it to him. And he always kept the place reasonably clean.

"It's right this way," he said, leading her through the house toward the basement.

"Thanks," the woman said. She seemed determined not to hurry. She kept looking around at everything.

Scratch said, "Has this got something to do with those murders I've been reading about?"

"Shhhh!" Grandpa hissed.

But Scratch felt desperate to know. What did the authorities think the murders were all about? Did anybody understand their purpose at all?

"I'd rather not say," the woman said, still looking everywhere.

Scratch couldn't stop himself from pushing the issue.

"Because it sure seems to me that the killer is trying to send some kind of message, whoever he is."

The woman stopped still and looked at him curiously.

"We don't care if he's sending a message," she said. "As far as we're concerned, he's just another psychopath. Could I see the basement?"

85

"Of course," Scratch said. He led her to the basement door and opened it, turning on the light. He offered to let her go down first.

"After you," she said rather politely.

He walked down the basement stairs in front of her. He wished he could see her expression. He wished he had some idea of what he was thinking. Anyway, he couldn't imagine that she'd see anything suspicious down here. It was just a perfectly ordinary basement with cinderblock walls—no furniture, even.

There was a large gas furnace in the middle. The woman started to walk around the furnace. While she was on its far side, Scratch's eyes lighted on a rusty steel pipe covered with cobwebs. Some plumber had left it there many years ago. Scratch's fingers itched with an irresistible urge.

He reached down for the pipe.

CHAPTER SEVENTEEN

Lucy came out from behind the furnace. Nothing was amiss in this basement. Actually, nothing was amiss in the house except that the man who lived here seemed unusually creepy. He was bending over, poking at something on the floor. But then he straightened up and just stood there watching her, looking rather stiff and awkward.

"I know, I know," he mumbled distractedly. "It wasn't a good idea."

Lucy was puzzled. He seemed to be talking to someone else.

"What?" she asked.

He looked up at her, more alert.

"The basement," he said quickly. "There's nothing in the basement."

"You're right, there isn't," she said, smiling pleasantly. "Thanks for your time. That's all I need."

"Time is important," he said.

She nodded in agreement and headed back up the stairs. He followed behind her, muttering softly to himself.

When they were upstairs again, Lucy took another good look at the homeowner.

"I'll be on my way now," she said. She handed him the flyer with Meara's picture on it.

Below the picture was a phone number.

"Hang onto this, and look at it again later on," she said. "If you remember anything, give us a call."

Then she left the house and went on with her search for whoever had held Meara Keagan captive.

CHAPTER EIGHTEEN

April felt wonderful. She knew that Joel had added something to the pot in the bong, and she was glad that he had. When she felt like this, she didn't have to worry about school or Mom or anything. She didn't have to remember being caught and held in a cage. She didn't have to think about helping her mom kill the guy who had held her. She knew she could trust Joel to take care of her.

He passed her the bong again.

They were in his car, parked deep in the woods, an out of the way place where no one would bother them.

"You know I really like you," Joel said. His words seemed to reverberate as he spoke.

"In fact," he said, turning to look her in the face, "April, I'm in love with you."

"I love you too," she whispered back. It was the first time she'd said that to a boy. So she said it again, louder, "I love you too, Joel Lambert."

He looked concerned. "I know your mom doesn't approve of me."

"That doesn't matter. She's just all uptight because she deals with so many creeps."

He laughed a little. "I suppose she does. Big FBI agent and all that. I'm sorry you've had to live with all that suspicion."

April felt a touch of protection toward her mother. "She does have to face a lot of violence. I've told you about the one who took me."

He grinned. "Yeah. That was actually pretty cool. What you both did, I mean." He kissed her. "You're a thoroughly cool girl."

He was pulling off her clothes and she knew that they were going to make love again. She was glad she'd been on birth control all year, even though it hadn't seemed important before.

She sighed happily and helped him get her undressed.

CHAPTER NINETEEN

Sherry Simpson didn't like how close the car was following behind her pickup truck. The driver had been behind her ever since she'd turned into the rural route that led to her family's farm. Now he had pulled up a lot closer, actually tailgating her.

It made her uncomfortable. It wasn't unusual, of course. Ever since she was a teenager, country boys sometimes did this to get her attention.

Back then it had been kind of fun. She'd gotten a kick out of driving away and leaving them in the dust. She knew these back roads very well, and it wasn't hard to get away from them. But now that she was in her late twenties, it wasn't fun anymore—especially at night.

She was driving home late because her bridge club had stayed to gossip longer than usual after their game was over. There had been a lot of laughter over how Gloria carried on about the new waitress at the Ohlman Diner. Gloria was obviously jealous of the new girl's attributes.

It had been a fun night with her friends, and Sherry hoped that it wasn't going to be spoiled by this loser who was tailing her. She could see his license plate in her mirror. It was a Delaware plate. She could make out most of the string of numbers on it.

I should report this guy to our local cops, she thought. *He's crowding me too much.*

But maybe he just wanted to pass her. After all, she was driving a bit slowly because of the wine she'd enjoyed with her friends. She couldn't exactly blame him for being impatient.

She was on a straight stretch, so she slowed down even more and pulled to the right, leaving plenty of room for him to get by.

Sure enough, he roared past her without so much as a glance in her direction. His car rounded a curve up ahead and disappeared behind the trees that lined the road.

Hope he knows these roads, she thought. *He's liable to end up in a ditch.*

A few seconds later she rounded the same curve, but then screeched her pickup to a stop. A car was stopped ahead of her, skewed sideways and taking up the middle of the road.

Was the driver drunk? Had he wrecked his car?

She picked up her cell phone, about to dial 911. But she could see by her headlights that the car wasn't wrecked or even in the ditch. A man was opening the hood and using a flashlight to look into the engine.

"I guess I'm stranded," he called out to her.

The man walked toward Sherry's car. He was still talking, but she couldn't hear what he was saying. She rolled down her window.

"Do you have a phone?" he asked. "Mine isn't working. I was stupid. I let the power run out, and I don't have a charger with me."

He flicked the light into her face and then away. Sherry hesitated. She was still holding the phone in her hand.

The man was now outside her window. He had a pleasant face, and his smile was somehow reassuring.

"I'm lucky you came along," he said. "I just need to call my brother to come help me. If I can use your phone, I'll help you get past my car. I'm sorry to block so much of the road. It startled me when the engine just made a loud noise and cut out. But I think you can get past with my help."

Sherry was about to hand him her phone. But then she noticed that he had one hand on her door handle.

She remembered bits of conversations among her friends earlier on ...

"Did you hear about that dead woman found in Redditch?"

"Yeah, and some woman was kidnapped up in Westree."

"Do you think it's some kind of serial thing?"

Sherry shuddered with fear. But she knew she couldn't show her alarm. She gave the man a big smile. But instead of handing him the phone, she slammed her pickup into reverse and pulled away from him. He held onto the door handle as long as he could, then yanked his hand away, disappearing from view.

She struggled to keep her pickup under control, slowing down to avoid swerving into the ditch beside the road.

Still in reverse, she maneuvered around the curve in the road, then spun the wheel to turn around. Stopping the pickup short of the ditch, she slammed it into drive and headed away.

She didn't drive very fast, hoping that he wouldn't try to follow. She reached for her cell phone, planning to dial 911. She thought she'd put down right beside her, but it wasn't there.

I must have dropped it on the floor, she thought.

She didn't dare stop to pick it up.

Just then came a smash of glass behind her. The back window had been broken.

He's in the truck bed! she realized.

An arm came through the broken window and reached around her neck.

CHAPTER TWENTY

The crook of the attacker's arm closed around Sherry's throat. Dazed and surprised, she lost control of the truck. It lurched into a ditch and came to a dead stop. In the violent jolt, the attacker lost his grip and his arm slipped back through the window.

Sherry's brain cranked into high gear as she assessed her situation.

The engine was still running. The truck was big and powerful, and with its four-wheel drive it probably wasn't hopelessly stuck. But she could hear her attacker scrambling in the truck bed, getting ready to attack her through the window again.

She thought quickly. What could she use as a weapon? She knew just the thing. She bent down and reached under the passenger seat until she found what she needed—her electric stock prod. She pulled it out and switched it on. Just as she was straightening up, the attacker's hand came slashing through the window again.

But even with her weapon, she was helpless inside the truck cab. If she tried thrusting the prod at him, he might actually break it, leaving her in even more danger than before. Still crouched over, she opened the driver side door and tumbled out into the ditch, holding the weapon safely away from her.

In a flash, he leapt out the truck bed and stood facing her, wielding a shovel that she'd left back there. She realized that he had used the shovel to break the back window. And now he had her at a disadvantage. She was lying on her back and he was standing over her, raising the shovel to strike.

She rolled away from him and struggled to her feet. She held the prod at her side, desperately seeking the opportunity to lunge at him with it. But it wouldn't be easy. The prod was only a couple of feet long, and the shovel's handle was much longer. He still had an advantage that way.

But just how strong is he? she wondered.

In the light that spilled from her headlights, she tried to assess his height and build. He was taller and heavier—her family had always made fun of how skinny she was, calling her "Beanpole." But after a life of farm chores and activities, she was wiry and stronger than she looked.

He took a swing at her head and she successfully ducked under it. She watched him draw back for another swing and readied herself, getting a firm footing. When the next swing came, she reached out with her free hand and caught the shovel by its wooden handle, stopping it in its flight.

Then with her other arm, she shoved the prod directly at his belly, making contact with soft flesh. The man writhed with pain from a shock about as powerful as a stun gun, then fell to the ground.

Sherry jumped back into her truck. She rocked the truck forward and back until it came loose from the ditch. Instead of trying to get back on the road, she plowed straight through the white wooden fence on the edge of a meadow.

She knew these fields like the back of her hand, and knew that her truck was big and strong enough to barrel straight across the terrain. She looked out ahead in the moonlight. She knew that another road lay on the far side of the meadow, about a quarter of a mile away.

She hoped he wouldn't be able to follow her in his smaller vehicle—or better still, that he wouldn't even try. But she wasn't going to slow down until she was far out of his reach.

CHAPTER TWENTY ONE

Riley and Bill were sitting in the local police station conference room, listening to Lucy and her team debrief them about their canvassing effort. Riley was disappointed that they hadn't brought in any suspects.

"Did you check everywhere you could?" Riley asked.

"More than a hundred residences in all," Lucy said. "Everything in the area where Jason Cahill says he hit Meara Keagan."

"You didn't come across anyone suspicious?" Riley asked.

Lucy shook her head. "I wouldn't go so far as that," she said. "This town sure has its share of strange characters."

Then, looking around at the five local cops at the table, Lucy added, "No offense intended."

The local cops laughed.

"None taken," the youngest cop said.

"Welcome to Ohlman, Delaware," the oldest said. "Eccentrics are the local industry."

"And not all of them were happy to talk to an FBI agent," Lucy added.

The oldest cop laughed again.

"The feds aren't too popular in these parts," he said. "The locals figure you're here to take all their guns away."

Lucy said, "Whenever somebody struck me as suspicious, I'd push them to show me their basement if they had one. Some folks didn't like it, but I can be pretty pushy."

"And you didn't find anything?" Bill asked.

"Oh, a few really big model railroads," Lucy said. "One guy has a huge collection of carnival glass. Another's got lots of antique firearms. It's a strange town, though, and folks have got a lot of imagination. I talked to a couple of kids who said there were some haunted woods nearby."

A cop who hadn't spoken yet said, "Yeah, kids around here love their ghost stories. I was like that at their age. I guess we all were. It's about all the excitement to be had in a one-horse town like Ohlman. Things get pretty boring otherwise."

Riley could see that Lucy was troubled about something.

"What are you thinking?" Riley asked.

"How sure are we that he's holding his victims in a basement?" Lucy said.

Riley thought for a moment.

"Not sure at all," she said. "For all we knew, Meara Keagan just imagined the whole thing with the clocks and the basement. It really does sound pretty bizarre. Maybe she'll remember better later on."

Bill was drumming his fingers on the table, looking more than a little impatient.

"Besides," he said, "we haven't ruled out Jason Cahill as a suspect."

Riley didn't reply. In her gut, she had pretty much ruled out Cahill. But in lieu of any leads, her gut wasn't enough to persuade Bill otherwise. Anyway, Cahill was still securely in custody. If he really was their killer, they'd prove it sooner or later.

At that moment, the door opened and an excited-looking young cop looked inside.

"He's struck again," the cop said. "Tried to abduct a woman on a rural road. Only this time the woman got away. We're bringing her in right now."

For the first time in quite a while, Riley dared to hope.

CHAPTER TWENTY TWO

Scratch was aching and bruised all over when he got home that night. As soon as he walked in the door, Grandpa started asking questions.

"Where is she? Where is the girl?"

"I didn't get her," Scratch said under his breath.

"What do you mean, you didn't get her?"

Scratch didn't reply. He just walked straight through the house toward the back door.

"I asked you a question, damn it!"

Without a word, Scratch stormed out the back door into the backyard. Then he hurried out onto the path into the woods at the far end of the yard.

"So what are you going to do now?" Grandpa asked.

Scratch still said nothing. The truth was, he had no idea what he was going to do. He was furious about botching the abduction out on the country road. He needed to vent his anger somehow.

When he reached the square clearing, he saw that the upright vent looked exactly the way it had before the woman's escape. He'd done a good job repairing it. He'd even pulled weeds up around it again.

But he didn't stop to admire his handiwork. He pulled open the flat, horizontal door to the fallout shelter. As he descended the steps, he heard the clocks chiming and ringing midnight.

"Shut up!" he yelled at the clocks as he walked through the door into the shelter. "All of you, just shut up!"

But of course the clocks didn't obey. Their faces actually seemed to be mocking him—especially one that was shaped like a huge eye that blinked with every chime. A hooting owl also looked and sounded even more hateful and contemptuous than usual. One that looked like the man in the moon seemed to be laughing at him.

He picked up the cat o' nine tails and beat himself on the back. But he didn't cry out his usual apology, his pathetic promise to do better. He was too angry for that.

After a few blows of the whip, he noticed two more faces—the girls who were still in the cage on the far side of the room. One was staring at him with hollow, skull-like eyes. He stopped whipping himself.

"What are you looking at?" Scratch yelled at them over the din of the clocks.

One girl just kept staring at him. The other lowered her head. She acted as if he wasn't even there.

"You!" he called out to her. "I asked you a question!"

But she didn't look up. He strode to the cage, unlocked it, and stepped inside. The one who had been staring at him made a move toward the cage door. He whipped her in the face sharply. She drew back and turned away from him, and he locked the cage door behind him.

Then he stood over the one with the lowered head.

"You!" he said again. "What's the matter with you?"

She didn't reply or look at him. He grabbed her by the hair and yanked her face up. She had the same empty, vacant expression as the other girl.

"Answer my question," Scratch shouted.

"Meara's gone," the girl said in a barely audible voice. "She went to get help. The police will come to save us."

Scratch felt a tingle of alarm at being reminded of the other girl's escape.

"Idiot!" Scratch said to the girl whose hair he was gripping. "Nobody's coming. Nobody's going to save you."

Now the other girl murmured in a harsh, determined voice, "Meara got out. They'll find us soon."

Scratch's fury was now out of control. He seized the head of the girl he was holding and snapped her neck.

*

Riley sat beside Bill in the police station interview room, looking across the table at Sherry Simpson. The healthy-looking brunette was dazed but uninjured. Riley knew that it had taken a lot more than luck for her to escape the killer's clutches.

"What can you tell us about the car?" Riley asked.

"A Subaru Outback, I think," Sherry Simpson said. "Pretty old."

"Excellent," Riley said, taking notes. "You're doing great."

"How about a license plate?" Bill asked.

Sherry closed her eyes.

"It was a Delaware plate," she said. "I saw the number. Let's see if I can remember."

She slowly recited four numbers.

"That's all I saw," she said. "Or at least all I can remember."

Riley looked at Bill, who looked back at her with a smile. She knew that they were thinking the same thing. The first four numbers of a Delaware license plate were quite possibly the final piece of the puzzle.

"I'll go have the staff run this," Bill said.

He got up from the table and left the room.

Riley said to Sherry, "Did you get a good look at him?"

Sherry knitted her brow in thought.

"I'm sorry, but it was dark. I saw him in my headlights for only a few seconds, and he looked sort of washed out, so I couldn't make out any detail. I couldn't tell what color his hair was or anything like that. Then when he was looking in my window, all I could see was that he had a nice smile. He fooled me for a moment."

Riley kept jotting down notes.

"What about when you were fighting him?" Riley asked. "What did you notice?"

Sherry paused to think some more.

"I think he was taller than me," she said. "Maybe five foot nine or ten. He was of medium build, in pretty good shape. He gave me quite a fight."

Then Sherry shook her head.

"I'm sorry," she said. "I wish I could tell you more. I should have paid more attention. Maybe if I'd taken a photo ..."

Riley patted her hand comfortingly. "It's all right, Sherry." She understood what the poor woman was feeling. It was often the most sharp and observant witnesses who expected most from themselves.

"No, it's not all right," Sherry said, her voice choking a little. "I should have done something after I'd shocked him, when he was dazed. I should have knocked him out. Or killed him. But I was just so scared and anxious to get away. Now he's still out there."

"Sherry, listen to me," Riley said firmly. "You're very brave and very smart. Three other women have died at his hands so far. But you got away. And with what you remember, we'll probably be able to catch him at last."

Sure enough, Bill poked his head inside the door.

"The license plate numbers did the trick," he said. "It's a Subaru Outback all right, a 2000 model. And the owner's name is Travis Kesler. He lives right here in town."

"Let's get a team together to pick him up," Riley said.

CHAPTER TWENTY THREE

A small team of local cops swarmed along beside Riley and Bill as they approached the large house. Lucy followed up at the end of the group. Everyone had weapons drawn.

Riley saw no lights in any of the house windows, but that wasn't surprising at four a.m. Her mind clicked away, analyzing the information they had gathered. It had turned out that Travis Kesler was a well-off and well-known Ohlman citizen. In the rush to set up his arrest, Riley hadn't had time to ask a lot of questions about him.

The house had three stories, and it surely had a basement. Riley had no reason to doubt that they'd found the right man. And yet she couldn't help noticing the big three-door garage adjoining the house. What kind of cars would she normally expect to find in an upscale garage like that? Maybe a Mercedes, a BMW, or a Porsche.

He doesn't seem like an old Subaru kind of guy, she thought.

However, DMV records had left no doubt that Travis Kesler was the owner of the car that Sherry Simpson had seen out on that country road. It was more than enough to carry out an arrest.

Riley and Bill climbed up onto the porch. She looked at Bill and he at her. She nodded, and they both drew their weapons. Bill pounded on the front door.

"FBI," he shouted. "We're looking for Travis Kesler."

A silence fell. Bill looked at Riley. She understood that he wanted to know whether to break through the door. She shook her head no. If Kesler was at home, he was possibly asleep. There were cops posted on each side of the house now, so there was no danger of him escaping through another door.

After a moment, Bill hammered on the door again. A light appeared in a window. The door opened, and a man clad in pajamas appeared. He was carrying a rifle.

"Put down the weapon!" Bill shouted.

The man peered out at them. The three agents all had their FBI jackets on and Riley was holding up her ID out for him to see.

"Okay, okay!" the man said, putting the rifle on the floor. "Now I see that you're really FBI. I didn't know, so I got my gun."

"Are you Travis Kesler?" Bill asked.

The man nodded.

"You're under arrest for the murders of three women. And the abduction of Meara Keagan. Turn around."

The man backed away.

"Wow. Wait a minute. This is some kind of mistake."

"Turn around, I said," Bill repeated.

Riley was studying him. He seemed about the height and build that Sherry Simpson had described. But did he really look as though he'd just fought a woman who had defended herself with a stock prod?

A woman's voice called out from the stairs.

"Travis, what's going on?"

Riley could see that she was wearing a robe and a nightgown. She was coming down the stairs.

"It's the FBI, Abby," Travis Kesler said. "I think they've got me mixed up with somebody else."

Then a child's voice called out from upstairs.

"Mommy, Daddy, who's there?"

Another child could be heard crying. Riley's head filled up with questions. Could Kesler really be holding his captives in a house with a wife and children? It made less and less sense by the second.

"It's all right," the woman yelled up the stairs at the children. "Don't worry. Go back to sleep."

There's something wrong with this picture, Riley thought.

With a silent gesture, Riley signaled Bill to put his cuffs away. Bill didn't look very happy to comply. Riley turned her attention to Travis Kesler.

"Mr. Kesler, do you own a 2000 Subaru Outback?" she asked.

"Yes," Kesler said.

"Could we have a look at it please?"

Kesler looked genuinely confused now.

"No," he said. "It's not here."

"Where is it?" Riley asked.

"My sister has it, I think. Maybe."

Bill looked incredulous. *"Maybe?"* he said.

"May we come in?" Riley asked the couple.

Kesler shrugged. "I guess," he said. "I've got to say, though, this is pretty weird."

Riley called to the cops outside, "Stand down." She nodded to Lucy, who stationed herself on the front porch.

101

Then Kesler and his wife led Riley and Bill into their spacious, tastefully decorated living room.

Riley said, "Mr. Kesler, your vehicle was identified by the victim of a near-abduction. Her attacker was driving it. It all happened just a few hours ago. The identification was solid. The victim remembered part of the license plate number."

"I don't see how that's possible," Kesler said.

"We thought Blair had it," his wife added.

"Blair?" Bill asked.

"Travis's sister," the wife said. "She works for him."

Travis Kesler and his wife both sat down, looking tired, shocked, and puzzled.

"I run a business—Kesler Services," he said. "We coordinate local attractions and the chamber of commerce when it comes to local tourism. Handle promotional activities of all kinds. It's a thriving business in this part of Delaware. Blair does office work for me."

Riley and Bill remained standing.

"Why do you think she's got your car?" Riley asked.

Kesler shrugged. "She doesn't own her own car. Never has. So she's free to borrow it whenever she wants. She has her own keys. I don't pay much attention to when she's got it. It's just a junky old thing—the first car I ever owned. But I'm sentimental enough to keep it. When Blair hasn't got it, it's parked out in the driveway. It's not there now, so I just figured ..."

His voice trailed off.

"Where is your sister now?" Riley asked.

"She said she was going to take some time off to visit friends in Long Island," Kesler said.

"And you thought she took her car to drive there?" Bill asked.

Kesler sat and thought for a moment.

"Well, I just figured," he said. "I don't know where else the car might be."

Kesler's wife added, "Sometimes she takes the train up there."

Riley's heart sank as the situation started to come into focus. The killer was smarter than she'd realized. He probably carried out all his abductions in stolen vehicles to avoid detection. He'd stolen Kesler's Subaru, and Kesler hadn't realized it.

We're back at square one, she thought.

At that moment, something seemed to dawn on Kesler.

"Wait a minute. Has this got something to do with those other killings? The women's bodies found in the area? Good God, do you think I'm involved with that?"

He had become quite agitated. But before Riley could explain anything, Lucy poked her head in the front door.

"Agents Jeffreys and Paige, I need to talk to you," she said.

Bill and Riley walked out the door. Lucy and one of the local cops were standing on the front porch.

"We just got a call from the station," Lucy told them. "Another body has been found."

CHAPTER TWENTY FOUR

The girl's emaciated corpse had a peculiar pink-orange glow in the early morning light. The sun was just starting to rise at Riley's back, and the river that lay beyond the body reflected a lovely golden glow.

One of these days, I'm going to enjoy a sunrise again, she thought.

She had no idea when that day might come. Meanwhile, the rest of the sky was clouding up, and Riley heard some thunder in the distance. It was going to rain before long. And she'd been up all night and was extremely tired. If she didn't get some sleep soon, she was afraid she'd start making mistakes.

This body lay only a few feet away from a road, where it had been easily spotted by an early morning driver. It was arranged much like the two others—face up with both arms stiffly positioned. There were scars on the girl's face, and Riley was sure that they would find long gashes on her back, the same as with the other three bodies.

Riley, Lucy, and Bill were standing beside Ohlman's police chief Earl Franklin, who was crouched beside the body.

"Aw, hell," Chief Franklin said. "I think I know who this one is."

He stood up.

"A local girl named Elise Davey ran off during the summer," he said. "She was seventeen. Her mother called me, said she'd run off in a fit of anger. It wasn't the first time. She'd run off two or three times before, once for several months. I wasn't surprised this time. Her home life is awful. Her mother's a drunk and her dad's abusive."

Chief Franklin looked deeply troubled.

"We looked for her, but not hard enough," he said. "I figured she'd taken off for some other state. She hitchhiked the other times she ran off. I should have known this time was different."

Riley was familiar with this kind of guilt. She'd experienced it plenty of times herself. She put her hand on Franklin's shoulder.

"How could you have known?" she said. "Don't beat yourself up about this. It won't help."

"Somebody's got to tell her folks," the chief said.

Riley turned around to Lucy.

"Lucy, get a ride back to town. Pair up with a local cop and break the news. Try to find out if they know anything. I doubt that they'll have any helpful information, but we've got to try."

"I'll get right on it," Lucy said, then walked away.

Riley took in the whole scene, trying to make sense of it. She, Bill, and Lucy routinely got called in on the atypical cases—the ones where the killers had their own warped agendas. This was definitely one of those cases.

But what is this guy trying to do? she asked herself.

Some of the atypical killers she hunted down took special care in how they displayed the bodies. So far, she couldn't find any rhyme or reason to what this new killer was doing with these corpses.

Just then a young man with a camera came running up. He snapped a picture.

"Hey!" Riley yelled. "This is a crime scene!"

The young man ignored her and kept snapping pictures.

"Come on, buddy," Chief Franklin said, trying to coax the insistent photographer away. "You've got no business here."

"Like hell I don't!" the man said. "I'm a reporter, and this is a major story. This is the fourth victim since May—not counting the woman who got away. And all of them got starved almost to death. What's with that, anyway?"

He knew a lot of details. Riley guessed that maybe he'd been tipped off by paid informants among the cops.

"What kind of a statement do you cops want to make about it?" the man asked.

He kept moving around the corpse taking pictures from different angles. Riley hated it when vultures like this guy made up their minds that getting a sensational story was more important than an ongoing investigation.

Her own sudden fury took her by surprise. She pushed the man violently away with both hands.

"Hey!" the man yelled, almost losing his balance.

Riley pushed him again, and he fell to the ground, dropping his camera. She stomped on it, crushing it under her heel.

"That was a thousand-dollar Nikon!" the man yelled, scrambling to his feet.

"Was it?" Riley said sarcastically. "Oh, I'm so sorry."

He picked up the ruined camera and backed away from her.

"I'm going to sue your ass but good, you crazy bitch!"

"Over a little accident like this?" Riley snapped. "I don't think so."

"What's your name, anyway?"

Riley flashed her badge at him. "Special Agent Riley Paige, FBI. That's spelled p-a-i-g-e. Be sure to get it right."

"I'm going to have that badge, lady!"

She was about to lunge at him again when she felt Bill's strong arm on her shoulder.

"Back off, Riley. Let it go."

Chief Franklin finally managed to lead the reporter away.

Riley called out to him, "Get some tape up around the perimeter! We'll have reporters all over us before we know it!"

Chief Franklin nodded back at her.

"What the hell was that all about?" Bill asked Riley.

"What do you *think* it was all about?" Riley said. "Bill, you know how these reporters can make a mess out of things."

"Yeah, but remember what you said to me about Dennis Vaughn? I could lose my badge, you said. Well, you could too. You know that Carl Walder's just itching for a chance to fire you again."

It started to dawn on her that Bill was right. Maybe the reporter wasn't going to say anything about the incident. But she doubted it. It was a lot more likely that she was about to become part of the story. Walder would be all over her about it.

But there was nothing she could do about that right now. She took a few deep breaths to calm herself down.

"I'm sorry," she said. "I'm tired, and I'm not thinking straight. Let's get back to work."

She and Bill walked back over to the body.

"What's his thing with hunger?" she asked Bill. "All the victims so far have been starved almost to death."

Bill shook his head.

"Maybe he experienced hunger once himself," he said. "Maybe this is some kind of revenge. Or maybe he just doesn't bother to feed them. Maybe it doesn't mean anything at all."

Riley felt sure that it did mean something—or at least that starvation served some kind of purpose. As she had done back in Mowbray, she closed her eyes and tried to imagine the scene from the killer's point of view.

It started to come to her again—a strange feeling that the killer wasn't acting alone. No, it wasn't that a partner had been here at the crime scene. He'd come here alone with the corpse. But this killer struck her as somehow incomplete—unable to create these strange displays entirely on his own.

He's following orders, she thought again.

But what were those orders? What was he told to do?

A hunch hit her hard in the gut, and her eyes snapped open. She looked at the emaciated corpse and its peculiar position.

"I know something, Bill," she said breathlessly.

"What do you know?"

"I know what these images mean."

CHAPTER TWENTY FIVE

Riley took out her cell phone, eager to show Bill what she meant. She brought up a photo of Metta Lunoe's corpse as it had been found back in May.

"Look at her arms," she told Bill, pointing. "Her right arm is raised above her head with her hand pointed straight up, her left down at an angle."

Then she brought up a photo of Valerie Bruner's corpse.

"Then in June, this corpse was arranged a little differently. Her right arm and hand were the same, but her left pointed down over her abdomen."

She followed with a picture of the victim found in the bandstand at Redditch. The FBI had identified her as a runaway teenager from Connecticut named Chelsea McClure.

"And on Monday, Chelsea McClure was found with her left arm and hand straight up and her right lower at an angle—a mirror image of Metta Lunoe."

Finally Riley pointed at the body at their feet.

"And now we have Elise Davey—in the same position as Chelsea McClure, except that her right arm extends a little higher."

Bill shook his head and shrugged.

"We went over all this before," he said. "I still don't get it."

Riley sighed a bit impatiently.

"What did Meara say about the basement where she was held captive?"

Bill considered for a moment. Then Riley saw a dawning coming over him.

"She said it was full of clocks."

Riley nodded enthusiastically.

"It's all about *clocks*, Bill. The killer is obsessed with them. He's even arranging his corpses to look like clocks."

Riley ran through the photographs again, commenting on them one at a time.

"That's right," she said. "It looks to me like Metta Lunoe was five o'clock, Valerie Bruner was six o'clock, Chelsea McClure was seven o'clock, and now Elise Davey is eight."

Bill scratched his chin thoughtfully.

"So he's trying to tell us something about time," he said. "But what?"

"That's what we don't know yet," Riley said. "But he held Meara Keagan until she escaped, and he tried to take Sherry Simpson. He's either still got captives, or he's going to take another, or both. And he's sure not finished killing."

A new wave of tiredness came over her. Now she was feeling a few raindrops, and the thunder was getting louder.

Riley said, "We'd better get the coroner over here to finish things up and take the body away. It'll be pouring any minute."

*

Scratch peered through the rain as he drove along the Six O'clock Highway well north of Ohlman. He'd told Grandpa that he was going out to look for a new girl. It was true, but he had other reasons for getting out.

Grandpa's complaining about his recent failures had become unbearable, and his back was too raw to whip himself anymore. Getting away from the house and the shelter was the only way to get away from Grandpa's voice.

He'd been listening to the radio since he'd left home. The murders were in the news now. Even the FBI had been brought in, and there was some fuss about a female agent who had broken a reporter's camera this morning.

At long last, the media had caught on to the fact that the killings were connected. It wasn't going to make things any easier for Scratch. Women were being warned not to hitchhike, and all of Delaware seemed to be on alert.

But that wasn't what bothered Scratch at the moment. Nobody on the radio was saying anything about the message Grandpa wanted to send. Was everybody so stupid that they didn't yet understand? Was even the FBI that stupid?

There's so much at stake, he thought. *The whole world's at stake.*

Even so, Scratch was feeling pretty good. He was happy with the new car he'd just stolen. This Ford was classier than the old Subaru he'd been driving. He was always careful not to use his own car when he was searching for a new girl. He was too smart to take the chance that someone would identify him that way.

Anyhow, it wasn't hard to steal cars around here. People often left the keys right in them, tucked above the flap or beneath the seat or in some other obvious place.

And despite the rain, Scratch felt somehow hopeful that he'd find just the right girl. The one he still had in the cage wasn't thin enough yet. She had been strong when he took her and hadn't wasted away as satisfactorily as most of them did. He would use her later. Right now he needed someone more appropriate and after all the bad luck he'd been having lately, his luck was due for a change. But it was more than just luck. He felt a new presence around him—some kind of protective spirit that wanted to keep him safe, wanted him to succeed. He wouldn't tell Grandpa about it. Grandpa would never believe it. Grandpa would never believe that he could do anything right.

One good thing was, it now seemed obvious that the Irish girl who escaped hadn't told the authorities anything. According to gossip, she was in the local hospital and her room was guarded. But maybe she wasn't conscious. Maybe she wasn't even alive. Scratch now felt sure that he had nothing to worry about from her.

He'd even stopped worrying about the woman with the truck who had gotten away from him last night. Whatever she'd told the authorities, it hadn't led them to him. Instead, they'd probably gone after the guy who owned the Subaru.

He giggled at the thought.

Serves him right for being so careless with the keys, he thought.

Just then, he saw that an expensive new sedan was pulled off on the highway shoulder. Its hazard lights were blinking in the rain. It had Washington, DC, license plates. As he slowed down and passed it, a woman's face stared out the window at him.

My luck's improving, all right! he thought.

He stopped his car in front of the sedan. It was too windy for an umbrella, so he slapped a cap on his head and got out. When he reached the other car, the woman inside rolled down her window.

"It's about time you got here," she snapped. "I called for help twenty minutes ago. You people are supposed to be efficient."

Scratch bowed toward her and smiled. "My apologies." he said. "We're a little shorthanded tonight."

"Where's the truck?"

"It got delayed, sorry," he said. "I can take you anywhere you need to go in my car."

"Well," she said. She seemed to think it over for a few seconds. "I'm certainly not going to sit out here waiting any longer."

"Of course, you don't have to. That's why we're here for you."

"I'll hold you people responsible for any damage to my car," she said.

"Of course, ma'am. Our people will take care of everything for you."

She got out of her sedan with her coat over her head. "Someone will have to answer for this shoddy service."

"Someone surely will pay for this," Scratch replied.

As he let her in the passenger side of his vehicle, he could see that she was extremely thin, as if she barely ever ate at all. His luck really was getting better and better. Some helpful spirit really was smiling down on him.

She's ready any time Grandpa wants, he thought.

He wouldn't have to starve this one before killing her.

"You'll be just fine," he told her.

CHAPTER TWENTY SIX

Riley napped fitfully while rain fell outside her hotel room. She was exhausted from having gotten no sleep at all the night before. Even so, she was too worried to fall into a deeply refreshing doze. Whenever she did drift off, she saw clock faces with times on them ...

Five o'clock ... six o'clock ... seven o'clock ... eight o'clock ...

But instead of regular clock hands, she saw emaciated arms pointed at the numbers on the clock faces.

What can it mean? she kept asking herself. *What kind of message is he trying to send?*

And how soon was another corpse going to turn up somewhere, pointing to yet another hour? Chelsea McClure girl had been found on Monday and Elise Davey just this morning, Wednesday. The killer was moving much faster now, and her experience had been that he wasn't likely to slow down.

What could possibly seem so urgent to him?

Just when she finally felt herself slipping off to sleep, her phone buzzed. She saw that it was a call from April. When she answered, her daughter's voice sounded agitated.

"What's wrong?" Riley asked.

"I didn't see Joel today," April said.

For a groggy moment, Riley couldn't remember who Joel was. Then it came back to her. Joel was April's boyfriend. The one that Crystal, Blaine's daughter, didn't like. The one that Riley had never met.

"Well, lots of kids miss school sometimes," Riley said, stifling a yawn.

April sounded almost frantic now.

"But he said he'd be there today," she said. "He definitely said, 'I'll see you tomorrow.'"

"When did he say this?" Riley asked.

"After school yesterday. We were ... we had a snack together after school."

Riley could hear a note of evasion in April's voice. Somehow, she felt pretty sure that "a snack" wasn't all that had happened after school yesterday. Her longstanding feeling that this boy was going to be trouble suddenly got a whole lot stronger.

"Have you tried to reach him?" Riley asked.

"Yeah, but he doesn't answer my texts or messages," April said.

Riley couldn't restrain a note of dry irony.

"I know what that's like," she said. Maybe now April had a better idea of how it felt to be deliberately ignored.

"This isn't funny, Mom," Riley said. "This isn't like him. Joel texts me all the time. I mean, like, constantly."

Riley didn't like the sound of that. Texting "all the time"—did that mean even during classes at school? Maybe Joel's absence meant that he was finally losing interest in April. If so, Riley was glad of it. Still, April really sounded upset.

"It hasn't been all that long," Riley said. "I'm sure you'll hear from him soon."

"But what if something's happened to him?"

"Like what?" Riley said.

April was almost crying now. "I don't know. Something really bad. Mom, I need your help. Can't you have somebody, some agent, check to see if he's all right?"

"You know I can't do that," Riley said.

"Why not?"

Before Riley could reply, she heard knocking on her hotel room door. She was sure that it was Bill, and that he had some news.

"I can't talk about it now," Riley said. "I'm on a murder case."

"Of course," April said, bitter and angry. "It's just my friend. Nobody important to you. Maybe if he winds up dead you'll get interested."

"April!" Riley said.

But April hung up. Now Riley felt emotionally rattled as well as exhausted. She got up and went to the door and let Bill in.

"We just got word that another woman has gone missing," Bill said. "She was driving alone down the Six O'clock Highway. She called for road service when her car started making strange noises. They told her to pull over and stay in her car until somebody got there. When help arrived, the car was empty."

Riley quickly tried to process this new information.

"Do we have any reason to think she was picked up by the killer?" she asked.

113

"No, but we don't have any reason to think otherwise, either," Bill said. "And there's going to be a mega-uproar about it. Have you heard of Wyatt Ehrhardt?"

It took Riley a moment to remember.

"Isn't he that new US representative from Minnesota?" she asked.

"Yeah, a real up-and-coming political star. He's up for reelection next week. And his wife is Nicole DeRose, the heiress and former supermodel."

Riley gulped as she realized the seriousness of the situation. "And now she's missing," she said.

Bill was pacing the room. "Right. Lucy's got a team checking various locations up and down the Six O'clock Highway, in case she just wandered off somewhere. But I don't expect them to find anything. Ehrhardt is on his way down from Washington right now. We've got to get down to the police station to meet him. I'll meet you out in front of the hotel."

Bill left the room. Riley put on her shoes and splashed some water on her face. Her mind boggled at how much more difficult the case was likely to become.

*

Just when Riley and Bill got out of their car and walked toward the police station, Wyatt Ehrhardt's chauffeured limousine pulled up. Ehrhardt stepped out, followed by a young woman with a briefcase. They entered the building quickly, and Bill and Riley followed.

A moment later, they were in the interview room. Riley, Bill, and Chief Franklin introduced themselves to Ehrhardt and the woman.

Cool and businesslike, the woman shook hands all around.

"I'm Rhonda Windhauser, Representative Ehrhardt's personal aide," she said.

Riley noticed that Ehrhardt was looking at the woman in an oddly proprietary sort of way. Rhonda Windhauser looked smugly pleased at her status. She was a voluptuous young brunette. Her dress was short and had a plunging neckline. In her gut, Riley felt sure that Rhonda Windhauser was more than just an aide—at least in the usual sense.

Ehrhardt was a youthful, energetic-looking man in his thirties. His tan and his coiffed hair were much too perfect for Riley's taste. She was surprised at her own sudden feeling of dislike for the man.

Maybe it was because he was a politician. Her last experience with a politician had been anything but pleasant.

A few months back, Virginia State Senator Mitch Newbrough's daughter had been murdered. Both narcissistic and paranoid, Newbrough had been convinced that the killing was politically motivated instead of what it really was—the work of a pure psychopath. He'd wound up wasting bureau time and resources on his wrongheaded theory. He'd also gotten Riley fired.

Riley hoped that Ehrhardt wasn't going to give her similar problems. But she had a bad feeling about him.

From what she remembered, Ehrhardt came from a working-class background and liked to brag about his common roots, his empathy for ordinary Americans. It seemed to Riley that his look didn't fit his message. She guessed that his haircut alone must have cost hundreds of dollars.

But what do I know about politics? she asked herself.

"Well," Ehrhardt said, "I take it we're waiting for a ransom demand."

Riley was startled by his matter-of-fact, straightforward tone.

"Why do you say that?" she asked.

"Well, that's the way these things usually go, isn't it?" Ehrhardt said. "I mean, my wife and I are famous, we have money. Somebody's going to demand a ransom sooner or later. I'm new to this kind of a situation. How are we going to handle it? Are we going to pay or not?"

Chief Franklin drummed his fingers on the table.

He said, "Congressman, I'm afraid your wife's abduction might be of a different nature. We don't know yet for sure."

Ehrhardt's eyes darted back and forth. "What do you mean?" he asked.

Riley, Bill, and the chief looked at each other uneasily.

Riley said cautiously, "Congressman, are you aware of a string of murders that have occurred lately in this part of Delaware?"

Ehrhardt looked rather blankly surprised.

"I don't think so," he said. "But I've been busy campaigning."

Rhonda Windhauser didn't look surprised at all.

"I read something about it," she said. "But I'm sure Nicole's disappearance was completely unconnected."

Riley was more and more mystified by their casual attitude.

"What makes you think that?" Riley asked.

"Well, those girls were nobodies, right?" the woman said. "Just kids mostly—and thought to be runaways at that. Nicole must have been targeted by somebody different. For a kidnapping, this is really well-timed. Whoever did it knows that Representative Ehrhardt doesn't want to make a big fuss about it right now. He's got to get right back on the campaign trail. He'll be glad to pay a ransom and end this quietly."

Then for the first time, a slightly distressed look crossed the woman's face.

"Wait a minute," she said to Riley. "What did you say your name was?"

"Riley Paige."

The woman shook her head and said nothing. Riley understood immediately. Rhonda Windhauser must have heard about Riley's little adventure with the photographer. The man's complaints had been in the news. So Windhauser probably wasn't happy to have Riley on the case.

Bill told Ehrhardt, "Given the nature of these recent abductions and murders, we really have no choice but to assume that your wife's disappearance is part of the same picture. We have to proceed on that basis."

Ehrhardt exchanged glances with everybody.

"Well, I can't tell you how to do your job," he said. "But I'm sure there's been a mistake here."

Rhonda patted him on the hand—a little too familiarly, Riley thought.

"Don't worry, Wyatt. We'll get a ransom demand any time now. We'll get all this sorted out."

It seemed to Riley like a weird reassurance. Since when did the loved ones of abductees look forward to ransom demands?

Rhonda looked at Riley, Bill, and Chief Franklin and added, "I'm assuming that you'll do everything you can to keep this out from the media."

"We'll do our best for now," Chief Franklin said.

Riley felt a new wave of uneasiness. How long could they keep this new development out of the news? So far, they hadn't had much luck in that department.

Bill leaned across the table toward Ehrhardt.

"Congressman, do you know where your wife was going at the time of her abduction?"

Ehrhardt shrugged slightly.

"Sure," he said. "Nicole was on her way down to Dwayne Prentice's house on the beach."

"I'm sure you've heard of Dwayne," Rhonda put in.

Riley vaguely remembered seeing someone by that name on TV—a political pundit of some sort.

"In fact," Ehrhardt continued, looking at his watch, "Rhonda and I are expected there too. Dwayne is holding a big strategy meeting tomorrow. We were just getting ready to leave DC when we got your phone call."

Something about this explanation didn't quite add up for Riley.

"Wait a minute," she said. "You just showed up here in a chauffeured limousine. What was your wife doing driving by herself?"

Ehrhardt and his aide exchanged glances.

"I assume that nothing we say leaves this room," Rhonda said.

Riley, Bill, and Chief Franklin all murmured in agreement.

"Well, Wyatt and Nicole have their little differences, like all married couples," Rhonda said with an artificial smile.

"We had a little spat this morning," Ehrhardt said. "She got mad and took off on her own without us—without me. You see, here's what happened—"

Rhonda cut him off before he could say more.

"It's nothing," she said. "We'd just rather not make a big deal out of it. Appearances matter a lot, especially when an election looks like it's going to be this close."

Riley felt a chill at the way Rhonda said those words.

"Appearances matter a lot."

So far, Ehrhardt and his so-called aide seemed a lot more concerned about appearances than they did about a woman's safety—or even her life.

A political marriage if ever there was one, Riley thought.

She remembered some of what she had read and seen on the news about Ehrhardt. Although from a working-class family himself, he'd married into a much higher level of society. In addition to being a well-known supermodel, Nicole DeRose was the heiress to the Vincent DeRose wine fortune.

In Nicole, Ehrhardt had found the perfect trophy wife. She was excellent eye and arm candy, and she had all the money he needed to fund his political ambitions. And what did Nicole get out of it? Well, considering Ehrhardt's rising political star, maybe she'd get to be First Lady some day.

Ehrhardt and Rhonda Windhauser struck Riley as possibly two of the shallowest human beings she'd ever met. They probably didn't have a moral principle between them. Was it just possible that Nicole's disappearance was merely a political stunt gauged to attract voter sympathy in the upcoming election?

Riley couldn't help but wonder.

"May I see a picture of Nicole?" Riley asked.

"Certainly," Rhonda said. And from her briefcase, she produced a portfolio full of photos of Nicole, many of them taken during her modeling heyday.

What struck Riley immediately was how unnaturally thin the woman looked. Anorexic or bulimic, she was sure.

The woman in these photos hadn't lived a happy life, no matter how filled with creature comforts. Riley wondered if Nicole DeRose Ehrhardt was about to meet an even more unpleasant death.

CHAPTER TWENTY SEVEN

Nicole rubbed the back of her head again. It still hurt from the blow she'd received after she'd gotten into that awful man's car. When she'd regained consciousness, she'd found herself in this horrible, vile-smelling basement caged alongside a beaten-up teenaged girl. All the space she could see beyond a chain-link barrier was filled with clocks.

The only sense Nicole could make of the situation was that she'd been kidnapped and was being held for ransom. Such episodes were not unheard of in a family as wealthy as hers. During a trip to Mexico, one of her cousins had gotten kidnapped by some kind of gang. Her family had quietly forked over a few hundred thousand dollars for her release. The media never found out about it.

Surely that's what was going on right now. Nicole wasn't especially frightened. But she was a bit angry. If Wyatt hadn't pissed her off earlier, she wouldn't have driven off by herself. They'd argued about this thing he had with Rhonda, that trashy aide of his.

She didn't mind that he was screwing around. They had an understanding, and she did plenty of screwing around herself. But they'd both agreed to keep it quiet and discreet. Why did he have to flaunt this stupid thing with Rhonda? It was like he wanted everybody to know about it. Did he really want a scandal this early in his political career?

But Nicole knew that it wasn't practical to waste time worrying about that now. She had to focus on her immediate situation. Who was this other girl, and why was she here? She'd seemed to be asleep ever since Nicole had regained consciousness. Nicole gave the girl a nudge, and she started to wake a little. She weakly lifted her head.

"Who are you?" the girl asked in a barely audible voice.

"Never mind who I am," Nicole said. "Who are you?"

"I'm Kimberly," she said. "I'm nobody."

The girl lowered her head.

"Well, you can't be *nobody*," Nicole said. "I mean, somebody kidnapped you. Your family must have money. What kind of ransom is he demanding?"

The girl looked up at her again and emitted a hoarse, grim chuckle.

"A ransom?" she said. "What do you think is going on here? He's not looking for a ransom. He's going to kill us."

The words took Nicole completely by surprise. Not that she believed it. It didn't make any sense.

"Well, he sure doesn't plan to kill *me*," she said. "I'm worth way too much alive. Don't you recognize me? I'm Nicole DeRose. I'm sure you've seen me in magazines or on TV."

The girl shook her head tiredly. She didn't seem the least bit interested in who Nicole was.

"He kills us all," Kimberly said. "I've seen him kill two of us already."

Now Nicole was starting to worry. But this just couldn't be true.

"He's not going to kill me," she said again, trying to convince herself.

The girl looked her up and down.

"Oh, he's going to kill you," she said. "I'll bet he kills you before he gets around to me."

Nicole felt a sharp tingle of fear.

"Why?" she asked.

"Because you're even skinnier than I am. He's been starving me ever since he brought me here, but he keeps saying I'm still not thin enough, I've got too much meat on my bones. But you ... Well, you're already as skinny as the others he killed."

Nicole shuddered. She looked at the girl carefully. Sure enough, as starved as Kimberly looked, Nicole was undoubtedly thinner. She'd been anorexic all her life. She'd never thought of it as an illness, though. She owed her modeling career to her unnatural thinness.

She tried to convince herself that the girl was just talking crazy talk. Why would anyone kill women just because they were thin?

At that moment, all the clocks started ringing and chiming. As they did, a man came into the room beyond the fence. Sure enough, it was the same man who had tricked her and caught her back on the highway.

He didn't look like a bad sort of guy. He was odd, though. As the clocks kept up their wild noise, he wandered among them, adjusting and resetting them. And he was talking quietly to himself.

She shouted above the din, "Hey, how long are you going to keep me here?"

He didn't reply, just kept mumbling and fiddling with the clocks. Pretty soon the noise started to die away.

Maybe I should try to make conversation with him, she thought.

It didn't seem unreasonable. For one thing, she'd grown up around antiques all her life. While a lot of these clocks looked kitschy and tacky, some of them looked like real collector's pieces.

"I really love these clocks of yours," she said. "Are those cuckoo clocks real Black Forest originals? And is that tall case clock a genuine Jacob Godschalk? Wow, that must be worth thousands of dollars."

He turned and looked at her. He started to talk again—but not to her. He seemed to be talking to somebody invisible in the room.

"You're right," he said. "She'll do perfectly."

To Nicole's alarm, he picked up a multi-tailed whip off a table and walked toward the cage. He had a threatening look in his eye.

"Look, we need to talk about this," she said fearfully. "Maybe you don't know who I am. I'm Nicole DeRose. I've been on the covers of lots of magazines. My family owns Vincent DeRose, the wine company. I'm married to Wyatt Ehrhardt—you know, the Minnesota congressman."

"Shut up," the man said, definitely talking to her now.

"Now wait a minute," she said. "You don't seem to get that I'm worth a lot of money. I'm not just some nobody. And if anything happens to me, you'll be in real trouble. But there's no need for trouble. You can get a million or more as a ransom. You've really hit the jackpot with me. I'll tell you who to call."

The man opened the cage and stepped inside.

"Shut up," he said again.

Then he lashed the whip toward her face. She turned away, screaming at the searing pain. She tried to run, but there was nowhere to go.

CHAPTER TWENTY EIGHT

When the interview with Wyatt Ehrhardt and his aide ended, a cop met Riley and the other participants outside the room. He looked extremely worried.

"We've got a problem—and a big one," he said. "There are reporters waiting outside."

Riley's spirits sank.

Several cops formed a makeshift guard unit around Ehrhardt and Rhonda and ushered them through a door at the back of the building. In a few minutes, the worried cop returned.

"That worked okay," he said. "We just rushed them straight out of the building, and their limo was waiting out back. But now reporters have the back door covered too."

So much for keeping this out of the media, Riley thought.

Whoever was leaking information was staying awfully busy.

She gazed around the police station. Cops and support personnel seemed to be going about their business in perfectly normal fashion. They were at their computers, on their phones, picking up cups of coffee, chatting. Nothing looked suspicious or out of place.

But then, Riley realized, tipping the media might be perfectly normal here. Someone might be getting regular payments or just doing a favor for a friend. After all, hot tips from a small-town police station were not likely to be as big a deal as they were now that a congressman was involved.

The cop who had met them said, "You can go out whichever way you want."

Bill shrugged and headed for the front door. Riley went along with him.

She could see that even in the still-falling rain, a cluster of reporters with cameras and microphones waited just outside the station. As soon as Riley and Bill stepped though the door, the media gang was all over them.

"What can you tell us about Nicole DeRose's abduction?" shouted one.

"Was she taken by the 'clock killer'?" demanded another.

Things were worse than Riley even expected. It sounded like somebody had even leaked her theory that the bodies were arranged like clocks.

"No comment," Riley shouted.

Riley and Bill pushed their way through the thick crowd of people and cameras, to no avail.

"You're Riley Paige, aren't you?" shouted one woman.

"Is it true you got fired from the FBI earlier this year?" yelled a man.

"Are you going to break any more cameras?" screamed another.

The situation seemed hopeless. Their car was parked half a block away. Riley felt her anger rising. She couldn't imagine how she and Bill were going to get away from these vultures without saying something that really shouldn't be said.

Suddenly, she heard a car horn honking. She turned and saw Lucy pulling up to the curb in a car. Lucy threw the door open.

"Get in!" Lucy shouted to Bill and Riley.

Bill and Riley scrambled into the car, and Lucy drove them away.

But Riley felt no relief at the rescue. The whole atmosphere surrounding the case had changed. Pressure was mounting by the minute. And Riley knew that it was the kind of pressure that didn't lead to solutions. It often led to terrible mistakes.

*

Nicole DeRose Ehrhardt had simply vanished. Lucy had organized the usual search teams to cover the area, showing her photo and asking for leads. Riley and Bill had managed to pick up their own car and join the hunt. They found no traces of the woman, no indication whether she had been picked up by a killer or by a more mercenary kidnapper. It was late in the day, and they still didn't know what kind of case they were working on.

When Riley and Bill found themselves media-free, they located a burger joint and ruminated about the case over burgers and beers. They still had no idea whether Nicole DeRose Ehrhardt was still alive or not. But they knew that the killer who had picked up the other girls had held them for a period of time. If he was holding her, they still had a chance to could find him before he killed again.

123

"I have to wonder," Riley muttered, "whether the congressman's wife staged this herself."

"You mean she might have gotten herself abducted?" Bill asked. "She couldn't be doing that to pry money out of him. It's apparently all her money anyhow."

"Maybe she just wanted to escape," Riley said, noting the touch of wistfulness in her own voice. "Maybe she had some charming friend pick her up and whisk her away to a more peaceful life. On an exclusive island somewhere."

Bill took a bite of his burger, considering the possibility.

"By all accounts she participated in his political career. Hell, she paid for it."

"I know. She probably paid in a lot of ways. And of course you're right. She must be as ambitious as he is. I think she'd have to be dedicated, or she wouldn't put up with him and with his pushy assistant."

Before they were finished with their meal, Bill's phone buzzed.

Bill said, "This is an email from Rhonda Windhauser." He read it aloud. "Congressman Ehrhardt has just had a fruitful conversation with Special Agent in Charge at BAU, Carl Walder. If there are no new developments tonight, we will meet again tomorrow morning to discuss the various options in this situation. Be at the following address—"

"Just forward it to me," Riley said.

"It's on its way," Bill said. "The meeting's not in Ohlman. It's out at the beach. Maybe we'll get a look at the ocean."

When they returned to their hotel rooms, Riley sent a text to April but got no answer. She was sure her daughter was still mad at her for not mounting a search for the absentee boyfriend.

Riley undressed for a hot shower. As the soothing water tumbled over her body, she felt sure that April's boyfriend would show up tomorrow. Then surely April would relax the pressure on her. But, Riley knew, the pressure with her current case was about to get much worse.

CHAPTER TWENTY NINE

April gasped when she saw Joel sitting on the bench just outside the school grounds. He looked just fine. But where had he been yesterday? What had happened?

"Joel," she cried, rushing over to him.

When he glanced up and saw her, he smiled as if nothing had happened. He was acting as if he hadn't just disappeared for a whole day.

"Where were you yesterday?" April cried. She could feel the tears about to burst out, but she kept them under control. "I was worried about you."

"I took some time off," he said.

"You didn't answer my calls."

He shrugged. "Like I said, time off."

April didn't know what to say or what to think. Why was he being so casual about this? She sat down beside him.

"What's the matter, Joel? Did I do something wrong?"

"Of course not," he said. He put his hand on her knee. "You're just fine. Always. But I had to meet somebody about an interesting purchase. I wanted to try some things out. I didn't think you'd want to be there."

Joel was looking directly at her now, studying her face and still smiling. Even so, he seemed distant somehow. She couldn't stand that.

He raised one hand and touched her hair. "You look as beautiful as always."

Even his compliments sound lame today! she thought.

April felt the tears building up again.

"Why are you so upset?" he asked.

"You said you loved me."

Now his voice started to sound downright cold. "I do love you, April. I want to be with you all the time. But there are some things you don't want to do, so I have to go on my own."

She knew he was talking about the drugs. She didn't even know what some of them were, new things and new names cropped up so often.

"So you tried out something new?"

"Something I hadn't been able to get before. It was a great experience. I'd like to share that kind of thing with you. Just with you. But you don't seem interested. That's cool, I won't force you. I'd never do that. But even so …"

April drew a deep breath. She'd faced this wall between them before. "You know I don't like to do much more than pot. I just can't screw up my life. My mom is depending on me to keep up in school. She has enough other stuff on her mind."

"Well," he said, "it's great that your mom can depend on you."

April wasn't sure how to take that. Joel didn't say anything more for several long moments and she just sat there waiting.

Then he looked at her and smiled.

"This stuff is by prescription anyhow. Sick people get them all the time. You know that doctors aren't going to give their patients something that would hurt them. It's a painkiller, and it can make you feel really good." He chuckled and added, "Kills all kinds of pain."

"How do you get it?"

"I know a guy who knows a doctor. It isn't easy to come by. But this way I can be sure it's safe to use."

"If it was really safe …" April's voice trailed off. She wanted to ask, *Wouldn't it be legal?* But she thought that would make her sound stupid.

"I thought you understood. I'm just trying to keep from being bored. I've been hoping you'd try it. I'd never give you anything that would hurt you."

April knew that Joel was really smart and he was so sweet to her. And good-looking. And popular. Lots of girls would die for the chance to date Joel.

April heard a bell ringing and knew she needed to get to her next class.

"Will I see you after school today?" she asked.

He shrugged.

"Got things to do today."

April felt a wave of panic.

He turned and looked at her.

"But maybe, if you stop being so uptight, we can get together."

It was time to make a decision. April was tired of resisting. What was being a "good girl" getting her anyway?

She smiled as she felt her last trace of reluctance vanish. She couldn't risk losing Joel.

"I'll try it," she said. "Whatever you want me to try, I'll try it."

CHAPTER THIRTY

Riley was filled with numb apprehension as Bill drove their car up to the big iron gate. Even from outside, she didn't like the looks of the little village called "The Dunes."

During her whole career, she'd never had a single good experience in one of these gated communities. She felt sure that this little excursion into the lives of the rich and privileged wasn't going to be any different.

Bill stopped the car, and a uniformed guard stepped out of the security hut.

"What's your business?" he asked.

Bill and Riley both displayed their badges.

"FBI," Bill said. "A routine visit."

The guard looked extremely suspicious. Riley couldn't imagine why.

"Let me see that," he said, holding his hand out.

With a reluctant look, Bill handed him his badge. The guard held it up to the sunlight and examined it.

Can he really wonder if it's fake? Riley wondered.

"What's your business?" the guard repeated, handing back Bill's badge.

"We're here to talk with Congressman Wyatt Ehrhardt," Bill said. "At Dwayne Prentice's house."

Now the guard looked more suspicious than ever. He stepped away to talk on his radio.

"What the hell's going on?" Bill asked Riley.

Riley shrugged. She had no idea.

The guard stepped back over to the car.

"Okay, you can go in," he said. "Turn right when you get to Ocean Drive. It's the last house you'll come to."

The gate swung open. Bill drove through it onto a wide street, between houses that loomed large above private yards. As they drove toward the ocean, the houses got larger and farther apart. Riley was sure that everything in sight would be priced in the millions.

They pulled up in front of a large modern house with lots of windows. A man standing outside the house stepped up to the car and checked their IDs. He too seemed a bit suspicious. But he waved them to a parking spot. Several other cars were parked there outside the house.

Bill pointed. "Look at that," he said.

Sure enough, one of the cars was a clearly marked FBI vehicle.

"What's this all about?" Riley asked Bill. "Weren't you and Lucy and I the only agents assigned to this case? I mean, aside from local police?"

"Looks like maybe not," Bill said.

At least Riley now knew the reason for the guard's suspicion a few minutes before. He'd already let some FBI agents through the gate. Small wonder that he'd wondered whether Bill and Riley were the real thing.

Riley and Bill got out of the car and walked over to the front entrance. A maid answered the door and ushered them into a huge room with a soaring ceiling. The room was lit by sunlight pouring into the enormous windows and a fire that was glowing in a wide stone fireplace.

Four people seated on large leather sofas rose to greet them. Two were Rep. Ehrhardt and his aide, Rhonda, who was as provocatively dressed as she'd been yesterday. The other two took Riley completely by surprise.

"Huang! Creighton!"

The names were out of Riley's mouth before she could think, and there was a note of dismay in her voice. From their expressions, Riley knew that they'd picked up on her displeasure.

Agents Emily Creighton and Craig Huang were both fairly new to Quantico, and both very young. They'd made rookie mistakes when dealing with the dolly killer several months ago. Riley was under the impression that Huang, the younger of the two, had grown into his job somewhat since then. She didn't know about Creighton.

Riley was well aware that they were favorites of Carl Walder. She was glad that Walder himself wasn't here. Even so, their arrival here meant that Walder was taking a direct interest in this case. This wasn't surprising. Ever the opportunist, he would naturally be interested in any case that involved someone with political clout.

But Riley knew that it didn't bode well, at least not for her. Walder was undoubtedly giving some thought to yanking her off the case—if he hadn't decided to do so already.

Both of the young agents greeted Bill and Riley in awkward mumbles.

"Please make yourselves comfortable," Rhonda said.

Bill and Riley sat down in deep leather chairs. Riley looked out a large window onto a patio and a big private pool. Beyond that lay a sand dune, and beyond that the ocean. The view was almost spookily pristine. She wondered if anybody ever walked on that beach or ventured into the ocean. Probably not. The house seemed too much a world unto itself.

Riley felt compelled to say something polite.

"Lovely house," she said.

But the truth was, she didn't find the place lovely at all. Despite the overall pine scent, she could almost detect the odor of unsavory money all around her. She remembered that the house was owned by a political strategist. Just what a political strategist had done to get this rich boggled her mind.

Rhonda asked Bill and Riley, "Would you like something to drink? Tea? Wine Whiskey?"

"They're on duty, Rhonda," Ehrhardt said.

"Of course," Rhonda said.

Bill and Riley both said that they were fine as they were.

"Sorry to make you drive all the way out here," Wyatt Ehrhardt said to Riley and Bill. "I just wanted to get an update, and I can't go anywhere else without getting mobbed by reporters. Agents Creighton and Huang showed up just a few minutes ago. I wasn't expecting them. I was hoping you could give me an update."

"I wish we had something new to tell you," Bill said.

Riley added, "The truth is, we don't know anything more than we did when we talked with you yesterday."

Ehrhardt looked worried. It was the same look of shallow concern that Riley had observed yesterday—as if he'd been rained out of a game of golf.

"This whole thing is really disruptive," he said. "We had an important strategy session scheduled for today, but everybody bailed when the news about Nicole got out. And it's just a few days before the election. Aren't we ever going to get a break? I don't understand why there hasn't been a ransom demand yet."

Riley could hardly believe her ears.

"Congressman, we talked about this yesterday," she said. "I'm afraid there's every likelihood that your wife's abduction is the work of a serial killer. We shouldn't expect a ransom demand."

Creighton and Huang cleared their throats and shifted about uncomfortably.

"What is it?" Riley asked them.

Creighton said, "We're afraid that Special Agent in Charge Carl Walder doesn't share your opinion."

Huang added, "He's convinced that this is an ordinary kidnapping that has nothing to do with the local killings."

Riley was aghast now.

"How does he figure that?" she asked.

Creighton shrugged. "Well, what are the chances that your 'clock killer' just happened to stumble across a congressman's wife? Isn't that kind of a coincidence?"

"Yes!" Riley said, almost shouting. "It *is* a coincidence! And when the two of you get enough experience under your belts, you'll know that coincidences really do happen. And Walder ought to have learned that a long time ago."

Out of the corner of her eye, Riley noticed Bill's anxious expression.

"Riley …" Bill began.

But Riley couldn't keep quiet. She turned to Ehrhardt and said, "Congressman, with all due respect, Agent Walder is a high-functioning moron. And we don't have time for this kind of crap."

"Riley!" Bill said more sharply.

But Riley continued. "It is extremely likely that your wife is in the clutches of a murderous psychopath. She needs to be found and rescued. We can't just sit around waiting for a ransom demand."

Riley heard Creighton speak sharply.

"Agent Paige, we'll handle this."

Stunned, Riley turned to look at the two young agents.

"What are you talking about?" she asked.

Huang said, "Special Agent in Charge Walder sent us down here to deal with the kidnapping. He doesn't want you to be distracted from your own case by it."

Riley's mouth dropped open. "Distracted from it? This *is* my case."

Bill spoke her name more forcefully than before. She turned and looked at him. His expression told her that it was time to shut up. She forced herself to do just that. Bill rose from his chair.

"My partner and I understand," Bill told Creighton and Huang. "We'll leave you to your work."

Then turning to Ehrhardt, he added, "You have all of our best wishes through this terrible ordeal."

Ehrhardt simply nodded, obviously shocked by the rancor in the room. Bill walked out of the house, and Riley mutely followed him. They got in the car and Bill started to drive.

"Jesus, Riley," he said. "Remember when you pulled me off Dennis Vaughn a few days ago? Well, now it's my turn to ask ... what the hell's the matter with you?"

Riley groaned aloud.

"Bill, don't tell me that you believe for a single second that Nicole DeRose's disappearance is a routine kidnapping."

"No, I don't. But that's not the point."

"What *is* the point?"

Bill took a long, deep breath.

"Think about what's going on here," he said. "Wyatt Ehrhardt thinks his wife has been kidnapped for a ransom. Therefore Walder thinks it too. I mean, Ehrhardt's a famous politician, how could he be wrong? Walder really is that much of a brown-noser, and he really is just that stupid. But we can't do anything to change that."

Riley looked silently out the window as the expensive houses went by.

Bill continued, "Walder and his minions are right about one thing. Coming out here was a distraction—a detour. We won't find any clues here. We've got to get back to Ohlman and crack this case."

Now the guard at the gate hut waved them through.

Riley sighed. "My ass really is in serious trouble now, huh?"

Bill chuckled bitterly. "A 'high-functioning moron'? Yeah, if that gets back to him—and you can be sure that it will—you're in trouble, all right. You were already in trouble because of that stunt with the camera. Walder definitely knows about that. And you know perfectly well that he's always itching for a chance to take away your badge."

They were out on the highway now. Ohlman was only about fifteen minutes away.

Bill added, "If you're wrong about Ehrhardt's wife, there will be hell to pay."

Riley didn't reply. The truth was she hoped that she *was* wrong. Even if it meant losing her job, she hoped that Nicole DeRose was the victim of a routine kidnapping, and that a ransom

132

would take care of everything. Riley couldn't stand the thought of another woman suffering the same fate as the other victims.

CHAPTER THIRTY ONE

The day had been unproductive, but even so Riley didn't get back to her hotel room until after 10 o'clock that night. They still weren't any closer to finding the killer or the women he was holding captive. To make things worse, she and Bill had been dodging reporters everywhere they went.

She sat down on her bed and looked at the text messages she'd been sending to April during the day. The last was still marked "delivered," not "read." April was going to some trouble to keep on ignoring her.

Riley dialed the house number and Gabriela answered.

"How are things at home?" Riley asked. "What's going on with April?"

"I don't know, *Señora* Riley," Gabriela said, her voice sounding uneasy. "She has been very odd, doesn't say much. She went to bed early."

Riley felt a prickle of worry.

"She hasn't been skipping school, has she?" she asked.

"No. She got home late on Tuesday, said she had to go to the library."

Riley could hear a note of doubt in Gabriela's voice. She felt the same way.

Gabriela promised to call if there were any problems, and they ended the call. Riley remained sitting on the bed, wondering if she could sleep. She had so many things to worry about. The case wasn't going well, and in any case, it looked almost certain that she was about to get pulled off of it. And she simply had no idea what to do about April.

Can things get any worse?

She was just getting up to undress for bed when her cell phone rang.

"Am I speaking with Riley Paige?" a woman's voice asked.

"Yes," Riley said.

"Ms. Paige, I'm afraid I have some serious news," the woman said.

Riley sat down again. From the woman's tone of voice, it sounded as if the call was unpleasant.

"My name is Gwen Bannister, and I'm a hospice worker in Moline, Virginia."

Riley knew that tiny little town in the Appalachian Mountains. She'd driven through it often to visit her father. He'd lived for years in a little cabin near there. She remembered how ill he'd looked the last time she'd seen him.

"It's about my father, isn't it?" Riley asked.

Gwen Bannister spoke quietly, as if she didn't want to disturb somebody. "He's in a hospice home here in Moline."

"What's he dying of?" Riley asked.

As soon as the words were out of Riley's mouth, she realized they sounded abrupt and callous. There was a pause.

"He's in the final stages of lung cancer," the woman said. "When it spread to the brain he didn't want us to notify anyone. He also refused radiation therapy. I'm afraid he hasn't got much time. I'd put him on the phone, but he doesn't have the strength."

Lung cancer, Riley thought. *I might have known.* She remembered his coughing when she'd last seen him. He'd been paler and thinner too. She'd seen that he was very sick, but she had known that he wouldn't talk about it.

"Has he asked to see me?" Riley asked.

"No."

It figures, Riley thought.

The last time she'd visited her father, they'd actually exchanged physical blows. She'd sworn to herself never to see or talk to him ever again.

Now was the time to decide once and for all. Even if she left right now, she might not make it to Moline before he died. Was she really going to pay her father one last visit when she was needed both here and at home?

She remembered his cruel words to her during that last visit.

"You ought to be grateful, you whiny little bitch."

She wasn't grateful. She had nothing to be grateful for. If she got to her father in time, what could she expect from him except more abuse? Why should she give him the satisfaction of cursing him with his dying breath?

"I can't come," Riley said.

"Are you sure?" the woman said.

She didn't sound surprised. Riley could imagine why. Tending to her father had to be a thankless job.

"I'm sure," Riley said.

"Would you like me to tell him anything for you?"

"No," Riley said. "Thanks for calling. Thanks for what you're doing."

"Well, your sister has been very helpful."

Riley hesitated. Wendy was there? Helping them at the hospice? She hadn't talked to her older sister in years, hadn't even known where she was. For a moment she had an urge to speak with her now. But it had been so long ... Riley realized she wouldn't know what to say.

"That's good," she finally said.

"Let me give you my number in case you change your mind," the woman said.

Riley jotted down the number and ended the call.

She went to the bathroom and looked at her face in a mirror. It wasn't a pleasant face to look at, at least not at the moment. She could see a strong resemblance to her father there. She gazed into her own eyes, looking for some hint of guilt or longing, some desire to see her father one last time. She came up empty.

Still, it didn't feel right to stay away.

One more thing to worry about, she thought as she got ready for bed.

*

Riley opened the case folder. The first photo that she saw was the horribly emaciated corpse of seventeen-year-old Metta Lunoe. She set it aside. Under it was a photo of the equally wasted corpse of Valerie Bruner.

She set that photo aside, but it was followed by another gruesome picture, Chelsea McClure. When Riley moved that one aside, she was faced with the awful image of Elise Davey. She hesitated for a moment. Surely that was all. Surely she just had to read the written reports now.

But instead she found another photo of another dead victim from a past case. She set that aside to find another dead victim, then another, then another ...

Soon she found herself knee-deep in photographs, all of them showing victims of cases she'd worked on.

She heard a grim chuckle, then a familiar gravelly voice ...

"Sure is a lot of dead people."

She looked up and saw her father. He, too, was standing knee-deep in the sea of photographs that stretched out to a distant horizon.

He didn't look sick. He looked much as he had when he'd still been strong and healthy. He was tall and gangly, and he wore a hunting cap and a red vest.

There was a grin on his lined, hard, weathered face.

"Guess you must be pretty proud of yourself. You sure did right by all these people. You found justice for 'em. Every last one. Doesn't stop 'em from being dead, though. But that's you all over, isn't it? You're no good for the living. The only folks you're of any earthly use to are all dead."

"What do you know about it?" Riley asked bitterly. "Are you even still alive?"

Daddy chuckled again.

"Well, that would be interesting, wouldn't it?" he said. "It'd give you a chance to do right by the living for a change. You'll have to hurry, though. That is if it's not too late already."

"I don't owe you anything."

"Oh, no. Nothing much. Just everything you are, and everything you're ever going to be, both the good and the bad of it. It'll be too late to thank me later. It's now or never."

Riley felt a familiar anger rising in her throat.

"You'll never get a word of thanks from me," she said.

Daddy threw back his head and opened his mouth as if to laugh. But instead of laughter, a harsh, ringing sound filled the air ...

Riley shook herself awake and groped for her phone, the dream still fresh and vivid in her brain.

"There's another body," Bill's voice said. "It's Nicole Ehrhardt."

Riley could still hear traces of her father's laughter.

"I'll be right there," she said and hung up. She went into the bathroom and splashed cold water on her face. They had all failed Nicole DeRose Ehrhardt and now her image would join the photos of the dead. And she knew that all hell was going to break loose over this death.

CHAPTER THIRTY TWO

Sometimes Riley hated being right. She was looking down at the body, which was laid out in a farm field about ten miles west of Ohlman. It was Nicole DeRose Ehrhardt, sure enough.

A familiar rumbling sound overhead forced her attention away from the body on the ground. She looked up and saw a helicopter circling overhead. It was a clearly labeled FBI chopper, and its pilot was obviously looking for a place to land.

Riley looked around at the others who had gathered at the crime scene. Agent Huang was on his phone. Despite the rising noise, she could see his lips say the words, "Yes, sir; yes, sir" over and over again.

Then Huang approached the group and said loudly enough to be heard, "Special Agent in Charge Walder is joining us."

Emily Creighton smiled brightly. Lucy looked worried. Bill shook his head and muttered something inaudible—a curse, Riley was pretty sure.

The chopper swung away, apparently having spotted a good place to set down nearby. Riley swallowed her dismay and turned her attention back to the dead woman. An ego like Carl Walder's was the last thing they needed flailing about right now. Maybe she had a few more minutes before Walder got here to gather information.

Riley took in the whole scene. A nice grassy smell filled the air. The field had been mowed yesterday, and fresh hay bales were stacked in an open shed near the road. Sometime during the night, the murderer had chosen this spot for the placement of the body.

The property owner had found her this morning and called the police. The area was taped off now, but even though it was barely dawn, a few reporters had already gathered outside the tape. Yesterday Chief Franklin had told Riley, Lucy, and Bill that he'd found and suspended the cop who had been leaking information to the media.

A lot of good that did, Riley thought.

The word was already out about the murders, and the damage was done. Reporters were keeping a close watch on FBI activities in the area and following them whenever they could.

Riley stooped down to examine the victim. Unlike the others, this one looked much like her photos. She hadn't endured weeks of starvation. But she'd been unhealthily thin already—anorexic, no doubt. Her collarbones stood out against her pale skin. The red mark of a whiplash defaced one high cheekbone. Her fashionable raincoat was torn and bloody.

The body lay in no obvious relationship to the edges of the field or any visible landmark. But like the others, it had not just been dumped. The woman's arms and legs were carefully arranged. The left arm stretched upward, the legs were straight, the toes pointed. The right arm extended straight out from the shoulder.

"Nine o'clock," Riley said.

"The next hour in the sequence," Bill added. "What do you think it means?"

Riley said nothing. She simply didn't know. But yet again, she had the feeling that whoever was here and had left this body was acting under orders—not altogether alone.

But Riley didn't have time to think it over now. The helicopter had landed, and Carl Walder was walking briskly toward them. He was looking straight at her, and his expression was anything but friendly.

"Agent Paige, I see that you're still trying to catch up with this case," he said.

Riley prickled with irritation.

Trying to catch up? she thought.

She gestured toward the body.

"It wasn't a kidnapping for ransom," she told Walder.

"No, apparently it wasn't," Walder replied.

Without another word, he kneeled down beside the body. He obviously wasn't going to admit that Riley had been right and he had been wrong. After a cursory look at the body, Walder stood up.

"Get the coroner," he said to Huang. "We can't leave this woman lying out here."

Huang looked startled by the order, but he made the call without asking questions. Riley, too, was startled that Walder would shut down the onsite investigation so quickly. They hadn't even had an evidence team on the site yet. Walder was usually a thorough if unimaginative investigator.

But Riley reminded herself that the man always had a tendency to fall apart when politically powerful figures were involved. After

139

all, he was a vain man with ambitions of his own. Riley had no idea what those ambitions might be or where they might end.

Walder yelled, "And somebody get those reporters away from here. Move the tape back."

Then he turned to Riley.

"Agent Paige, I would have preferred to talk to you privately in my office, but under these circumstances, I can't put this off."

He led Riley a short distance off. Bill followed, blatantly ignoring Walder's attempt at confidentiality.

"A complaint has been registered about you," he said.

Riley rolled her head. "Yeah, I know. The reporter and the camera. Look, the bastard was intruding upon the privacy of a murdered woman."

"That's no excuse for what you did," Walder said.

Riley took a deep, long breath.

"You're so very right, sir," she said, trying not to sound sarcastic. "It won't happen again."

"It definitely won't happen again on this case," Walder said. "I'm taking you off. Effective immediately."

Riley stared at him. She'd been more or less expecting this. Still, she was surprised at his brazenness. Walder was pissed about a lot more than her breaking a reporter's camera.

She managed not to smirk. "This is about what I said about you yesterday, isn't it?"

Walder's face reddened.

"I wasn't here yesterday. I have no idea what you said."

Riley was on the brink of calling him a high-functioning moron all over again. Bill stopped her with a poke of his elbow.

Riley looked into Walder's beady eyes. She understood everything now. He was punishing her for two things—for calling him a moron, and for being right about Nicole Ehrhardt's abduction. Riley wondered which of the two had offended him more.

"You can't take her off the case," Bill told Walder. "Riley's got a better handle on this case than anybody."

Walder sneered.

"I guess you're talking about her 'clock theory,'" he said. "Yeah, I've heard about it. So has everybody else, courtesy of the media. You should have kept your mouth shut, Paige. Your theory's probably wrong, anyway."

140

"Now wait a minute—" Bill began. But Riley silenced him with a gesture. There was no point in explaining to Walder that Riley wasn't at all responsible for the information leaks. He surely knew that already, and he didn't care.

Walder continued, "You will return to BAU and work in your office until further notice. You and I will confer about your future assignments. I'll be returning by helicopter this afternoon. You can go back with me then."

Riley's voice was shaking with rage as she replied, "Thank you, but I drove my own car here. I'll drive home."

Bill trotted along beside her as she strode away.

"Riley, let's talk him out of this," he said.

"You know we can't do that," Riley said. "You stay, try to keep Walder from screwing things up more than necessary."

"I'll keep in touch," Bill said.

Bill fell behind, and Riley plunged among the reporters, shouting "No comment" to every question they asked. When she got past them, she saw the coroner's wagon approaching along the road.

Nobody was going to learn much from the crime scene—not with the rush job that Walder was doing. Fortunately, Huang had been taking pictures, and she would make sure that Bill sent them to her.

As she got into her car and started driving, she thought about her father dying up in the Virginia mountains. Or maybe he was dead already. If so, she felt pretty sure that his spirit was gloating over her humiliation.

"Go ahead and gloat, you miserable bastard," she muttered aloud. "I'm not through yet."

CHAPTER THIRTY THREE

When Riley got home later that day, she sensed that trouble was in store. April hadn't responded to a single text message or accepted a call since Riley had gone to Delaware. Something was going on, and she wasn't sure she was ready to deal with it.

It was late afternoon, and April ought to be home from school by now. But Gabriela met her at the door and Riley could tell from her expression that all wasn't well.

"*Señora* Paige, I wasn't expecting you," Gabriela said.

"I thought I'd be in Delaware a while longer," Riley said.

She had stopped at the BAU on her way back to pick up photographs and make sure that she had all the files about the case. Walder wouldn't approve, of course, but Riley was determined to keep tabs on what was going on.

"I am glad you are here," Gabriela said, wringing her hands. "April is being ... odd."

Riley set her travel bag down.

"Is she at home?" Riley asked.

"Not yet," Gabriela said. "She said she would be at the library, just as she said on Tuesday."

Riley could tell that Gabriela didn't believe the excuse. Riley certainly didn't either.

This isn't good, Riley thought.

After all, April was supposed to be grounded for two more days.

The doorbell rang. For a moment, Riley thought it was April, who had forgotten her keys. But when she opened the door, Blaine's daughter, Crystal, was standing outside. She was gangly like April, and about the same height, but her complexion was paler and freckled. She was carrying a few books.

"Hi, Ms. Paige, Gabriela," Crystal said. "Is April at home? I thought maybe we could study together."

Riley was happy to see Crystal. She thought that April's new friend was a good influence. It was nice having Crystal and Blaine right next door.

"No, she's not," Riley said. "In fact, we were just wondering when she'd be back. Would you like to come in?"

Crystal smiled and came inside. Gabriela offered her some lemonade.

"I'd love some," Crystal said.

Riley and Crystal sat down in the living room, and Gabriela brought lemonade for both of them. Riley noticed that Crystal looked worried.

"April told Gabriela that she'd be at the library," Riley said.

Riley could tell by Crystal's expression that she didn't believe this excuse either. Did Crystal know something that she didn't know? Riley knew better than to pry very hard. She remembered what it was like to have a best friend in high school. Things could go really badly if parents tried to play them against each other.

"Have you met April's boyfriend yet?" Crystal asked.

Riley wondered if Crystal was giving her a hint as to April's possible whereabouts.

"No, and I think maybe it's time I did," Riley said. After a pause she added, "You said a few days ago that you didn't like him."

Crystal took a hesitant sip of lemonade.

"Well, what all has April told you about him?" Crystal said. Riley could feel that she was testing the waters.

Riley shrugged. "Hardly anything. Except he's about her age."

Crystal's eyes widened. Riley wondered what was wrong.

"Is he in any of your classes?" Riley asked.

Crystal just stared at her for a moment.

"Ms. Paige, if I say anything, do you promise not to tell April I said it?"

Riley nodded.

"He's not April's age," Crystal said. "He's more like seventeen. And he's not in school. He was a sophomore last year, but he dropped out. I don't think he flunked out or anything like that, although I think he stayed behind for a year earlier on. Actually, he's pretty smart. It's just that ..."

She fell silent again.

"I'm sorry, Ms. Paige," Crystal said. "You'll have to ask April about anything else."

Riley fought down the urge to ask a flood of questions. The situation certainly sounded serious. But she understood. Crystal had just violated April's trust. She'd done so with the best intentions, because she was worried about April, but Riley couldn't expect her to say much more.

But there was one thing she really had to know.

"Do you think April's with him right now?" Riley asked.

"I don't know. The truth is, April doesn't tell me much about what she does with him. She's gotten a lot more secretive since they got together. That's part of what I don't like."

Crystal fell quiet. She still looked upset about something, Riley thought. She was concerned about April, of course, but Riley sensed that it was about something else as well. Riley felt a maternal tug of concern. She wondered if maybe she should ask what was bothering her.

I'm not her mother, she reminded herself.

"I guess maybe you think I'm overprotective," Riley said with a small laugh.

"Oh, not at all!" Crystal said, smiling. "You're a terrific mom! A lot better than mine …"

Her voice trailed off rather sadly. Riley wished she'd tell her more about her mother. She knew that Blaine was divorced, and she remembered him mentioning that she drank and was bipolar. But how involved was she in Crystal's life?

Crystal managed to smile again.

"Anyway, April and I are both lucky. We've both got *one* parent who really cares."

Crystal got up from her chair.

"I'd better go on home and get my homework done," she said. "Please tell April to call me when she gets home."

"I'll do that," Riley said, showing Crystal to the door.

Riley stood outside for a moment and watched the girl walk the short distance to the next townhouse. She wondered what their relationship might become in the near future. Was she going to get involved with Blaine? Was she going to wind up Crystal's stepmother, and was Blaine going to be April's stepfather?

Riley sighed. It wasn't an unpleasant thought. But it was too soon to tell. And maybe a life like that was too much to hope for.

Meanwhile, she saw that it was after four-thirty, and April wasn't home yet. It wasn't shaping up to be a good day. First, she'd been fired from a case. At least she knew that Bill would keep her updated about that. But now it was obvious that something was seriously wrong about April. What was she going to do?

Riley sighed, wondering if she was any good at anything.

She took her travel bag upstairs and put it in her bedroom. Then she stepped across the hall to April's bedroom. It was a mess, of course, but no worse than usual.

No cause for alarm, she told herself, sitting on the edge of April's bed.

She knew that she was easily alarmed when it came to her daughter. Ever since April's abduction by Peterson, she'd tended to panic whenever she didn't know where April was. Now was one of those times. Was April in some kind of danger at this very moment because of this new "boyfriend"? Might he even have kidnapped her?

Riley took a few deep breaths, trying to convince herself that she was being irrational. Somehow that was proving difficult.

She noticed that April's laptop computer was lying on her bed. Riley wasn't surprised. April usually took her tablet computer to school instead. But right now, the laptop began to tempt Riley. She'd always tried to respect April's privacy.

I'd better keep it that way, she told herself sternly.

But the temptation grew stronger. It even seemed justified. April had been lying to her about Joel all along. Surely April had forfeited her right to privacy this time. And for all Riley knew, this really was an emergency.

With trembling fingers, Riley flipped open the laptop and turned it on. Of course, the first thing it asked for was a password. Riley decided to make a wild guess.

"JOEL," she typed.

The desktop suddenly appeared. It seemed almost too easy and obvious.

She clicked onto April's Facebook page. The page and profile looked innocent enough. At a glance, it looked just the same as it did whenever Riley was logged on to Facebook. April's profile picture was a simple selfie, and her cover photo was a bunch of flowers.

But Riley knew that the page would be different now. Whenever she was on her own computer, April's settings blocked her from seeing all kinds of things that she could see right now—for example, a photo of April and a boy sharing a sloppy kiss. The tag showed that the boy was Joel Lambert. Riley clicked on the name, and his page appeared.

There was another selfie of a dark-haired, square-jawed, rather handsome-looking boy. The cover photo showed him smoking a bong, surrounded by wreaths of smoke.

Riley tingled all over with alarm. She knew it was time to put a stop to this relationship right now. Riley checked the boy's personal details. She noticed that Joel had posted both his home phone and address on his page. It seemed a little careless of him. But apparently, Joel didn't mind putting that information out there for close friends like April.

She took out her cell phone and started to dial the number. But she changed her mind before she finished. Instead, she walked straight downstairs and headed for the front door.

"Are you going out, *Señora*?" Gabriela asked, stepping into the living room.

"Just for a few minutes," Riley said. "I'll be right back."

And so will April, she thought as she walked out the door and got in her car.

*

Although Joel Lambert didn't live far from April's school, the neighborhood wasn't a good one. As Riley pulled her car in front of his house, it reminded her disturbingly of Dennis Vaughn's house in Redditch—a rundown little place with peeling paint and a sagging front porch.

Is April really in there? Riley wondered, getting out of her car.

She walked up onto the porch and knocked on the door sharply. She waited for a few long seconds before knocking again. She knocked a third time, and then Joel Lambert appeared, wearing jeans and a T-shirt. He looked surprised to see Riley.

"What do you want?" he asked.

"I'm here looking for my daughter," Riley said, crossing her arms.

Joel looked puzzled for a moment.

"Your daughter?"

Then he smiled. It was a calculatedly charming smile that barely hid the trace of a chronic sneer.

"Oh, you're April's mom! And you're FBI, aren't you? That's so cool. Can I see your badge?"

Riley didn't reach for her badge. She sensed that the kid was trying to stall her. Through the screen, she could see April's backpack on a beat-up brown couch.

"I want to see April," Riley said. "And don't try to tell me she's not here."

Just then April stopped into view. She forced an extremely awkward smile.

"Hey, Mom!" she said. "What're you doing here?"

Riley simply frowned at April.

"May I speak with your parents?" Riley asked Joel.

"Sorry, they're not here," Joel said. "They're both at work."

Riley brushed past Joel into the house. It was thoroughly trashed inside. Riley wondered if there were any parents in Joel's life. This kid might well be on his own. She sniffed, trying to detect if there was a smell of pot. But the air was so thick with other disagreeable odors that she really couldn't tell.

"April, go get in the car," Riley said.

"But Mom—"

"Go. I'll be right there."

April sulkily walked past Riley out the door.

Riley stared daggers at Joel.

"I want you to stay away from my daughter. Do you understand?"

Joel responded with a look of exaggerated surprise.

"Whoa, what's the matter? We weren't doing anything illegal. Hey, I really wish you'd show me your badge. I'd love to see it. I've never seen a real FBI badge before."

Riley stepped toward him, grabbed him by the arm, and forced it behind his back.

"You are going to stay away from her," she said firmly.

"Or what?"

Riley twisted his arm until he let out a cry of pain. She pushed him face first against the wall.

"I'll make your life hell," she said. "You'll be damned lucky if all I do is arrest you. Do you understand?"

"Yeah," Joel said, sounding scared now.

Riley let go of Joel and walked out of the house. She got back in the car and started to drive home.

"What was that all about?" April asked.

"Maybe that's what you should tell me," Riley said, her jaw clenched with anger.

April tried to sound nonchalant. "Oh, I get it. This is because I told Gabriela I was going to the library. I can explain. Joel's house is almost on the way to the city bus stop. I ran into him on the way, and we got to talking, and I forgot about the library. And I forgot about the time."

"You're lying," Riley said sharply. "You've lied about a lot of things. That kid isn't your age. And he's not in school with you. He isn't in school at all."

"Did I ever say he was? How do you know that, anyway?"

Riley didn't reply. Her head was exploding with questions. What was going on here? Were the kids doing drugs, drinking, having sex? Whatever it was, Riley was sure it was nothing good, and possibly illegal and dangerous. The only thing she knew for sure was there was no point in asking any questions right now. April would only keep right on lying.

"What did you say to Joel when I went to the car?" April asked uneasily.

Riley fought down the urge to start yelling at April.

"Never mind what I told him," she said. "Just remember, you're grounded."

"Yeah, but just for a couple more days, right?"

"Huh-uh. For the foreseeable future."

April's voice broke into a high-pitched whine.

"That's not fair! What if I've got to go to the library?"

Riley shook her head and stifled a sarcastic laugh. She drove in silence for a couple of minutes, then heard April's phone buzz. After a few moments, April cried out.

"Mom! I just got a text from Crystal! We've got to go there! We've got to go to her house!"

"No way," Riley said. She figured April was just trying to distract her from current issues.

"You don't understand!" April said. "Her mom came over! She's in real danger!"

Riley suddenly remembered that Crystal's mother was bipolar and alcoholic. Maybe that was why Crystal had seemed so uneasy a little while ago. Maybe she knew that her mother might be coming over.

Which meant her life could be in danger.

148

CHAPTER THIRTY FOUR

Riley could hear a woman shouting from inside Blaine's house. For a moment, she and April stood outside the door, wondering what to do.

"I shouldn't be here?" the woman's voice yelled. "You've got a hell of a nerve! I belong here as much as you, you spoiled brat!"

Then came a loud crash of something breaking.

Riley grabbed the doorknob and tried to open the door. It didn't move. It was locked.

"Open up!" Riley yelled.

Instead, she heard the woman screaming again.

"I'm your mother, goddamn it! I'll show you a thing or two about belonging!"

April grabbed Riley by the arm.

"Mom, we've got to get in there!" April said.

"I know. Give me a moment."

Riley thought fast. She had a lock-picking kit in her purse, but using it might take too much time. Shooting the lock with her pistol could be dangerous both to the people inside and to her and April. Instead, she grabbed a seldom-used credit card out of her wallet and wedged it between the door and the frame right next to the doorknob.

As the noise inside raged on, Riley pushed the card against the latch. She wiggled it against the sloping surface of the latch until she felt it move. She hoped that the dead bolt wasn't also locked. It wasn't, because when she bent the card away from the doorknob, pushed open easily.

"Wait here," Riley told April.

She stepped into the house. Flowers and pieces of a broken vase were scattered all over the floor. Riley saw a woman wielding a table lamp over Crystal, who was cowering against a wall.

Without a word, Riley rushed over to the woman, swung her around to face her, then pushed her away from Crystal. The lamp crashed to the floor.

The woman stared back at Riley.

"What the hell?" the woman snarled. "You get out of my way!"

She lunged, trying to get past Riley toward Crystal. Riley side-armed her and pushed her violently backward into an upholstered chair. Crystal's mother started to rise from the chair, but Riley raised her fist.

Riley heard Crystal's voice yell, "Don't hit her! Please!"

Still holding her fist high, Riley hastily assessed the situation. The woman was cringing now, ready for the blow. More physical force seemed unnecessary and there was no need to draw her weapon. It would only further traumatize Crystal.

Besides, Riley could see that Phoebe Hildreth was no longer a threat—at least not to her. But she'd arrived just in time to save Crystal from serious injury.

Quailing in the chair, Phoebe yelled, "Crystal, call the cops! We've got an intruder!"

Riley pulled out her badge.

"I am a cop. I'm FBI."

Phoebe gave her a drunkenly baffled look.

"FBI? Who called the FBI?"

"I live next door," Riley said, putting her badge away.

Phoebe looked Riley over with bloodshot eyes.

"Really?" she said with a sarcastic smirk. "And you have a key? Isn't that just so neighborly."

Riley studied the woman. She remembered that Blaine had said he had married her too young, and for all the wrong reasons.

He'd said, *"I thought Phoebe was the most beautiful girl I'd ever seen."*

Riley saw a lot of sad history in her ravaged appearance. There was still just a trace of that youthful beauty there. But years of heavy drinking had taken a terrible toll on her once lovely face, which was now puffy and heavily lined. She was overweight, and she looked years older than she must actually be.

Riley heard April call from the doorway, "Mom, Crystal's dad just got here."

Riley got out her phone to call 911. At that moment, she heard Blaine's voice.

"Riley, don't. Please. No police."

Blaine came inside, followed by April. Sobbing, Crystal threw herself into her father's arms.

"I got your text," Blaine told Crystal comfortingly. "I'm here. Everything's going to be all right."

Now Phoebe simply looked exhausted and weak. Whatever had been fueling her rage just a few moments before had suddenly slipped away, leaving an empty shell. It was hard for Riley to believe that this pathetic, damaged woman had ever been a physical threat.

April was standing in the doorway, staring at the scene in stunned silence.

Still holding Crystal tightly, Blaine said, "Riley, call a cab, okay? We'll send her home."

Still in the chair, Phoebe was staring at Blaine and Crystal. Riley could tell that the sight of their devotion to each other was too much for her. Phoebe dissolved into helpless tears, crying like a little girl.

*

A short while later, Phoebe was in a cab on her way to her sister's house, where she lived. April and Crystal had gone upstairs to Crystal's room. Riley and Blaine sat across the kitchen table from each other.

"Thank God Crystal texted me," Blaine said, staring into a hot cup of tea. "Thank God she texted April, too. If you hadn't gotten here when you did ..."

His voice trailed away, horrified at the thought.

Riley took a sip from her own tea and said, "Blaine, I'm not sure sending her home like that was the right thing to do. Maybe the police should have picked her up."

Blaine shook his head wearily.

"She's not usually physically abusive," he said. "She knows better. That's why she lost custody rights when we divorced. I had no idea she was coming over today. It's been nearly six months since we've even seen her. I'd thought she was doing okay living with her sister."

Blaine fell silent for a moment.

"I'll have to get a restraining order if anything like that happens again," he said.

Riley took Blaine by the hand.

"I think the time to do that is now," she said.

Blaine nodded. His eyes filled up with tears, and he couldn't seem to speak. But Riley could sense what he was feeling. She remembered something else that he had once told her.

"I kept thinking I could rescue Phoebe."

151

Riley knew that now Blaine was feeling guilty, toward both Phoebe and his daughter. As far as Riley was concerned, he was in no way to blame for what had just happened, or for the ruin that Phoebe had become. She also knew that she couldn't talk him out of feeling guilty. She'd felt the same way too often herself.

April came down the stairs.

"Crystal's okay now," she said.

Riley squeezed Blaine's hand tightly.

"Are you going to be all right now?" she asked him.

Blaine nodded silently.

"Just call me if you need anything at all," Riley said.

Riley and April left and walked next door to their own townhouse.

Riley felt tired, but she knew that her own family troubles were not over yet. She had a lot of questions to ask her daughter.

*

Gabriela looked glad to see Riley and April when they stepped inside the door. But she obviously picked up on the silent tension between the two. She only asked. "What do you want to do about dinner?"

"We'll just get sandwiches for ourselves," Riley said. "Thanks, Gabriela."

Gabriela headed downstairs to her own apartment. Riley and April went into the kitchen, where Riley started pulling things out of the refrigerator to make simple sandwiches. April stood and watched silently for a few moments.

Then April said quietly, "Thanks for what you did for Crystal."

Riley didn't reply. What had just happened at Blaine's house wasn't the issue right now.

"You could help with sandwiches," Riley said.

"I don't think I want one," April said.

Riley went ahead and worked on her own sliced turkey sandwich.

"You're really mad at me, aren't you?" April said.

Riley took a long, deep breath.

"Never mind about whether I'm mad at you," she said. "You'd better answer some questions."

She could hear April gulp with anticipation.

"Like what?" April asked.

Riley looked her daughter straight in the eye.

"Like what you haven't told me about that boy. You were at his house, which is a mess. Who are his parents? Where were they?"

April glared back at her. "I've never met his parents," she said. "Why should I? He said they both work. I guess they don't make a lot of money and don't have a maid to keep the house clean."

"Why did he drop out of school?"

"He's been working part time but he said he needs to make more money. I think he's looking for a full-time job."

"Where does he work part time?"

"I don't know. It isn't his fault his parents aren't rich and he has to help out."

"How did you meet him?"

April crossed her arms and her eyes darted back and forth.

"He was around school at the beginning of the year and we just started talking." April drew a deep breath. "You wouldn't understand, but he's actually interested in what I have to say. He likes spending time with me."

"Does he do drugs?"

April blinked hard.

"No," she said.

"You're lying," Riley said. There was no doubt in her mind about it. She hadn't been an FBI agent all these years for nothing. And she knew he daughter well enough to tell.

"I'm not lying," April said. She lowered her head.

"Look at me," Riley said.

April slowly lifted her face and looked at Riley.

"What about telling Gabriela you're going to the library? You were lying about that."

April made no answer.

"Did he tell you to lie about that?"

"Of course not."

April's whole face trembled. "I need time ... I need my own life." She looked away again. "So what are you going to do? Ground me forever?"

"I'll ground you for as long as it takes. I'll ground you until I'm absolutely sure that you're through with Joel."

April's eyes widened and her mouth dropped open.

"What?" she gasped.

"You heard me."

"That's crazy! I mean, when is that going to happen? You think I'm lying all the time! You don't believe anything I say! So how are you ever going to be sure I'm through with Joel?"

Riley stared hard at her.

"That's what we've got to work on," she said.

April slammed her hand on the table so hard that the food and utensils jumped.

"You've got to be the worst mom in the whole world," she yelled. "You're even worse than Crystal's mom."

"April!"

"No, really! She can't help being like she is. You can. But it's that goddamn job of yours, I guess. It's ruined you. You just don't know how to trust anybody. You have no idea how to be a mom, or any other kind of human being."

Riley was speechless. April stormed up the stairs to her room and slammed the door behind her.

CHAPTER THIRTY FIVE

Scratch sat crouched outside the cage staring at the only girl left inside. He thought her name was Kimberly. It felt odd, having kept her here all this time and still not being sure of her name.

"Do it," the girl said in a hoarse whisper. "Do it now."

Scratch knew that she meant killing her. He wished he could comply. But of course, he couldn't kill her until Grandpa said so. And Grandpa wasn't saying anything at all right now.

Scratch knew that Grandpa was mad, of course. He'd been mad for days now, ever since the Irish girl had gotten away. Scratch still wondered what had become of her. And Grandpa wasn't the least bit happy that Scratch's most recent captive and kill turned out to be a politician's wife. It had put their whole project at even greater risk.

Whenever Grandpa was quiet like this, Scratch felt desperately alone.

"I wish you'd talk to me," Scratch said to the girl. "Do you want to spend the rest of your life not talking like this?"

The girl said nothing.

Scratch felt sad enough to cry. He knew he was failing in the great mission that Grandpa wanted to fulfill.

Was anyone going to understand the message? Would all these girls starve away and die for nothing?

When everybody was dead, who would there be for him to talk to? Grandpa might then be angry enough never to speak to him again. Grandpa might simply go away. Scratch would be all alone, the only living human in the whole world.

Unless …

A dim hope started to come over him. Maybe—just maybe—it was part of Grandpa's plan that there would still be a living girl in this cage, even after the destruction came. If so, maybe she could be his companion. Maybe they could start the whole world over again together. Maybe that was what Grandpa really had in mind.

And maybe this girl—the one who never seemed right to kill, who never got quite skinny enough—was the one who would stay with him. Maybe she would be his.

If so, would *she* ever talk to him, even when he was the only man alive?

But he mustn't dare to hope. There was only one thing he knew for sure—that three more girls must be killed.

CHAPTER THIRTY SIX

That evening, Riley still felt absolutely miserable. She was staring blankly at something on the muted TV but April's words of anger were still ringing in her ears. When the phone rang and she saw that the call was from Bill, she answered breathlessly.

"Bill! Give me some news!"

She heard Bill breathe a heavy sigh.

"I've got news," Bill said. "But you're not going to like it."

Riley sank back in her chair, bracing herself for whatever Bill was about to say.

"Walder's convinced that Meara Keagan can get her memory back," he said. "So he's called in a psychiatrist to hypnotize her."

"He's what?" Riley gasped.

"It gets worse," Bill said. "The shrink they're getting is Leonard Ralston."

She could hardly believe her ears.

"That's crazy," she said. "Ralston's a quack. The last time Walder brought him in on a case, he got the wrong guy to sign a confession."

Bill let out a bitter chuckle.

"Yeah, well, you and I both know Walder doesn't let little things like that bother him. Ralston's written bestselling books. He's done his hypnotism thing on TV talk shows. Walder just loves celebrities. They can do no wrong as far as he's concerned."

Riley moaned aloud.

"What can I do, Bill?" she asked.

"You can do exactly nothing. I'll do everything I can to get you back on the case. Meanwhile, you've got to keep your distance. You could make things a lot worse for yourself."

"Yeah, I know," Riley said. "I'll stay put."

A silence fell between them.

"So how are things at home?" Bill asked.

Riley could tell by his tone of voice that he wanted to talk about something, anything, other than the case. She understood the feeling. And it seemed like an opportunity for her to open up to someone she had often trusted with her life.

On the other hand, was she going to burden Bill with all the details about her ugly, petty situation here at home? He'd had to

157

deal with his own share of domestic nastiness, including a bitter separation and an ongoing custody struggle over his two sons. And through it all, he'd been haunted by a case that made him feel like a failure. No, now was not the time.

"Things are okay," she said.

"Good. Well then, I'll keep you posted."

Riley thanked him and ended the call. She sat on the couch staring at the silent TV. She didn't know what show was on. But from the looks of it, it was some kind of a sitcom with the usual snarky dialogue between parents and children. The plots always involved lighthearted squabbles that were easily resolved in a half hour between commercials.

Are there really any families like that? she wondered.

Until today, she'd thought that Blaine and his daughter had a pretty flawless life together, right next door. But that illusion had gotten shattered in a big way. She closed her eyes and remembered looking into Phoebe's ravaged face. Now that the whole scene was over, she could give herself over to pity for the poor woman. And now, remembering the desperation in those bloodshot eyes, Riley had the strangest feeling that she was looking in a mirror.

She remembered what April had said before storming upstairs.

"You're even worse than Crystal's mom."

It wasn't true. It couldn't be true. Phoebe had long since failed at everything she'd hoped to do in life. Riley was at least hanging on by her fingernails. But she knew deep down that she had more in common with Phoebe than she wanted to admit.

We're both disappointed, she thought. *Disappointed with ourselves.*

Riley had wanted to give April a better life than she had. She hadn't wanted anyone to make April feel as small and useless as her own father had made her feel. She'd wanted April to have a happy childhood with a loving family—not like the emotionally empty years she'd passed being raised by her aunt and uncle.

But was the life she'd given to April any better than her own? The promise of a happy two-parent household was gone, and now a Guatemalan maid was more of a mother to her daughter than Riley was. Worse still, Riley couldn't keep April safe from the risk and danger that permeated her own life. After her captivity, April knew almost as much about violence and cruelty as Riley did. And April had even helped her mother kill the man who attacked them. Why should a teenager have to live with an act like that?

Small wonder she thinks I'm a terrible mother, Riley thought.

Was there anything in life that was in her control, that she could do something about?

Suddenly she remembered Jilly, and the last phone conversation they'd had together. The poor girl had felt lonely and unwanted. Maybe if they could talk again now, they could make each other feel better.

She quickly calculated the time difference between Virginia and Arizona. It was a little after five o'clock there. She figured it wasn't a bad time to call.

She picked up the phone and dialed the number for the teenage shelter in Phoenix. Once again, Brenda Fitch answered the phone.

"Hi, Brenda, this is Riley Paige."

"What can I do to help you?"

Riley was taken a little bit aback. Brenda's voice sounded tentative and cautious.

"Well, I was wondering if Jilly was around," Riley said.

There was a short pause.

"Yes," Brenda said.

"Could I talk to her?"

A longer silence fell. Riley's heart pounded. What could be the matter?

Finally, Brenda said haltingly, "Riley, I—we—all of us appreciate what you did for Jilly by bringing her here. You probably saved her life. It's just that—"

Silence again.

"What?" Riley asked.

"Well, Jilly was terribly upset after the two of you talked last time."

Riley's spirits sank as she remembered.

"Couldn't I come to live with you?" Jilly had asked. *"I won't be much trouble."*

Jilly had cried when Riley said no. Riley felt a desperate need to put things right between them.

Brenda said, "She told me she didn't think she wanted to talk to you anymore."

Riley felt a tightness in her throat.

"Couldn't you ask?" Riley said. "Maybe she'll change her mind. I promise not to upset her this time."

"How can you promise that?" Brenda asked.

The question stopped Riley cold. Brenda was right. How was this time supposed to be different? She still couldn't say that Jilly could come and live with her. Talking to Riley would just hurt her all over again.

"She's going through a really rough time," Brenda said. "I just don't want to make things any worse."

"I understand," Riley said.

She almost asked Brenda to send Jilly her love. But no, that didn't seem like such a good idea. Just knowing that Riley had called might get Jilly's hopes up for something that could never happen.

"Maybe it's best not to mention that I called," Riley said.

"I think so too," Brenda said.

"But is it okay for me to call you once in a while, just to find out how she's doing?"

"Of course."

Riley and Brenda exchanged goodbyes, and the call ended.

Riley fought down a sob. She just couldn't let herself feel like this. She more than half wanted to jump into her car and drive straight down to Delaware. But Bill was right—she'd only make trouble for herself without helping at all.

Meanwhile, all she wanted to do was numb the pain.

She walked to the kitchen and pulled down a bottle of scotch from a cabinet. She opened it and poured herself a large glass. She picked up the glass and took a small sip. The burning in her throat immediately felt comforting. She gulped the rest of the glass down and poured herself another.

CHAPTER THIRTY SEVEN

Riley spread the photos of victims on the coffee table, then took another gulp of scotch. She'd put the bottle and the glass in front of her, and she expected to go on drinking for a while. It felt good. And right now, she was experiencing a familiar buzz of lucidity that she got when she had imbibed just enough but not too much. She knew it wouldn't last long. Why not take advantage of that feeling to pore over case materials?

She spread the photos of all the murder victims across the table. Again, it struck her as painfully obvious that the corpses' hands were in clock positions. But not everyone agreed.

She remembered what Walder had said.

"Your theory's probably wrong, anyway."

Was it possible that she was only imagining it? Maybe right now was the time to figure it out for sure.

But before she could put the materials in any kind of order, the phone rang. She saw that it was an unfamiliar number. She was tempted not to answer, but for some reason she decided otherwise.

The voice on the line said, "Riley, this is Wendy."

Riley half-recognized the voice and knew the name. But her mind stumbled over who this caller was.

"Your sister," the caller added.

Riley gulped hard.

"Hello," she said. "It's been so long."

"Yeah, it has."

A cascade of confusing emotions poured over her. Not the least of them was guilt. Wendy was ten years older and had left home when Riley was still a kid. She had made just one attempt to reach out to Riley years ago. Riley never replied to her letter. She didn't know why, and she regretted it. Since then, she hadn't known anything about Wendy's life or her whereabouts.

And now she remembered that the hospice worker in Virginia had told her that Wendy was with her father.

Wendy said, "The hospice gave me your number. I've been here for a couple of days."

"I know," Riley said. "They said you were being really helpful."

Wendy didn't reply. Riley swallowed hard.

"He's dead, isn't he?" she said.

"Uh-huh," Wendy said. "About an hour ago."

Riley had no idea what to say. Any questions that came to mind seemed stupid and clichéd. Did he die peacefully? Was he in pain toward the end? Did he say anything? Riley didn't really care, and she couldn't act like she cared.

She suddenly felt no emotions at all. But her head was swimming a little. She hoped she wouldn't sound like she'd been drinking.

"We're going to have a funeral in two days," Wendy said. "A small service."

Again, Riley made no reply.

"I've notified some of his marine buddies," Wendy added. "A couple of them might be there, but I'm not sure. They sounded surprised that he'd died. I don't know why. Maybe they thought he'd never die. Or maybe they thought he'd died a long time ago. Who knows?"

Riley knew that Wendy was tiptoeing around a question. It seemed best just to answer it outright.

"I can't come to the funeral," she said.

Wendy sounded taken aback by Riley's bluntness.

"There won't be any other family there. Everybody we're related to has died or moved away or …"

Her voice trailed off. In her mind, Riley finished her sentence.

"… or just plain hated his guts."

She thought it best to keep that thought to herself.

"I can't be there," she said again.

"Oh."

Neither Riley nor Wendy said anything for a moment.

Wendy began, "I was hoping—"

Riley interrupted her.

"No, Wendy, I just can't," she said. "I'm sorry to be like this, but I can't. Thanks for calling. I wish you well. And thanks for being there for Daddy. Goodbye."

"Riley, wait," Wendy said.

There was such a strong note of urgency in Wendy's voice that Riley didn't hang up.

"I'm sorry," Wendy said.

Riley was completely taken by surprise.

"Sorry for what?" she asked.

A moment passed before Wendy replied.

"I can understand if you still hate me," she said, her voice choking now.

Riley was completely shaken now.

"Hate you?" she gasped. "I don't hate you. I never hated you."

"I don't see how you could help it," Wendy said. "I mean, the way I left you like that all those years ago ..."

Wendy's voice trailed away. She sounded as if she were so overwhelmed by emotion that it was hard for her to speak.

Finally she said, "You were just so little. You were five, and I was fifteen. And I told you I was just going to stay overnight with some friends. You were too little to wonder why I'd packed so many things. I didn't say goodbye."

After another pause, she added, "I feel like I abandoned you."

Riley was shocked beyond belief. She realized that she remembered absolutely nothing about that moment, when Wendy had left for good. But somehow it seemed wrong to say that.

"You didn't abandon me," Riley said. "Daddy hit you."

Riley heard Wendy let out a single sob.

"It wasn't your fault," Riley said. "Nothing was your fault."

Wendy replied with an uneasy laugh.

"Thanks for saying that," Wendy said.

"I mean it."

Neither of them said anything for a moment.

"Well, I've got to go," Wendy finally said. "I've got a lot to do here. And I hope—"

Wendy seemed unable to finish the sentence.

"You take care of yourself, Riley."

Wendy ended the call. Riley sat there wondering what she was going to say she hoped for. Perhaps that they could get together sometime, or at least stay in better touch? But how was that even possible? They'd never had any kind of relationship, had never been real sisters. Was it possible to change that now?

Riley realized that she was shaking all over. A momentous force in her life had just passed away, and she had no idea what to feel. The truth was, she couldn't get it through her head that Daddy was really dead. She could still hear his voice loud and clear.

She distinctly remembered him saying, *"It'll be too late to thank me later. It's now or never."*

But she realized that he hadn't said that in real life. It was in a recent dream.

Now, under her breath, she repeated what she'd said in the same dream.

"You'll never get a word of thanks from me."

She swallowed down the rest of her glass of scotch and poured herself another. The phone rang. Riley was sure that it was Wendy again. She was glad. Maybe they could end their conversation on a better note.

"I'm glad you called back," she said.

She heard the sound of harsh laughter.

"That's nice to hear," a man's voice said. "I get lonely listening to the sound of my own voice."

She recognized the voice at once. It was Shane Hatcher, a prisoner at Sing Sing. He'd been incarcerated there for several decades, serving a life sentence for a number of brutal murders he'd committed as a youthful gangbanger. In prison he'd become something of a criminology expert, and he had helped Riley with a couple of cases. But he was a manipulative and dangerous man, and Riley had hoped she was through with him.

"I don't want to talk to you," Riley said.

More than even with her sister, Riley hoped that he couldn't detect a note of intoxication in her voice.

Hatcher laughed again.

"Oh, come on, Riley. Don't be like that. I've missed you. And you've missed me too. Admit it."

Riley wanted to tell him, no, she had absolutely not missed him. But was that altogether true? Some part of her was perversely drawn to Shane, like a moth to a flame. It wasn't physical attraction—not that at all. She could never love a monster like that. It was just that he had a brilliant but evil mind, and he fascinated her, and she couldn't help but want to understand him better. That was why he terrified her so deeply.

"I hear your daddy hasn't been well," Shane said.

Riley's skin prickled all over.

"Where did you hear that?"

He chuckled some more. "Oh, I get around."

It was a joke, of course. But Riley didn't laugh. This worried her. How did he know about her father's illness? Doubtless he'd used the Internet to find out. Hatcher probably knew how to get all kinds of information that way. And now it seemed that he must be keeping obsessive track of her.

So what kinds of things might a cunning man like Shane have found out about her online? Her birthday? Her Social Security number? Where she lived? Her yearly income? The terms of her divorce settlement? Worst of all, what might he know about April?

She felt queasy all over at the possibilities.

"So how's your daddy doing?" Shane asked. "Do you think he'll pull through?"

There was a sarcastic edge to the question. Shane obviously suspected otherwise. Riley said nothing.

Shane chuckled darkly.

"Oh. He died, huh?"

Riley still said nothing.

"Well, I'm sure you got a chance to clear up your differences before he moved on to a better place," he said, his sarcasm thickening. "That's something. That's all that matters. I'm happy for you both."

The words stung. Riley knew they were supposed to. Shane knew perfectly well that there could have been no such reconciliation. He was somehow fascinated by her relationship with her father. The last time she'd seen Shane, he'd told her, *"You don't give your daddy enough respect."*

And, *"You should listen to your daddy."*

Now he was going to try to play on her feelings of guilt. But that wouldn't work. She didn't have any feelings of guilt.

She almost ended the call at that very moment. But it was as if Shane knew her intention and kept right on talking.

"Wait a minute. Let's chat a bit. Let's catch up. I hear you're working on a case in Delaware. And I hear you've got some kind of 'clock' theory about him. Tell me more. You know how much I love this kind of thing."

"I'm not telling you anything," Riley said.

Shane chuckled again.

"You should come up and see me in Sing Sing," he said. "We could kick around some ideas. You know I could help."

Riley bristled with anger and frustration. The truth was, he just might be right. Her past visits to him had been painful but productive. He'd supplied vital insights into the minds of two killers. His advice had helped her a lot.

But this had to stop. Even behind bars, he was too dangerous to deal with.

"Don't call me again," she said.

With a tone of mock hurt, Shane said, "So you're not going to come see me?"

"No."

Riley abruptly ended the call. For a moment, it felt good to have had the last word—"no." Then she stared at the telephone apprehensively. Was he going to call back right away? If so, it wouldn't be enough to simply ignore whatever message he left.

She relaxed a little as minutes passed and no call came. Still, she doubted that she'd gotten free of him for long. Although he said otherwise, Shane Hatcher was *not* a man who could take no for an answer.

She sat down to look at the photos again, but her mind wasn't clear. Now she was simply drunk. She felt dizzy, and her eyes were losing focus, and she couldn't put together a complete idea. She lay down on the sofa, closed her eyes, and fell into a troubled sleep. Images of emaciated corpses filled her dreams.

*

Riley awoke to the smell and sound of sizzling bacon in the kitchen. She realized that Gabriela was cooking breakfast. Riley's head was splitting. She sat up and looked down at the coffee table, where she saw the photos from last night and an open bottle of scotch and a partially drunk glass.

She carried the glass and the bottle into the kitchen. She put the bottle back in its cabinet and poured the remaining scotch in the glass into the sink.

Gabriela was hunched over the stove, humming a song. Riley felt horribly ashamed and embarrassed. Gabriela couldn't have helped but notice Riley passed out on the couch when she came upstairs this morning.

"*Buenos días,* Gabriela," Riley said shyly.

Gabriela turned around and smiled at her.

"*Buenos días, Señora* Riley."

There wasn't a trace of judgment or reproach in Gabriela's smile. It was full of silent sympathy and understanding. As she

166

often did, Riley felt a surge of gratitude to have such a warm and kindly woman in her life—and in April's life as well.

Riley walked back in the living room just in time to hear a wail of despair from upstairs. A few seconds later, April came galloping down the stairs, sobbing uncontrollably.

"What's wrong, honey?" Riley asked.

April paced and spoke in an accusing voice.

"Joel just called. He's breaking up with me. And it's really, really final. I hope you're happy. It's all your fault. He says you're crazy. He says he doesn't want to be mixed up with a girl with a crazy mom like mine."

Riley managed not to smile. She remembered how she'd roughed him up and given him an ultimatum to stay away from April.

"I'll make your life hell," she'd promised. *"You'll be damned lucky if all I do is arrest you."*

Apparently Joel had gotten the message.

Riley hugged April and sat down with her on the couch. She handed April a box of tissues. Gabriela silently came in with coffee for both of them, then went back into the kitchen.

"Why did you have to do that?" April blubbered. "Coming to get me like I was a little kid. It was so humiliating."

Riley patted her on the back. April pulled away from her.

She said, "Well, if you don't want me to treat you like a little kid, you'll have to act more like an adult. I came to get you because you were grounded. You weren't supposed to be out. I had every right. And when I saw him and that place where he lived ..."

Riley paused for a moment.

"That boy's wrong for you," Riley said. "He's too old for you and—he's just wrong for you."

"That's not up to you to decide," April sobbed.

Riley chuckled a little. "Actually, it *is* up to me to decide. You're fifteen years old."

"So how long am I grounded for now?"

Riley fought off the temptation to say something like, *"Until you're thirty."*

Instead she said, "That's completely up to you. Prove to me that you don't need to be grounded. When you start acting grown up enough to make these kinds of decisions, be my guest, make your own decisions. It really gets pretty tiring."

Riley put her arms around April, and April didn't pull away.

"Am I wrong?" Riley asked quietly.

"Huh-uh," April muttered, crying in Riley's arms.

Riley hugged April.

"Then come on," she said. "Gabriela's got breakfast ready."

*

Little was said between Riley and April over breakfast, but Riley got the strong feeling that things were back on the right track. After they had finished eating, April went back upstairs to shower and get dressed. Today was Saturday, so she planned to get together with Crystal and do homework.

Riley went back in the living room and noticed again the materials on the coffee table. She was sure that she was right about the women being posed to indicate hours on a clock. She looked at the photos again.

Five ... six ... seven ... eight ... nine ...

Her theory was right. The killer was obsessed with time. And how long did they have before he decided to mark the hour of ten? Another woman's life depended on someone finding out.

Nobody else seemed to believe her theory, but nobody else had come up with any leads to the killer either. They weren't even close to catching him.

Riley tingled all over with a renewed sense of urgency. It didn't matter that Walder had taken her off the case. It was her job to prevent more women from suffering so horribly and dying at this killer's hands.

She knew she had to get back to Delaware.

CHAPTER THIRTY EIGHT

Meara closed her eyes and concentrated on following Dr. Ralston's directions. He had hypnotized her several times now. She never remembered exactly what he said to her when she was hypnotized, but after each time, she seemed to remember something about her captivity that she hadn't before.

She found these sessions a little creepy, but she didn't want to tell him that. He was trying to help. And he was a nice man.

"Relax now," the doctor's voice was saying yet again. "Relax your toes, your feet, your legs."

As he guided her along, Meara began to feel like she was floating in air rather than lying in the hospital bed. As all her muscles went soft, she could no longer feel the cast on her leg. It felt nice to escape from that uncomfortable, itchy thing.

"Now I want you to go back to that place you've talked about," the doctor murmured. "That basement with the clocks."

The scene started to take shape around her—a scene that she'd described to Dr. Ralston before. She was in a fenced area in a gray room. She could see clocks nearby. All kinds of clocks.

"I'm scared," Meara said.

"Don't be. It's like I've told you before, you are safe at all times. Nothing will harm you. This place may seem real, but it's all in your mind now. Are you there?"

Meara's fear seeped away, and she was comfortable again.

"I'm here," she said.

"Good," Dr. Ralston said. "Are you alone?"

It struck Meara as odd that Ralston asked this same question every time he hypnotized her. But she gave the same answer as always.

"No," she said. "Three other girls are here. Chelsea, Elise, and Kimberly."

All was quiet for a moment. Meara knew what Dr. Ralston was going to ask next. She hoped that she could answer this time. The other times, she had been too frightened to remember.

"Do you see the man who held you captive?"

Meara's breath quickened. For the first time, she could make out his image. He was standing just inside the fence staring at the other girls.

"Yes," she whispered. "I can see him."

"What does he look like?"

The picture became sharp and vivid. Meara reminded herself not to be frightened.

"He's white. In his thirties. Not really tall but very strong. Medium build. Dark straight hair. His eyes are dark. And wild looking, like a crazy person. They always seemed black to me. Like the devil's. My grandmum always said the devil has black eyes."

"You mean he has brown eyes?" Dr. Ralston asked.

"Yes."

Then something horrible came back to her.

"He's killing one of us! He's killing Chelsea! He's breaking her neck!"

She almost started crying.

"Don't worry, Meara. It's only a memory. It can't hurt you. Today you will be able to tell me something else new. You will tell me how you left this room. Look around you and tell me where you got out."

In her trance, Meara looked all around the gray room. Something kept drawing her eyes upward. That had happened before, but she had never seen exactly what was up there. Today it was a little different.

"I see a glow of light up high," she said.

"Up high?" Dr. Ralston. "Do you mean a window?"

At his suggestion, she saw it vividly—a rectangular window at the top of the wall, with sunlight pouring through its panes.

"Yes, it's a window," Meara said.

"So you climbed up to a high window and got out of the room?"

"Yes, that must be it," she said.

She tried to remember how she had done it. Was she able to reach the base of the window from the floor, then pull herself up with her arms? Was she even strong enough to do that? If not, how had she gotten up there? But Dr. Ralston didn't seem to be worried about such details. She decided that she needn't worry about them either.

"Wonderful!" Dr. Ralston said. "Now picture yourself outside the window. You have escaped the room where you were held. You are free. Look around you. Tell me what you see."

A few moments passed, but nothing came.

"It's all gray, like a fog," she said.

Dr. Ralston kept talking in his soothing, comforting tone.

"That's fine. Breathe deeply. Just relax. Nothing can hurt you. Just keep looking around."

She felt happier now. She wondered—was it because she remembered getting free, or because the memories were coming easier, and much more clearly? It was probably a bit of both, she figured. Anyway, it was a very good feeling. It was the best feeling she'd had in a very long time.

"Are you tired?" Dr. Ralston asked. "Do you want to take a break?"

She thought for a moment. But she didn't want to disappoint anybody, especially not Dr. Ralston. Especially when she was feeling more and more confident by the moment.

"No," Meara said. "Let's keep going. I want to keep going."

*

After her drive back from Fredericksburg, Riley parked in front of the police station in Ohlman. She wondered what kind of situation was awaiting her here. The only thing she knew for sure was that she wasn't going to be welcomed with open arms. Quite the opposite.

Before she got out of the car, she texted Bill.

I'm in Ohlman. Where can I meet U?

Bill replied, *????*

Riley smiled. Of course he was surprised.

U need my help, she texted.

Bill's response came quickly.

Walder's going to go ballistic.

Riley hesitated. Walder was here? He had said he was going to leave in his helicopter yesterday. He must have decided to give the case his personal attention now that an important figure was involved.

She knew Bill was right. Walder would have a fit but she didn't care.

Where can I meet U? she typed again.

The message was immediately marked "read," but Bill didn't reply. What did that mean? Riley guessed that he was probably in

171

some situation where texting wasn't convenient. As likely as not, it was a meeting right here in the police station.

She got out of the car and strode into the station, then headed straight for the conference room. She knocked. A voice said, "Come in."

She opened the door, and sure enough, a meeting was going on. Bill was seated at the table, as were Lucy Vargas, Emily Creighton, and Craig Huang. So were Carl Walder and the local police chief, Earl Franklin. At the head of the table sat Leonard Ralston himself.

Walder jumped up from his chair, looking anything but pleased to see Riley.

"Agent Paige, what part of 'you're off the case' don't you understand?" he snapped.

Riley flashed him a mock-pleasant smile as she took a seat beside Bill.

"You folks just go on like I'm not here," she said. "I'll catch up on my own."

Leonard Ralston stared at her for a moment. She'd met him a few times, and she'd never showed him much respect. He had the youthful good looks and tousled hair of a TV personality. In fact, she'd seen him on talk shows, hawking his many books about all the criminal cases he'd solved with his hypnotic prowess. Riley had never found any of those stories very persuasive.

A voice recorder was on the table in front of him.

"Start the recording where you left off," Walder told him, sitting back down.

Bill whispered to Riley, "We left off with her remembering how she escaped. She climbed up through a window to get out of the basement."

Ralston pushed the button and the recording resumed.

The first voice she heard was Ralston's.

"Are you tired? Do you want to take a break?"

Riley then immediately recognized Meara Keagan's Irish-accented voice. She sounded sleepy and hesitant, obviously in a hypnotic trance.

"No. Let's keep going. I want to keep going."

Then came Ralston's voice again.

"Do you see houses? Buildings?"

Riley's skepticism kicked in hard. Those sounded like leading questions.

"Yes," Meara replied. *"A building. A big building. I got out through the window of the building. The building must have a basement."*

For all her fogginess, Meara sounded eager. Riley could visualize what was going on. She'd seen Ralston demonstrate his prowess on TV. It always seemed to work best on young women. Ralston cut a dashing and charismatic figure, and it seemed to Riley that women sometimes felt an unconscious desire to please him.

"How tall is the building?" Ralston asked.

Meara's reply came without delay.

"Four stories, I think. No, five. I'm pretty sure it's five. I can see that it's right on the Six O'clock Highway."

Meara's voice continued.

"It has a place to eat. Yes, a restaurant, there on the ground floor, above the basement. It has a gift shop. I think there are clocks in the gift shop. Cuckoo clocks...all kinds of clocks. Some with dancing dolls."

Ralston turned off the recording and looked around the room smugly.

"That's as far as I've been able to get her so far," he said. "But with another session—"

"I don't think that will be necessary," Walder said. "This information is exactly what we need. Excellent work, Dr. Ralston."

Ralston leaned back in his chair, smiling that photogenic smile of his.

"I must say, I'm pretty proud of these results," he said. "And knowing that it helps your investigation—well, it's a validation of my work."

Walder drummed his fingers on the table.

"So now we know that the women have been held in a five-story building with a restaurant and a gift shop. A gift shop with *clocks* in it. And it's on the so-called Six O'clock Highway. It shouldn't be hard to find."

Emily Creighton nodded in enthusiastic agreement. But Riley detected a level of uncertainty among the others. As for herself, she certainly felt more than a little bit doubtful.

"There's something wrong here," Lucy said. "We've canvassed all over Ohlman, looking for the lair. I'm sure there aren't any five-story buildings in this little town."

Walder thought for a moment.

"Well, then it's not in Ohlman," he said, sounding as if he'd come to a very sage conclusion. "Show us a map of the area, Chief Franklin."

Franklin brought up a map on the room's large monitor. He pointed to a stretch of highway. As soon as it appeared, Franklin spoke up.

"Hold it. I know the place she's talking about. It's called the Serenity Café and Gift Shop."

He pointed to a place on the map.

"It's a touristy place up north along the Six O'clock Highway. It's closer to Westree than here. I've been there a few times. The gift shop has got clocks in it. And the guy who owns it—well, I don't know his name, but he looks exactly like Meara's description of the killer. Medium build, dark hair, brown eyes."

Walder snapped his fingers triumphantly. "Bingo. We've found him. The killer's keeping his women close to where Meara Keagan was first abducted."

Riley couldn't believe her ears.

"Wait a minute," she said. "This doesn't make sense."

"No one asked for your opinion, Agent Paige," Walder said. "In fact, it's time for you to leave."

But Riley ignored him. She pointed at the map.

"The place you're talking about is miles north of here. Meara got hit by a car right near here. How did she get this far south?"

A silence fell in the room.

Finally, Emily Creighton said, "She didn't remember anything after she got out of that basement. Maybe she hitchhiked. Doesn't that make sense? She wanted to get as far away from where she was held as possible. The driver may never have known anything about her, what she'd been through. And now she doesn't remember that part."

Ralston said, "Well, with maybe a little more work—"

"I said that won't be necessary," Walder said.

Craig Huang was looking far from convinced.

"Maybe we'd better track down that driver before we jump to conclusions," he said.

Walder snapped at Huang in a scolding tone.

"We don't have time for that, Agent Huang," he said. "He's likely to be holding other women in that basement. He might be getting ready to kill one as we speak. Chief Franklin, how soon can we get a search warrant?"

Franklin didn't have to stop to think.

"I'll call Judge Weigand right away. I can get it in minutes."

Walder nodded enthusiastically.

"Great. Do it. Then get a team together. We're going to put this bastard away once and for all."

The meeting broke up, and everyone started preparing for the raid.

Bill took Riley aside.

"Riley, you've really got to get out of here," he said. "Go back home. Walder will fire you for sure if you don't."

Riley didn't reply.

"Didn't you hear what I said?" Bill said.

Just then Walder's voice called out, "Agent Jeffreys! Get over here! Help us plan the raid."

Bill shook his head at Riley and walked away.

Riley had already made her mind up. She sure has hell wasn't going home. She wanted to be there to see what became of this raid. Maybe if it was the disaster she expected, someone would listen to what she knew about this killer.

CHAPTER THIRTY NINE

In her own car, Riley followed the group of police vehicles speeding on their way north. She had no idea how the raid was going to end, but it was too important for her to miss. She didn't care what Walder had to say about it—or even Bill, for that matter.

Orders be damned, she thought.

After a while, the vehicles pulled off the Six O'clock Highway onto a service road lined with small businesses. Sure enough, standing among them was a five-story building. On the bottom floor was a sign that clearly read Serenity Café and Gift Shop.

Riley slowed her car as the vehicles ahead of her parked in front of the building. Led by Walder and Chief Franklin, Bill and Lucy got out, followed by Emily Creighton and Craig Huang and several Ohlman cops, all well-armed and wearing Kevlar vests. Riley had also put on her own vest before the drive.

When she stepped out of her car, Walder caught sight of her right away. He stared daggers at her but said nothing. She knew he didn't want to make a scene about it right now, with locals and tourists on the site.

There'll be time to fire me later, she thought wryly.

It was early on a Saturday afternoon, and the little business strip was fairly busy. Pedestrians stood staring at the cops' ominous approach. Some hurried away, while others stayed to watch from a safe distance.

While the local officers took positions, Riley joined up with Bill, Franklin, Lucy, Creighton, and Huang alongside the building. There was a row of basement windows along the ground.

"It does have a basement," Walder announced. "This could be the place."

But the panes were too filthy to see inside.

Questions started coming into Riley's mind. In this fairly busy area, how likely was it that captives were being held in that basement? Meara's description of her captivity made no mention of being bound and gagged, only caged. And other women had been caged with her. Wouldn't their screams have been heard? Still, it looked like the basement was big, taking up the building's entire foundation. In such a large space, Riley had to admit that it wasn't completely impossible that women had been held there.

And as deeply as she disliked Walder, she hoped that he was right this time. With a quick raid, whoever might be imprisoned down there could be set free. Still, she was worried about how hastily this operation had been set up. Even if this was the right place, things could very easily go wrong.

Walder starting giving orders.

"Jeffreys, Vargas, Creighton, Huang—we're all going in the front."

He glanced again at Riley. From his expression, Riley knew that he realized that commanding her to stay out would only hold things up. And he knew there was no point in trying to talk her out of joining them.

Weapons drawn but held low, the seven agents walked around to the front of the building. The gift shop was to the left of the restaurant, and items for sale were on display in the window. Riley looked them over. In the recorded interview Meara had described *"Cuckoo clocks...all kinds of clocks. Some with dancing dolls."*

Sure enough, there were clocks here. They looked cheap, but the plastic cuckoo clocks seemed to fit Meara's description. And there were some dancing dolls on top of music boxes. Could this be the right place after all? She hurried to catch up with the others.

Their weapons still lowered, the group followed Walder through the front door. The stout hostess at the front podium turned pale and gasped with shock when she saw them. The quaint, touristy café was almost full of lunch customers, some of whom reacted with alarm. One woman actually screamed and an elderly man looked like he might be in danger of a heart attack.

"There's no cause for panic, everybody," Walder yelled. Then, turning to Craig Huang, he said, "Get the customers out of here in an orderly manner."

Huang moved among the tables, carrying out Walder's order.

Walder called out, "Who's the owner?"

A frightened-looking man stepped forward. Riley immediately saw that he more or less matched Meara's description of her captor—white, medium height, strong build, dark hair, brown eyes. On the other hand, she'd glimpsed at least two male customers who could fit that description just as well. It was a pretty ordinary image.

"I'm the owner," the man said.

"What's your name?" Walder barked.

"Ike Middleton," the man said.

Walder pushed the man so that he stood with his arms against the wall.

"We've got a warrant to search the premises," Walder said. "How do we get to your basement?"

"The door's in the back, all the way through the kitchen in the back room," Middleton said. "But I don't understand. Will somebody tell me what's going on?"

Walder didn't reply. Emily Creighton began to frisk him for weapons.

"Creighton, Vargas, hold him right here," Walder said. "Jeffreys, let's you and me go downstairs."

Riley noticed that Walder was simply ignoring her, making no attempt to keep her out of the action. That was just as well, since she had no intention of not going down to that basement with them.

She followed Bill and Walder through a pair of swinging doors into the kitchen, where a couple of cooks and a busboy stood slack-jawed with shock. Then they pushed through another pair of swinging doors into a back room with a dishwasher, where they found the basement door.

"Holster up," Walder said, putting away his own gun. "We won't need weapons."

Bill obeyed, and so did Riley. Even though she agreed with Walder this time, she thought he sounded much too sure of himself. Indeed, the whole operation smacked to her of overconfidence.

Walder opened the basement door and turned on the light switch. Then he led the way through the door. They walked down the wooden stairs into a large, musty, gray basement. Gift items, including three clocks, hung on the wall next to the stairs.

At the bottom of the stairs, they found themselves facing a maze of stacked-up boxes resting on wooden pallets.

"Let's split up," Walder said, pointing in different directions for Bill and Riley.

Riley went in her designated direction, following a narrow aisle between stacks of boxes and then along a far wall. She found absolutely nothing but more boxes. She turned back and rejoined Bill at the base of the stairs.

Then they heard Walder call "Here!" His voice cracked with excitement.

Riley and Bill hurried to join him.

Walder was standing in front of an area that was separated by a tall chain-link fence. The gate was secured by a padlock.

The area beyond the fence appeared to hold more boxes.

"It just looks like storage for costlier items," Bill suggested.

"Something must be hidden beyond those boxes," Walder growled.

He drew his gun and blew the padlock off the gate.

CHAPTER FORTY

Walder yanked the gate open and charged on inside. As Riley and Bill followed, he disappeared behind a pile of boxes. Then they heard him yell.

"Damn it!"

Riley caught up with Walder and looked around. There was nothing back there at all—just a patch of bare, concrete floor in an empty, cobweb-infested corner. Riley knew that there was nowhere else to look in this basement. She glanced at Bill, who just shrugged.

Walder put his gun back in his holster.

Frantic footsteps were storming down the stairs. As Riley and the others came out of the fenced area, Emily Creighton rushed toward them, her weapon drawn. Craig Huang was standing on the stairs, also prepared for action. Riley realized they had heard the shot fired when Walder destroyed the padlock.

"Is somebody down?" Creighton asked sharply.

Walder shook his head.

"Holster up," he said. "We're fine."

But he didn't look fine. He stared at the floor, his teeth clenched in anger. Riley was pretty sure that he was remembering what he'd said at the station.

Bingo. We've found him.

And also what he'd said when she'd expressed her doubts.

"No one asked for your opinion, Agent Paige."

Walder was so furious and embarrassed that he couldn't even look at the others, especially not her.

"Come on," Walder growled. "Let's get out of here."

They went back up the stairs, then through the stock room and kitchen into the restaurant. Lucy Vargas was still holding Ike Middleton at gunpoint with his hands against the wall.

"Let him go," Walder said to Vargas.

Lucy holstered her gun, and Ike Middleton stepped away from the wall, looking thoroughly shaken.

Riley shared in the disappointment at not finding any captives. At the same time, something new was bothering her. Meara hadn't simply imagined the existence of this place. Everything here fit her description perfectly—the five-story building, the restaurant, the gift shop with clocks and dancing dolls. Could this place still somehow be connected with her captivity?

While Walder offered his abject apologies to Ike Middleton, Riley went to the front door and looked out over the people scattered outside. They all stared at her with puzzled, frightened expressions.

"It was an unfortunate misunderstanding, folks," she called out. "We're terribly sorry. If you'll just hang around for a few moments, we'll wrap things up."

A baffled murmur passed among the onlookers.

Riley saw the stout hostess standing nearby and walked up to her.

"You work here, don't you?" Riley asked.

The woman nodded.

"What's your name?"

"Louise Bader."

Riley took her gently by the arm.

"Come on inside," she said. "Maybe you can help us with something."

They went back into the restaurant. Ike Middleton was sitting alone at a table, still looking thoroughly stunned. Walder was huddled in conversation with Bill, Lucy, and the other two agents. Riley led the hostess over to them and introduced her.

Then she turned to the owner.

"Mr. Middleton, perhaps you could also join us."

The owner walked up to the group with a slightly unsteady gait.

Riley took out her cell phone and brought up a picture of Meara Keagan.

"Does this face look familiar to either of you?" Riley asked.

Middleton scratched his head.

"I don't know," he said. "I'm afraid my memory for faces really sucks."

But Louise Bader's face showed a flash of recognition.

"I've seen this picture before," she said. "When was it? Oh, yes—it was Tuesday or Wednesday, some cops came around looking for some woman. I didn't recognize the face then, but …"

She peered more closely at the photo.

"Oh, my God. I think I *do* recognize her now. There was a young woman who came in here with friends a couple of weeks ago. Her hair was different and she was wearing glasses, which was

181

why I didn't recognize her in the photo last time. She had some kind of accent. Ike, do you remember now? She was really nice. We both noticed her and talked about her."

"Yeah," the owner said. "I think the way she talked sounded Irish."

The agents all glanced at each other.

"Thanks so much," Riley said to the man and the woman. Then she led her colleagues aside.

"That explains it," Riley said. "Meara Keagan came in here at least once for lunch. Then came the trauma of her captivity. When Ralston hypnotized her, her memories got mixed up. She thought she'd been held captive here."

Walder stared into space for a moment.

"Okay," he said. "We'll just have Ralston give it another try."

Riley's mouth dropped open.

"With all due respect, sir—" she began.

"Respect seems to be in pretty short supply, Agent Paige," Walder barked. "I ordered you off the case. You're not even supposed to be here."

Riley knew she ought to shut up, but she just couldn't.

"You're making a big mistake, sir."

"Nobody wants your input, Paige."

Riley felt her face flush with anger. She clenched her fists at her sides.

"Damn it, sir, Ralston's a quack! He sent us on a wild goose chase. If he hypnotizes Meara again, he's just going to get more false memories. We don't have time to go chasing after more bad leads."

Walder was seething.

"What the hell are you even doing here? I ordered you to go back to BAU, and I meant it. But here you are, interfering in this investigation."

"Interfering!" Riley gasped with disbelief.

Walder barked, "Agent Paige, at this moment, your whole future with the Bureau is hanging by a thread. You get out of my sight. Right now. Do it, or I'll take your badge and your gun. And the next time I hear from you, you'd better be nowhere near Delaware."

Riley was shaking all over with rage. There was a whole lot more that she wanted to say. But she knew that Walder was always at his worst when his vanity was wounded. And his vanity had taken a real body blow just now. For him, the worst part had to be knowing that he was wrong and that Riley was right. But he'd never admit it. And Riley knew better than to push him any further.

She turned around and walked out of the restaurant. She strode past the baffled onlookers and got into her car. She sat at the wheel for a moment, trying to decide where to go or what to do.

All she knew for sure was that she wasn't going back to Virginia. Not now, when women's lives were at stake, and Walder was making a mess of things. It was up to her to track down the killer once and for all.

She started the car and took the Six O'clock Highway back to Ohlman.

*

Riley spent the rest of the day wandering through the tiny little town, hoping for her gut instincts to kick in. But her mind kept coming up empty. Ohlman looked as innocent and innocuous as any town she'd ever seen. She knew that cops had canvassed the area without finding a trace of the killer.

Why do I think I can do any better? she thought miserably.

Night fell, and despair really started to kick in. Starting with her drive from Fredericksburg that morning, she'd passed a long, discouraging, and tiring day. She worried that her judgment was about to fail her. But she couldn't give up. Not now.

As the darkness deepened, Riley found herself walking along the Six O'clock Highway right on the edge of town. There wasn't a car in sight. Somewhere along here, she knew, Meara had been hit by the drunk driver. Whatever Walder's opinion might be right now, Riley still felt sure that Meara had been held captive near here.

If so, the killer was nearby. Probably right now. But what was he doing? What was he thinking?

Riley thought back to what Meara Keagan had told her in the hospital, back before Ralston had been brought in to hypnotize her. She'd remembered being held in a cage, where she and other girls were beaten and starved.

For whatever reason, the killer kept the girls alive for a time before killing them. He also seemed to keep more than one of them at any given time.

183

Riley wondered if he might be looking for another captive right now. Maybe he needed to replace Nicole, whom he'd killed, and Meara, who had escaped.

Riley mulled the possibility over. She remembered that Nicole DeRose Ehrhardt had been abducted right along this highway. So had at least two of the killer's younger victims, probably while hitchhiking.

A crazy, desperate idea started to form in her mind.

Just then she saw approaching headlights in the distance. She pulled her jacket tighter around her, hoping that she might look like any ordinary hitchhiker.

Of course, Riley knew that she couldn't pass as one of the teenagers the clock killer had taken. And she'd never been as skinny as Nicole DeRose Ehrhardt. But it was chilly out, and maybe her jacket and cap might conceal the fact that she was much too robust for the killer's taste.

The car slowed as it came toward her, then stopped just ahead of her. Riley's pulse quickened as she trotted up to the car. Then she saw that the driver was an elderly woman.

The woman leaned over to the window.

"Honey, you shouldn't be out here," she said with concern. "Hitchhiking's illegal, you know. Besides, it's especially dangerous these days. Haven't you heard about the killer that's loose around these parts? Anyway, get in. I'll take you someplace safe."

"It's okay," Riley said evasively. "I'll walk the rest of the way."

The woman gasped in disbelief.

"The rest of the way *where*? Lord, girl, didn't you hear what I said? It's dangerous out here."

Riley pulled out her badge.

"It's okay, ma'am," she said. "I'm looking for the killer."

The woman looked a bit confused.

"But shouldn't you have someone with you? A partner or something?"

Riley smiled ironically. Yes, of course she should have someone with her—at least within hearing distance. But that wasn't an option right now.

"I'll be okay," she said. "Please move along now."

"Good luck," the woman said. She rolled up her window and drove away.

A moment later, there wasn't a car in sight. Riley knew that she was going to need more than a little luck tonight.

*

Scratch drove along the Six O'clock Highway with low expectations and a sinking spirit. He had only one captive left back in the shelter—the one whose name he thought was Kimberly. Grandpa still wasn't happy with her. Even after weeks of near-starvation, she just wasn't skinny enough.

Besides, Grandpa kept saying that they needed two more girls in addition to Kimberly.

"Three more hours, three more girls," he kept telling Scratch.

The pressure was unbearable. Scratch was painfully aware of the importance of the mission. The future of humanity depended on Grandpa's message getting through. It looked less and less likely that it was going to happen. And of course, it was all Scratch's fault.

But the worst part of it all was the loneliness. How long had it been, Scratch wondered, since anyone in the world had said a single kind word to him? Grandpa was always cruel, and always had been. But lately, Grandpa had been saying less and less, which felt even worse. Scratch had always known he was worthless. But what was he going to do if even Grandpa decided he was too worthless even to abuse and insult?

Soon, most of the human race would be dead. Maybe there wouldn't be anybody left alive at all. What would life be like for Scratch, all alone in that gray place, all alone in the whole wide world, without even Grandpa to talk to?

Scratch still clung to a desperate hope that maybe one more girl would be left alive, and that she'd find it in her heart to care about him after the destruction came.

But he kept remembering those words of Grandpa's.

"Three more hours, three more girls."

Three more girls had to die. If he wanted a girl of his own, a girl to keep, he'd have to catch three more girls, in addition to the girl he thought was named Kimberly. And girls were getting scarce. Scratch couldn't turn on the TV or the radio or check the Internet without seeing warnings about Delaware's "clock killer." Girls all through the area were on their guard.

185

He didn't know how much time he had left, but he knew that time was running out.

Just then, his headlights fell upon a human figure walking along the side of the road. At first, he couldn't tell much about who it might be. In chilly weather like this, the person was pretty well bundled up.

But then the person turned around to face him. Scratch's heart quickened and his spirits rose. It was a woman, all right. And now she held out her arm and stuck out her thumb.

A hitcher! he thought.

As he slowed his car, he reached behind his seat to make sure that the length of two-by-four was ready. It seemed a shame that he'd have to knock her out cold. He really wished he could talk with her a little. He really was so terribly lonely.

But now was no time to take chances. He had a terrible duty to fulfill.

CHAPTER FORTY ONE

The headlights blazed in Riley's face as the car slowed toward her. Whoever was driving wasn't bothering to dim their lights. She had to shield her eyes. By the time the car slowed to a stop beside her, she was nearly blinded.

Riley could hear the passenger window roll down. Then she heard the driver's voice.

"Where are you headed?"

Riley couldn't really see the driver, but it was a man's voice.

"Ohlman," Riley said.

She heard him chuckle a bit.

"Me too," he said. "We're practically there already. Hop in."

Her vision still full of bright spots, Riley groped her way into the car. She wished she could get a good look at the driver. But it was going to take a few moments for her eyes to adjust.

"Where are you coming from?" the man asked.

"Westree," Riley lied.

The man said nothing. The bright spots started to go away, and Riley's vision got clearer. Once again, she remembered Meara's description—medium height, strong build, dark hair, brown eyes.

The man at the wheel fit that description perfectly. But then, so had the owner of the restaurant. So did a lot of men.

"Hey, you must be pretty cold," the man said. "I've got some hot tea in a thermos."

Keeping his left hand on the wheel, he reached back between the seats with his right. Riley remembered that Meara said her captor had knocked her out cold.

Before the driver could grab whatever he was reaching for, Riley pulled out her gun and pointed it at him.

"Put your hand back on the wheel," she said.

The man let out a yelp of alarm and quickly obeyed.

"Jesus, okay! Okay!"

Holding the gun steady, Riley looked back between the seats, trying to see what the man might have been reaching for. It was too dark for her to make anything out.

"I have a little cash on me," the man said. "Not much, I just got back from a trip. But if you'll just let me reach for my wallet—"

"This isn't a holdup," Riley said.

With her free hand she pulled out her badge and showed it to him. The man looked thoroughly dumbstruck.

"Drive me straight to the Ohlman police station," Riley said.

The man drove on without saying another word.

*

In only a few minutes, the man parked the car in front of the police station. Riley held the gun on him as they entered the station. A couple of cops were standing in the front area. The huskier of the two called out, "Hey, Rufus! What's going on?"

His hands still raised, the man shrugged nervously.

"I'm getting brought in by the FBI, I guess," he said.

"Do you know this man?" Riley said to the huskier cop.

The cop chuckled.

"Sure, I do. This is Rufus Crim."

The thinner cop added, "We've all known each other since we were little. Hey, what's going on?"

Riley felt more unsure of herself by the moment. A fresh wave of exhaustion swept over her, and again she wondered whether her judgment might be off. Still, she was sure that the killer was likely to be somebody that everybody in Ohlman knew.

Bill burst into the front area from inside the station.

"Riley!" he yelled. "What the hell is going on?"

"This might be our killer," Riley said.

The huskier cop chuckled again.

"Not a chance," he said. "Rufus hasn't been anywhere near here for three weeks or more."

Riley turned to the man and asked, "Is this true?"

"Yeah," Rufus said. "I've been down in Miami, visiting relatives. I flew into Philadelphia today, then drove down here from there. I can show you the tickets. What's this all about, anyway?"

Bill let out a groan of frustration.

"For Chrissake, let him go, Riley," Bill said. "He's not our man."

Riley holstered her weapon, feeling crushed and embarrassed.

"I'm sorry," she told Rufus. "I'm really sorry."

Bill took Riley aside and said to her quietly, "What's the matter with you? Have you lost your mind?"

Riley said nothing. She more than half-wondered the same thing.

"Walder's going to suspend you for sure," Bill said.

"Is he here?" Riley asked.

"No, but we just called him, and he's on his way over from his motel," Bill said. "Another girl was just taken captive. Come on. Lucy's interviewing her boyfriend."

Bill and Riley hurried down the hall to the conference room, where Lucy was already talking to a distraught-looking teenager. They sat down at the table with Lucy and the boy.

Lucy told them, "This is Russell Bingham. His girlfriend, Mallory Byrd, was abducted a little while ago. He just started telling me what happened."

Russell was a scrawny, long-haired kid with downy fuzz on his chin. He was trembling all over.

"Mallory and I were out hitchhiking," he said. "I know it was stupid, but we thought it would be fun. We live up in Bowdon, and some friends of ours were having a party here in Ohlman. So we spent the day hitching down the Six O'clock Highway. We figured out pretty soon that drivers—guys, anyway—were more likely to stop if they thought Mallory was alone. I'd stay out of sight off the road, and then when somebody stopped for her, I'd get in too."

He paused for a moment, shaking more than before.

"Well, it got dark, and we were pretty close to Ohlman, and I was out of sight behind some bushes and Mallory was standing by the road when a car pulled up. I could hear the driver's voice telling Mallory to get in, and he sounded nice and all. I stepped out from hiding, and Mallory had already gotten in. She was opening the back door for me. But when the guy got a look at me ..."

He shuddered deeply.

"Well, he started driving, and I tried to jump for the back door, which was still open. The car grazed me as it went by and knocked me down, and I heard Mallory screaming. Both the doors hung swinging open, but I guess the car was going too fast for Mallory to jump out."

He clenched his hands together anxiously.

"Anyway, there I was lying on the ground, and as soon as I could, I called the cops on my cell phone."

Lucy gently put in, "You didn't get the license plate? The make of the car?"

Russell Bingham shook his head.

"I should've," he said. "I was just so shaken up."

"We understand," Lucy said. "Give me a moment to talk with my colleagues alone."

The boy nodded. Lucy led Bill and Riley out into the hallway.

"Did the girl have a cell phone?" Riley asked. "Couldn't it be tracked?"

"We tried that already," Lucy said. "The cell phone was found on the shoulder of the highway. The driver must have thrown it out of the car after he'd gotten away with the girl."

Before Riley could ask Lucy any more questions, she heard an angry shout down the hall.

"Special Agent Riley Paige!"

Carl Walder was striding toward her, looking angrier than she'd ever seen him.

"I heard about the stunt you just pulled, bringing in an innocent man," he barked.

"I'm sorry, sir, but—"

"I don't want to hear it," Walder said. He held out his hand. "You're suspended. And if I have my way, you'll never serve on the Bureau again. Give me your badge and your gun, right now."

Riley was horrified but not surprised. Without a word, she gave him her badge and her gun.

"Now I want you to get away from here," Walder said. "I don't give a damn where you go, as long as it's far away."

"I'll do that, sir," Riley said through clenched teeth.

She walked rapidly down the hall toward the front entrance. Bill raced to catch up with her.

"Riley, I *told* you—"

Riley didn't stop walking.

"I know, I know," Riley said. "I was an idiot. You'd better get back there and away from me if you want to keep your job."

"But what are you going to do now?"

Riley didn't reply. The truth was, she had no idea. She stormed out the front door, leaving Bill behind, and headed straight to her car. She got into the driver's seat and just sat there, trying to think things through. She'd been on the move all day, so she didn't even have a motel room to go back to.

Walder's words rattled through her brain.

"And if I have my way, you'll never serve on the Bureau again."

She had to fight back the tears. Her attempt to serve as bait to catch the killer had failed. But now that she had a moment to think about it, it was more a case of bad luck than stupidity. The killer had, in fact, been out looking for a victim. He'd just happened to pick up Mallory Byrd instead.

Bad luck for me, Riley thought miserably. *Worse luck for Mallory.*

Now she found herself wondering whether she should just drive on home. For all she knew, she was desperately needed there. In any case, it was time to check in. She dialed the house number, and Gabriela answered.

"Buenas noches, Gabriela," she said. "How are things going there?"

Gabriela's voice sound cheerful.

"Good," she said. "Much better. Crystal was here earlier, and April did homework with her. April watched TV for a while and went to bed."

Riley breathed a sigh of relief.

"Thanks, Gabriela. Let me know if there are any problems."

"I'll do that."

Riley ended the call and sat staring ahead. She remembered something else that Walder had said.

"I don't give a damn where you go, as long as it's far away."

An idea came to her. There was a place she could go, and a man who might be able to help. She'd sworn never go to there or see him again. But now she was just desperate enough to change her mind. She started the car and drove north into the night.

CHAPTER FORTY TWO

Riley hated her visits to Sing Sing. Just getting through all the security protocols was demeaning and humiliating. There were the usual pat-downs, the removal of all jewelry and any other kinds of metal, including belt buckles, and the drug-sniffing dogs.

At least it stopped short of a strip search, she thought.

She had arrived in Ossining, New York, before dawn. She'd napped in her car, hit a doughnut shop for breakfast, and then notified Sing Sing officials that she wanted to see the prisoner. She'd cleaned up and combed her hair, but she still felt disheveled.

Now she was wondering whether she'd made a terrible mistake in coming here. But there was no point in turning back—not now.

By the time she got through the screening and was escorted to the visiting room, just about everything she'd brought with her had been taken away. All she had was a folder full of photographs of the murder victims. She hoped that it would be enough.

The guard led her into the familiar little room with cream-colored walls and a barred window. Shane Hatcher was already sitting at the battleship-gray table, a pair of small reading glasses perched on his nose.

He was a vigorous-looking fifty-five-year-old African-American. At a glance he didn't look especially threatening, but Riley knew better. During his youth as a gangbanger, he'd been known as "Shane the Chain." He'd beaten his victims to death with chains in murders so brutal that he would likely never be released from prison.

He smiled at her.

"Sit down," he said, a note of irony in his voice. "Make yourself at home. I wish I could offer you something, but as you know already, mine is a rather Spartan lifestyle. I'm sure you understand."

She sat across the table from him. They stared at each other for an uneasy moment.

"I'm sorry for your loss," he finally said.

It took Riley a moment to realize that he was talking about her father's death.

"It's no loss at all," Riley said in a tight voice.

"Oh, it is, it is," Hatcher said in a surprisingly gentle voice. "He made you what you are—both the good and the bad of it. Now there's a big empty place in your life. Maybe you haven't felt it yet, but you will. Did you go to his funeral? No, I don't imagine you did. How does that make you feel?"

Riley didn't reply. Even so, she got the strange feeling that Hatcher was asking out of genuine sympathy. She hoped that she was wrong. She didn't like the idea of any emotional connection between them.

"Let's get down to business," she said.

"Yeah, let's do that. So why are they calling this guy a 'clock killer'?"

Riley opened the folder and spread the photos across the table.

"Well, it's my own theory, and not everybody agrees," she said, pointing at the pictures. "But look at the positions of these bodies—the way the arms are pointed. It looks to me like the arms are supposed to be clock hands. See? Five o'clock, six o'clock, seven o'clock, eight o'clock, nine o'clock."

Hatcher peered through his glasses with great interest.

"Oh, yes," he said. "I see it, yes. You're absolutely right, and anyone who says otherwise is a fool. But there's more."

He pointed at arrows that had been printed on each of the photos.

"What do these mean?" he asked.

"They indicate north," Riley said.

She got a tingling feeling that something was about to pop into place.

"Well, turn them all in that direction," Shane said.

Riley twisted the pictures around so that all the arrows pointed directly away from her. She remembered the strange feeling she'd had at the crime scenes—that although the bodies had been precisely posed, they hadn't been laid out in any sensible way with their surroundings. But now she started to see that she was wrong.

"Now imagine that the table's a map of the area, with north pointed away from you," Hatcher said.

Riley pictured the locations on the table and placed each photograph in its proper place. She gasped a little. Now she could see it perfectly.

The photos formed the lower part of a clock face, with each of the bodies positioned exactly like hour hands pointing in the

193

expected directions—five o'clock, six o'clock, seven o'clock, eight o'clock, nine o'clock.

But even more important, now she could see that the town of Ohlman was at the very center of the clock face. It looked like she'd been right all along. The killer was surely based in Ohlman.

"He's even more obsessed with time than I thought," Riley said.

"And he's trying to send a message," Hatcher added.

"Yes, but what's he trying to say?"

Hatcher leaned back in his chair and smiled a sinister smile.

"Tell me, Riley, what time is it right now?"

Riley's watch had been taken away, so she had to think for a moment.

"Well, they let me into the prison at eight fifteen, and it took a good half hour to get through security, so ..."

"That's not the kind of time I'm talking about," Hatcher said.

Riley didn't understand. Hatcher began to speak in a strangely casual tone.

"I'm really looking forward to the end of the world. I mean, what has the world ever done for me? I want to be awake when it happens. I want to enjoy it. I wish I could see the expressions on people's faces."

Hatcher leaned across the table toward her, his eyes alive with interest.

"This is not your garden-variety psychopath," he said. "He's a madman, pure and simple. There's nothing sadistic about him. In fact, he's trying to help us all. In his twisted mind, killing women is just an unfortunate necessity. It's the only way to get his message out."

He leaned back in his chair again.

"But you've got insights of your own," he said. "Tell me what you've got."

Riley thought for a moment.

"I've got this feeling—that he doesn't act alone. That he acts under orders."

Hatcher smiled knowingly.

"Oh, you're so right," he said. "But you're going to have trouble bringing his accomplice to justice."

"And why is that?" Riley said.

"His 'accomplice' doesn't exist."

Riley felt a flood of understanding.

"He's schizophrenic," she said. "He hears voices—or maybe just one voice. That voice tells him what to do. Following that voice's orders is the only purpose he has in life."

Hatcher rapped his knuckles on the table.

"Congratulations," he said. "You're catching on. My, we do make a good team, don't we? My brain and yours working together, they're a formidable combination. We should work together more often. Maybe make it an official investigation team. Think the FBI might go for it? No, I guess not. You're not exactly in good standing with the Bureau right now, are you? I mean, you did show up at Sing Sing without your badge."

Riley felt a sudden chill. He knew that she'd been suspended. But how?

Obviously detecting Riley's alarm, Hatcher said, "Come on, Riley. I could feel it when you came in here. I know you. In some ways, I know you better than you know yourself."

Once again, Riley heard a note of concern in his voice. It worried her. What kind of bond was this cold-blooded killer forming with her? Was it affection, admiration, or both, or something else entirely? Whatever it was, she didn't like it. She wanted nothing to do with it.

She put the pictures back in the folder.

"I'm leaving," she said.

"Wait a minute," Hatcher said. "We've got a standing agreement. I always get something out of our meetings. Let's talk a little. Conversation's hard to come by on the inside, believe me. How's that daughter of yours? She's fifteen, isn't she? That's a tough age. Things can go very bad."

The chill Riley had been feeling deepened. She had the uncanny sense that she didn't have any secrets at all from this useful but terrible man.

Still, she knew that Hatcher had his own code, his own sense of fair play. She mustn't violate it. She owed him a little something more.

"What do you want?" she asked.

"The same as the first time we met," Hatcher said. "You tell me something about yourself—something you don't want to people to know. Something you wouldn't want anybody else to know."

A strange feeling came over Riley—an inexplicable urge to confide in him. She knew it wouldn't be wise. But she couldn't fight it.

"I envy my sister," Riley said. "Wendy's her name. I haven't seen her for years, and I have no idea what kind of life she's got, but ... I envy her."

Hatcher said nothing. He just smiled.

"Daddy hit her so much, she ran away," she said. "She was fifteen, I was five. She got away. I didn't. But it's not so much that she got away ..."

She remembered something that her father had said about Wendy not long ago.

"I only hit her with my hands. Bruised her up a little on the outside, that's all. Didn't hit her deep enough."

Then he'd added, *"I never laid a hand on you. I hit you a lot deeper than that. You learned. You learned."*

Struggling to keep her voice calm, Riley said, "Daddy didn't get a chance to *shape* her."

Hatcher nodded with an awful understanding.

"But he made you everything you are today."

Riley felt the air go out of her lungs.

That can't be true, she thought.

But she couldn't think about it right now. She had to get out of here. She had to breathe.

"I've got to go," she said. "I've got to solve this case."

Hatcher let out a rather mocking sigh.

"Yes, I suppose you do. Get it done quickly. Get it out of the way. You've got other troubles coming soon. You'll need to give them your full attention."

Riley resisted the urge to ask him what troubles he was talking about. Maybe he really knew something, or maybe he was just trying to lure her into conversation.

"Besides," he added with a wink, "it's not the end of the world. Or maybe it is. You should think about that. It's staring you in the face, but you don't see it."

She got up from the table and started to walk away.

Hatcher called after her, "Watch yourself, Riley Paige."

She turned to look at him. His expression seemed genuinely worried. She couldn't imagine why. And she didn't want to.

"I won't come back here to see you again," she said.

Now Hatcher smiled an inscrutable smile.

"You might not have to," he replied.

Riley left the room without asking what he meant. By the time she was outside the building, she was hyperventilating. Visiting Hatcher was always nerve-racking. This time was no exception.

She remembered his words:

"You might not have to."

And she tried not to wonder what they meant.

*

Tiredness kept sweeping over Riley all during the drive south. She hadn't gotten any sleep at all for about twenty-four hours except for a short nap in the car before going into Sing Sing. And with fresh ideas about the case buzzing through her mind, Riley was finding it hard to keep her mind on her driving. She needed a change of pace.

She remembered that there was a ferry from New Jersey to Delaware. She decided to take that rather than stay on the road. The hour-and-twenty-minute trip across the Delaware Bay might give her time for some clear thinking. Or at least to get a little rest.

She pulled up the directions on her GPS system and headed for Cape May. When she pulled into the terminal, she was glad to see that there weren't a lot of cars in line for the next ferry. She didn't have to wait long before the handsome white boat loaded and then pulled away from the dock. Most other passengers headed up the stairs to the passenger decks, but Riley walked to the bow instead.

The air was crisp and clear. Gray-blue water swirled past the bow into white streamers on both sides. As the boat moved away from the dock and beyond the breakwaters, it passed a white lighthouse. The rippling gray-blue water was restful to Riley's mind.

She turned and glanced up at the decks overhead. She knew that food was available there, even a bar. She hadn't even had breakfast today, but somehow she didn't feel hungry. What she wanted was quiet. She went back to her car and got inside.

She closed her eyes, but knew she wouldn't be able to go to sleep. She didn't really want to. Hatcher had said some things that she knew were important, but that she didn't yet understand. He'd spoken in riddles, as usual. Now it was time to parse out his meaning.

She remembered what he'd said just before she left.

"It's not the end of the world. Or maybe it is. You should think about that. It's staring you in the face, but you don't see it."

Now it was time to see it. She kept her eyes closed and breathed deeply. Then it came to her—an image that she seldom thought about.

It was the so-called Doomsday Clock—a symbol used by *The Bulletin of Atomic Scientists* to show how close humanity was to a global catastrophe. In the days of the Cold War, the clock indicated the danger of a worldwide nuclear holocaust. Nowadays it also warned of the perils of climate change.

Whenever the situation seemed especially dangerous, the scientists moved the minute hand a little closer to midnight.

Now Riley understood Hatcher's hint. The killer was keeping his own version of a Doomsday Clock. He was using women's bodies to warn the world that its end was near. According to his own way of keeping time, midnight was when he thought it was going to happen."

Riley realized that the implications were enormous. If the killer followed his ongoing pattern, he needed to kill three more victims—one for ten o'clock, another for eleven o'clock, and the last for midnight. Now that Riley understood the clock image, she ought to be able to locate on a map just where the killer planned to leave these final victims.

But I'm not going to let it come to that, she thought.

She knew that Shane Hatcher was right about one other thing—this killer was a flat-out madman with crazy delusions. But who was he taking his orders from, really?

She remembered what Hatcher had said.

"His 'accomplice' doesn't exist."

Somehow that didn't ring true for her. It was too glib, too simple. Riley knew that Hatcher's insights were hardly infallible. He had his limits. There was a flaw in his considerable talents as a criminologist. He was too clinical, too cold, too intellectual. He couldn't empathize, couldn't get under a killer's skin like she did.

And now it was time for her to do just that.

She closed her eyes again and let herself slip into that familiar dark part of her own mind. There she got an image of him—an image that he seemed to hold of himself. It was a grotesque, surreal picture of a man building an enormous clock, using women's dead bodies as hands.

The women were part of a message—not people but items, clock parts. He bore the women no animosity, but his dehumanizing of them was total.

As the clock took shape, it began to tick, the corpse hands began to move, and an alarm sounded—an alarm warning of an apocalyptic midnight soon to come.

That's how he sees himself, Riley thought. *But how did he get that way?*

She turned the question over in that dark part of her mind. An image quickly flashed before her. It was a little boy watching an older man at work in a dimly lit workshop. The man was using delicate tools to build an actual clock out of thousands of precision pieces. The boy watched anxiously. The man didn't mean him well, but everything in the boy's life depended on him. It was absolutely crucial that he understand every move the man made.

Her dark musings were interrupted by the deafening roar of the boat's horn. It was announcing the ferry's arrival in Lewes, Delaware.

In an inkling, the image was gone. But Riley wasn't disappointed. She'd gotten the exact insight she'd needed.

Her next stop would be Ohlman—the clock's center, its hub, its axle. And she knew what she had to do.

CHAPTER FORTY THREE

As she pulled into Ohlman, Riley felt in her gut that she was closing in on the killer. The store's website proudly called itself "Ohlman's only watch and clock repair service." She thought it might also be a madman's lair.

The place she was looking for was easy to find. She saw the sign for Gorski Jewelers as soon as she turned onto Main Street, and she parked her car right in front. When she got out and approached the place, she tried to guess whether or not the building had a basement, but she couldn't tell from outside.

Unfortunately, a CLOSED sign hung on the door.

Riley let out a moan of discouragement. She'd completely forgotten that it was Sunday. In a little town like this, there probably wasn't a single store open along Main Street. Practically everybody had gone to church that morning and was now spending the afternoon with their families.

It was jarring to think of the horror that lurked in the heart of this wholesome community—perhaps right in front of her at this very moment.

She wondered whether the killer was religious. It was entirely possible. Schizophrenics often suffered from religious delusions. If so, did he refrain from torture and murder on Sundays? Riley doubted it.

There was a phone number on the door. Riley pulled out her phone and dialed it. She got an outgoing message with an elderly woman's voice.

"You've reached Gorski Jewelers, and this is Irina Gorski. Please leave a message at the tone."

After the tone, Riley said, "If you're there, please pick up the phone. This is an emergency."

There was a click, and the same woman's voice answered.

"An emergency? What on earth are you talking about?"

Looking through the glass door, Riley saw a tiny, white-haired woman at the back of the store. She was holding a telephone and staring straight at Riley. She realized that this was who she was talking to.

Riley felt deflated. She wasn't looking for a woman, much less an elderly one. Could Irina Gorski possibly have anything to do with the murders? She had to find out.

Riley rapped on the window and said into the phone, "Please let me in, Ms. Gorski. My name is Riley Paige, and—"

Riley was about to say she was an FBI agent. But if the woman asked her for her ID, she had none to show her.

Instead, she simply said, "I'm hunting for the 'clock killer.'"

The woman's eyes widened with interest. She opened the door and let Riley in.

"Are you some sort of detective?" she asked.

"Something like that," Riley said. "I've got a, uh, strong personal interest in the case."

The woman looked at Riley attentively. Then with a wink, she said, "What can I do to help you rule me out as a suspect?"

Riley was sure that this diminutive old woman had nothing to do with the murders. Even so, there was a question she had to ask.

"Do you have a basement?" she asked.

"No, just this one floor," the woman said.

Riley looked around. The shop was very small, and she saw no doors that might open to a basement. Still, she had a strong feeling that she had come to the right person for information.

"Could we talk?" Riley said. "I've got a few questions you might be able to answer."

"Certainly," the woman said, leading Riley behind the counter to a couple of chairs. "Have a seat."

Riley sat down.

"Ms. Gorski, do you know anyone in town who is obsessed with clocks and time?"

Irina Gorski's brow knitted with thought.

"That's an interesting question," she said. "No, not anymore. But a long time ago ..."

She paused as if reaching back into her memory.

"There used to be a strange fellow in town—Tyrone Phipps was his name. He operated a shop out of his house, on the main floor. He was the last true clockmaker in this whole area. A 'horologist,' he called himself—that's someone who studies and measures time. Oh, he really was obsessed with time."

Riley's attention quickened.

"Tell me more about him," she said.

Irina Gorski scratched her chin thoughtfully.

"Well, he had other obsessions, too. He had this thing about the Cold War. He was always sure that a nuclear holocaust was about to happen, and that it would be the end of the world. I remember the Cuban Missile Crisis back in 1962—well, you weren't even born, I guess. It very nearly happened. The end of all of us."

She shook her head at the memory.

"And Tyrone was running from door to door, knocking and yelling, 'Are you ready? Are you ready?' Well, when he came around to my place, I said, 'Are *you*?' I mean, what a question! What could anybody do to prepare for the end of civilization?"

She let out a sad little sigh.

"What happened to him?" Riley asked.

"Well, he died—I'm pretty sure it was 1989. Yes, it was the year the Berlin Wall fell, and the Cold War was over. But folks say that he never changed his tune even on his deathbed. They say his very last words were, 'Are you ready? Are you ready?' A very strange fellow."

Riley's heart was beating faster. She felt sure that she was about to get the break she needed.

"Ms. Gorski, did Tyrone Phipps have any children?" she asked.

The woman sighed.

"Yes, and that's a sad story, I'm afraid. He and his wife, Megan, had one daughter, Anita. His wife died in a car wreck when little Anita was barely a year old. Anita grew up to be a sad, messed-up girl, got mixed up with the counterculture. You know, hippies, the whole 'sex, drugs, and rock and roll' scene. When she was just eighteen, she had a baby boy, Casey. Nobody ever knew who the father was. She pretty much abandoned Casey to her father's care. She died of a drug overdose a few years later."

Riley could barely contain her excitement now.

"Whatever happened to Casey?" she asked.

"Why, he still lives here—in his grandfather's old house, where the clock shop used to be. The address is One-Twenty Lynn Street. An odd boy—although he's actually grown up now. He seems to live off his grandfather's inheritance, doesn't work for a living. He never really bothers anybody, just keeps to himself."

Then a worried look crossed the woman's face.

"But—oh, dear. Do you think maybe Casey … I mean, the murders—"

202

"What do *you* think, Mrs. Gorski?"

The woman thought for a moment.

"I don't know what to tell you. He's such a strange fellow. I just don't know."

Riley got up from her chair.

"Ms. Gorski, thank you so much. You've helped me more than I can say."

Irina Gorski looked at Riley with concern.

"I'm glad," she said. "But you be careful, dear."

"I will."

When Riley got back in her car, the first thing she did was call Bill on her cell phone. Bill answered sharply.

"Riley, where the hell are you? Please tell me you're back in Virginia."

Riley suppressed a chuckle.

"You know me better than that, Bill. I'm right here in Ohlman. And I've found him. I've found our killer."

Riley heard Bill groan.

"Riley, I'm not listening to this. You've gone off the rails. Go home. You'll get into even more trouble."

Riley's tone grew more insistent.

"Bill, listen. I'm serious. I know what I'm talking about. His name is Casey Phipps. His grandfather was a clockmaker. Time is a family obsession."

Bill was silent for a moment. Riley felt sure that she had piqued his interest.

"He lives at One-Twenty Lynn Street," she said. "All we've got to do is go pick him up. Can you meet me there?"

There was another pause.

"If Walder finds out about this, he'll have a fit. I've got to stay here at the station so he doesn't catch on. But I can send Lucy."

"You do that," Riley said. "I'll meet her there."

Riley drove straight to One-Twenty Lynn Street and parked nearby. It was a fair-sized wood frame house with a swing on the front porch. As she parked, she saw two boys in the street throwing a baseball back and forth. They were both about nine or ten years old. A little girl, about seven, stood on the sidewalk watching them.

Again, Riley felt jarred by the sight of such innocent playfulness in such close proximity to terrible evil.

Almost immediately, she saw Lucy approaching in her car. Lucy parked and trotted over to Riley's car and got in the passenger's side.

She pointed to the house.

"Is that the house you're talking about?"

Riley nodded.

"Oh, Riley, I hate to say this, but this is a mistake. We canvassed this whole neighborhood. I checked this house myself. The guy who lives here's a little odd, but I'm sure he's not our guy."

"Did he let you look in the basement?" Riley asked.

"Yeah, and he was nice about it, too."

Riley struggled with a moment of self-doubt. But no, Irina Gorski's story still had her completely convinced. The man who lived here, Casey Phipps, was their killer. And as far as the basement was concerned ...

Well, Lucy must have missed something, Riley decided.

Perhaps she'd overlooked a door leading into another room. Riley just had to take a look there herself.

"Let's go," she told Lucy.

They got out of the car and walked toward the house. The little girl trotted up to them.

"Don't go there," she said, pointing to the house.

"Why not?" Riley asked.

One of the boys throwing the ball called out.

"The guy there's weird," he said. "We stay away from him."

The other boy said, "Except on Halloween when he gives away candy."

"How do you mean, weird?" Riley asked the boys.

"He talks to himself," the first boy said.

The little girl stomped her foot.

"He does *not* talk to himself! He talks to the ghosts!"

The first boy yelled, "Shut up, Libby. People will think you're crazy."

The girl named Libby spoke to Lucy and Riley in a hushed, urgent tone.

"My brother says there's no such thing as ghosts. But he's wrong. I've heard them. And the man who lives here talks to them."

The little girl's words added to Riley's sense of certainty. Casey Phipps sounded like exactly the man they were looking for—

a man who talked to ghosts. Riley thanked the girl, and she and Lucy walked up the sidewalk toward the house.

CHAPTER FORTY FOUR

"It's her again!" Scratch whispered to Grandpa as he peeked from behind the window blind. *"That FBI woman! And she's brought someone with her."*

There was a knock on the door.

"What should I do?" Scratch said.

"What do you think?" Grandpa snapped. *"Let them in, for Christ sake."*

Scratch opened the door, hoping he didn't look as terrified as he felt.

The woman who had been there before—the one with the dark complexion—held out her badge. She spoke in a very polite voice.

"Sir, you probably remember me," she said. "Agent Lucy Vargas."

Scratch's mouth had gone dry, and his reply sounded a little hoarse.

"Sure, I remember," he said.

"This is my colleague, Agent Riley Paige."

Scratch looked the other woman over. She was the older of the two, with dashes of gray in her dark hair. Oddly, unlike the younger woman, this woman didn't seem to have a gun.

"What can I do for you?" he asked the women.

"Well, we've just got a few more questions, if you don't mind," the younger woman said, smiling. "Could we come in?"

"Sure," Scratch said.

The two women came inside. The older one looked all around the living room with keen interest.

"I hear that this place used to be a place of business," she said. "Wasn't your grandfather a clockmaker?"

Grandpa's voice sounded indignant.

"Not a clockmaker, damn it. A horologist."

Scratch forced himself to smile.

"Actually, Grandpa liked to call himself a horologist. Why do you ask?"

The older woman didn't reply. Her gaze made him most uncomfortable, as if she could see right through him.

"I wonder if I could look in your basement," she said.

"Why?" Scratch asked. "Your, uh, colleague went down there last time."

206

"I'd just like to have another look," she said with an unsettling smile.

Scratch stood there dumbly.

"Let her go!" Grandpa whispered. *"We've got nothing to hide. Not here."*

Scratch was liking this less and less by the second.

"Go ahead, be my guest," he said. "It's right back there through the kitchen."

The woman disappeared into the kitchen. Scratch could hear the basement door open, followed by her footsteps going down the stairs.

Now the younger woman was poking around, peeking into his bedroom and his kitchen. While she was turned away from him, he reached down to pick up the whip, which was lying beside an upholstered chair. He'd been using it on himself a lot lately. He thrust it out of sight behind his back just as the woman came back into the living room.

"So this was really a clock shop?" she said.

"Yeah," Scratch said.

"So where are all the clocks now?"

Scratch almost said that they'd all been taken out to the shelter. But Grandpa stopped him.

"Lie, you idiot!"

Sweat was breaking out on Scratch's forehead. The woman was asking too many questions. And he couldn't think of a single lie to tell.

"I don't know what to say," Scratch said aloud.

"Idiot!" Grandpa said.

"I'm sorry," Scratch said. "I just don't know what to say."

The woman stepped toward him, looking at him strangely.

"Are you talking to me?" she asked.

It was too much for Scratch to handle. The woman was only a few steps away. He swung the whip out and struck her in the face with it. She let out a gasp of pain and bent over, fingering her face. Scratch slammed the butt of the whip against the back of her head. She crumpled to the floor and didn't move.

"Now look what you've done!" Grandpa snarled. *"They'll come looking for her."*

"I'm sorry!" Scratch said.

His mind went into overload, filled up with images of how the room used to look when he was a child—full of clocks ticking everywhere, all over the walls. They began to chime and ring the hour.

He slashed the whip across his own back, hoping to make the madness stop.

"There's no time for that," Grandpa said. *"We've got to take care of the other one. You know what to do."*

The phantom sounds and images faded away. Yes, Scratch knew exactly what to do. When he was little, Grandpa used to punish him by locking him up in the basement. The windows were boarded over, so when the lights were out, it was pitch black down there.

He walked back to the basement door, switched off the light, and shut the door behind him. In the darkness, he heard a surprised outcry from the woman.

Suddenly, the whole situation made sense to him. Grandpa had been very wise to lock him up like that. Scratch knew every nook and cranny of the basement, light or no light. He had his whip, and the woman was unarmed.

She'd never get out of the basement alive.

CHAPTER FORTY FIVE

Riley was fingering a paneled section of basement wall, trying to detect if there might be a hidden space behind it. But the wall seemed solid.

She also noticed something vaguely unsettling. It took a moment for her to put her finger on it. Then she realized—it was a complete absence of natural light. There was only a single light bulb lighting the whole basement. Why wasn't there at least a little light spilling in from upper windows? But now she saw that those windows were all painted over, and had been for a long time.

A realization was dawning on her. She couldn't quite get hold of it. Somebody had been held here. Somebody had suffered here.

Suddenly, she herself was plunged into total darkness.

"Hello?" she called out.

There was no reply, but she could hear footsteps coming down the stairs.

It was him, she realized. He had been tormented here, and he had tormented the women in some similar place. And there was still more to the suffering …

An uncanny, icy horror overcame her—a terrible sense of *déjà vu.*

I've been here before, she thought with a shudder.

But when? And where?

She felt her body sag against the wall. Memories that Riley thought she'd shaken off came flooding back.

She was trapped in complete darkness in a little makeshift cage. She crouched in the crawlspace, awaiting the return of the monster with the propane torch. She couldn't see her captor but she could hear him breathing. She knew that soon the light of a flame would break through the darkness …

Riley tried to snap herself out of the memory into the desperate present. She had suffered PTSD attacks after being held by the killer named Peterson, but they had let up in recent months.

Get a hold of yourself, she thought.

But she was paralyzed with irrational fear, crouched in a damp corner. She didn't hear the footsteps anymore. The man had reached the bottom of the stairs and his feet just made faint shuffling sounds on the concrete floor. Someone was there in the dark with her. She was sure that he could hear her gasping breath.

She knew that she had to pull herself to her feet, get out of this corner. But she simply couldn't move.

Then came a whistling in the air. She had no idea what it was until she felt a swift, searing pain across her face. She remembered the scars all over the dead women's bodies, their faces as well as their backs. Meara, too, had been marked by the blows of this multi-stranded whip.

Riley's terror abruptly morphed into fury. She wasn't going to let those victims' pain go unpunished.

As the whip whistled down toward her for a second blow, she reached out and grabbed hold of it in the darkness. She yanked her attacker forward, heard his body slam into the wall beside her. Then the whip fell limp in her hand.

She scrambled out of the corner, realizing that she and her attacker had just switched places. He now had his back to the wall and she had his whip in her hand. She didn't stop to think about what to do next. She lashed out with the whip, not knowing where it might make contact.

She heard a wild scream of pain. It felt good—dangerously good—to be inflicting the same pain on him that he he'd inflicted on his victims. She lashed again, and again, and again, until the screaming faded to a desperate whimper. Then she stopped. Surely, she thought, she had beaten him into cowering submission.

She groped forward to find the killer.

Suddenly, he struck her hard, lunging low at her legs and tackling her. She could feel that he was strong. But he was unskilled, unaccustomed to resistance from his victims. With all the force of her well-toned body and her ferocious will, she leapt back to her feet and seized him by the arm. Knowing he was disoriented by now, she swung his body as far and as hard as she could.

She heard and felt the terrible impact of his head smashing against the wall.

Riley staggered backward, breathing hard. At that very second, she was blinded by the brightness of the basement light.

She heard Lucy's voice call out from the top of the stairs.

"Riley!"

"I'm here, Lucy," Riley yelled back, gasping for breath. As her eyes adjusted to the light, she could see the man's body twitch his last ounce of life away. He was bleeding from the blows of the whip, and his head bore the ugly, bloody marks of its fatal impact.

In a moment, Lucy was by Riley's side.

"What did you do?" Lucy asked.

"I gave him his own back," she said.

She looked at Lucy, who was rubbing the back of her head. Her face had also been cut by the man's whip.

"He really knocked me out for a few minutes there," she said. "I guess he thought I was dead. But I'm tougher than he figured."

"He won't hurt anybody ever again," Riley said.

"I just called for backup—not that we really need that now," Lucy said with a pained smile.

Then Lucy shook her head, looking ashamed.

"Riley, how could I have been so stupid?" she said. "I was here. I talked to him. I should have known it was him. But when I didn't find any women down here, I ..."

Lucy's words faded away and her expression darkened with worry.

"Where are the women?" Lucy asked.

The question jolted Riley like an electric shock. Casey Phipps was dead, but his captives still had to be rescued. Now she was sure that he had never held them down in this basement. But they still had to be trapped somewhere. And they desperately needed help.

"I've got an idea," she told Lucy.

CHAPTER FORTY SIX

Riley hurried up the stairs with Lucy close behind. She went out the front door and saw that the children were still in the yard next door. The little girl was watching the boys play ball.

Riley knelt down beside the girl. The child looked at their cut faces with alarm.

"What happened to you?" she asked.

"Don't worry about us, Libby," Riley said. "We're fine. But I need your help. You told me that you'd heard ghosts talking."

The girl nodded, looking a little frightened now.

"Could you take me to where you heard them?" Riley asked.

"I'm scared to," Libby said.

"Don't be," Riley said. "You're a brave girl. And they're not really ghosts. They're women who need our help."

Just then, Riley saw police cars approaching from down the street.

"You stay here and tell them what happened," she told Lucy.

She said to the child, "We've got to hurry."

*

The little girl led Riley around the back of the Phipps house and through the backyard. She pointed out a path that led into a wooded area.

"Show me," Riley said. "You're doing great."

The child led Riley into the woods. Bushes encroached thickly on all sides of the path, and Riley pushed branches out of the way they hurried along. After about a hundred feet, the path opened onto a large square grassy area. Two periscope-like objects poked out of the ground.

Now Riley understood. Years ago during the Cold War, Tyrone Phipps had built a secret fallout shelter, hoping to survive the nuclear apocalypse he so obsessively awaited.

Riley looked quickly around until she spotted a small, rectangular mossy spot. She pulled away the moss, which had been laid down to hide a horizontal door.

"Stay right here," she told Libby. "I'll be back soon."

Libby nodded. Riley pulled the door open and called down a short flight of stairs.

"Is anybody here?"

A piercing scream cut the air.

"Here! Help us! We're down here!"

Riley almost smiled at the sound. It meant that the women were still alive. She hurried down the steps into a strange room filled with clocks, with a chain-link cage at the far end. A young woman had thrown herself against the links, gripping them frantically, screaming at the top of her lungs.

"Help! Help! Get us out of here!"

Riley knew that the screaming woman was Mallory Byrd, who had been taken just yesterday and was not yet weak with starvation. But bloody streaks showed that she had felt the sharpness of her captor's whip.

The other woman, the one Meara had called Kimberly, was lying in a fetal position. She looked more dead than alive. Riley spotted a key ring lying on a table. Picking it up and opening the lock, she flung the cage door open and hurried inside.

Mallory threw herself upon Riley in a spasm of wild gratitude.

"It's okay," Riley said. "He can't hurt you again." She reluctantly pushed Mallory aside and went to check on Kimberly. She lifted up the poor woman's head. She looked like a baby bird in a nest awaiting its mother.

The sight was so pathetic that tears began to run down Riley's face. She had some idea of what this woman had endured, and she again felt a deep satisfaction that the man was dead. She hugged Kimberly, being careful not to hurt the fragile creature.

"It's all right now," Riley said. "Everything's going to be all right."

CHAPTER FORTY SEVEN

Riley sat with Lucy on the porch steps of the Phipps house, recovering from their ordeal. After an ambulance had come for the women in the fallout shelter, Riley had walked back through the woods to the house. Soon the medical examiner would be here to pick up Casey Phipps's body.

Lucy was still berating herself for not realizing earlier that Casey Phipps was the killer.

Riley put a comforting hand on Lucy's shoulder.

"We're all only human," she said. "He had the whole town fooled. Nobody knew."

Lucy looked into Riley's eyes.

"Yeah, but if you'd been here doing the canvassing, would you have known right away?"

Riley smiled grimly.

"Probably," she said. "But I've been doing this for a long time. Give yourself some time. Like a couple of decades, maybe."

Just then a vehicle pulled up and parked in front of the house. Bill and Carl Walder got out and Bill charged toward Riley. He almost threw his arms around her, but then he saw her wounds.

"Shit, Riley," he said. "Are you okay?" he asked.

Riley was relieved. A hug would have been quite painful at that moment.

"I'm fine," she said.

"I wish I'd been here. I wish I'd been able to—"

He didn't finish his sentence. Riley understood what he was thinking. For months now, this case had been eating away at him inside. And now the whole thing had come to an end, and he hadn't even been here.

Riley touched his face gently.

"It's okay, Bill," Riley said. "We all did it together. You can sleep easier now."

Just then she heard a voice call out.

"Agent Paige!"

She saw Walder striding toward her, his face bright red with anger. His arms were stiff at his sides, and Riley could see that he was holding something in each hand. He walked straight up to her and for a moment he just stared at her.

Then he handed her back her gun and her badge.

"Good job," Walder said in a tight, bitter voice.

Then he walked away without another word.

It would be nice, Riley thought, if that was she last she'd see of him. But she knew she'd never be so lucky.

And that he'd always be looking for an excuse to fire her.

CHAPTER FORTY EIGHT

April was walking alone in the night. The streetlights cast their eerie glow on a world nearly empty of activity. She felt like a scared little girl. She hated the feeling. She felt ashamed of it.

I don't want to feel like that anymore, she thought.

But she was determined not to go back home—not now, maybe not ever. For now, at least, she was sure she wouldn't be missed. Gabriela was in her basement apartment, and April was sure she'd slipped out the front door without being heard. And of course Mom wasn't even at home.

She kept telling herself that she hated Mom and didn't want to see her again. Whatever Mom had said to Joel, he had refused to see April since then. What business did Mom have, wrecking her life like that?

Anyway, she was sure that Joel still loved her as much as she loved him. What did Mom know about love? As far as April could remember, Mom hadn't ever loved anybody like she loved Joel. Certainly her mom and dad had never felt anything like that kind of love.

She couldn't shake off her fear. She'd walked far enough from home now that even the idea of walking back was scary. But she had to go somewhere.

She saw a few cars moving along a wider street up ahead. Maybe she could hitch a ride, get somebody to drive her home.

Or maybe I could get somebody to drive me far away, she thought.

But the thought of getting a ride from a stranger also scared her. She felt fear well up in her throat and tears burning her eyes.

She took out her cell phone and dialed Joel's number. She hoped that he'd finally answer after a whole day of ignoring her calls.

To her relief, she heard his voice say, "April?"

She sputtered, trying to keep from sobbing.

"Joel, I'm outside alone, and I need you to come and get me."

"Where are you?" Joel asked.

April looked up at the nearest street signs and told him.

"I'll be right there," he said.

216

*

When Riley walked into her house that night, the first thing she did was to call out to Gabriela downstairs.

"I'm home, Gabriela."

Gabriela called back, "*¡Qué bueno!* Did you solve the case?"

"I did. Is everything okay here?"

"Everything's fine."

Riley thanked Gabriela and sat down in the living room. She felt deeply satisfied by her day's work. The two young women she had rescued were in the hospital. They didn't have any life-threatening injuries, but it would take time for Kimberly to get back to full health. They would both need counseling to deal with the trauma they'd been through. Still, they were going to be fine.

Most important, Casey Phipps was dead.

It's over, Riley told herself.

She took special pleasure in fingering both her badge and her gun.

Lots of people had wanted to give her their congratulations, including the mayor of Ohlman. But she hadn't waited around for that. She'd driven straight home.

Now she looked at her watch and saw that it was just turning midnight. She was glad she wasn't in a room full of clocks noisily announcing the hour.

She was just thinking about fixing herself a drink when her cell phone rang. Riley saw that the call was from the teenage shelter in Phoenix. When she answered, she heard the worried voice of Brenda Fitch.

"Riley, I'm sorry to bother you so late … but have you heard anything from Jilly? I mean, has she called you or anything?"

Riley's heart jumped up in her throat.

"No. Why? What's wrong?"

She heard an anxious sigh.

"Jilly left here last night. We don't have any idea where she went. We're really worried."

Riley was too stunned to say anything.

Brenda said, "If you hear anything from her, would you please let us know right away?"

"Of course," Riley said. "And please keep in touch with me about her."

217

They ended the call and Riley plunged from feeling wonderful to miserable. What had happened to Jilly? With no place to go, no family to care for her, where could she possibly be except back on the streets at the mercy of predatory men?

But there was nothing she could do about it right now. Nothing at all. Still, there was one thing she could do to make herself better. She went upstairs to look in on April, who was surely asleep by now.

But when Riley opened the door, April's bed was empty.

She rushed downstairs in a panic, calling out to Gabriela in the basement

"Gabriela! April's gone!"

Gabriela came dashing up the stairs in her nightgown.

"But I thought she was in bed!" Gabriela said. "She went up to bed at the usual time."

"You look through the house," Riley said. She ran out onto the back deck and turned the floodlights on. April wasn't in the back yard.

She came back inside to find Gabriela in as much of a panic as she was. She picked up the phone and dialed April's number. There was no answer at all—not even April's usual outgoing message.

"Maybe she's at Crystal's house," Gabriela said.

Riley felt a surge of desperate hope. She dialed Blaine's number. Crystal answered the phone.

"Crystal, is April there?" Riley demanded.

"Isn't she at home?" Crystal said.

"No," Riley gasped.

Crystal didn't sound groggy, as if she'd been asleep. She sounded as if she were already worried and upset.

"We had a fight this afternoon," Crystal said. "It was about Joel. I shouldn't have told her what I thought about him. She said we're not friends anymore."

"Okay, Crystal," Riley said. "Please call if you hear anything from her."

As she ended the call, Riley knew better than to hope for that. Something had gone seriously wrong. She wondered whether to call the police and get an Amber Alert out. But that wasn't an option—not yet, anyway. April must have walked out on her own. She wasn't kidnapped this time. Riley couldn't report her as a runaway until after some time passed.

I've got to go look for her, she thought.
She decided to start at Joel's house.

*

April felt very mellow. The pill Joel had given her had wiped away all of her anxieties. She was so glad to be here with him. This time they weren't at his house but at some friend's house.

She and Joel were stretched out together on a bed. A few other people walked by the open door.

April watched as he manipulated her cell phone.

"What's your password?" he asked.

She smiled. "What do you think?" she said.

He smiled back. Of course it was easy for him to guess that it was his own name. He punched in the password.

"What are you doing?" April asked.

"Turning off the GPS. We don't need your Nazi-mom storming in here."

April giggled.

She started to say that she would have to get home soon, because Gabriela would panic if she found her gone. But she found that she didn't really care about that. Besides, she was having trouble saying anything complicated.

In a few moments Joel put down the phone.

"All safe now," he said.

Just then a man April didn't know peered in through the open door. He had a questioning look on his face, and she saw that he held a wad of cash in his hand. He looked over April as if she were something to be bought, and she didn't like the look.

"Soon," Joel told him.

The man went away.

"Soon what?" April asked.

"Nothing," Joel said. "Nothing for you to worry about."

April lay back and watched as Joel struck a match and lit a candle on a little table next to the bed. His face looked beautiful in the warm light. She tried to focus on what she'd just been worrying about, but already her mind drifted onto other things.

April just watched as though she was in a dream.

"I feel like a point of light," she said.

"You're glowing," Joel said, smiling. "And soon you're going to feel like a star in the sky."

She watched contentedly as Joel puttered about, heating something in a metal spoon over the candle flame.

She felt that she was watching from a distance as he wrapped something around her arm—and then pushed the needle into her flesh.

Then she let out an astonished gasp as she felt her body disappear. She'd never felt anything like this in her life. She didn't want to quit feeling this way.

Not ever, she thought.

COMING SOON!

Book #5 in the Riley Paige mystery series!

Blake Pierce

Blake Pierce is author of the bestselling RILEY PAGE mystery series, which include the mystery suspense thrillers ONCE GONE (book #1), ONCE TAKEN (book #2), ONCE CRAVED (#3) and ONCE LURED (#4). Blake Pierce is also the author of the MACKENZIE WHITE mystery series and AVERY BLACK mystery series.

An avid reader and lifelong fan of the mystery and thriller genres, Blake loves to hear from you, so please feel free to visit www.blakepierceauthor.com to learn more and stay in touch.